REMEMBERING DEMONS

THE GOD CYCLE: BOOK ONE

J. CORNELIUS

ACKNOWLEDGMENTS

First and foremost, a resounding thanks to you, dear reader. The fact that you have this book in front of you and are willing to trust me with your time is an honor and a dream come true.

I grew up reading fantasy and sci-fi classics: Friedman, Zelazny, Tolkien. I've loved it for as long as I can remember. I think I may owe my aptitude for languages to my eagerness to be reading all those wonderful stories. There are so many aspects of fantasy and sci-fi that I love, but above all, what truly did it for me was the license to fabricate profound ideas about a world, sometimes even our world, and play with them... page after page after page. I was always drawn to new ideas, which is why I make a living as a basic researcher, and why I am fascinated with modern theoretical physics and what it implies about how the world works.

I never dreamt that I would be writing my own stories... but perhaps it should come as no surprise that what eventually drew me to writing—was an idea.

With time, it just sort of took root. But since I obviously could not possibly write a book, I did the only sensible thing: I ignored it. Until one day, I didn't. That's really all it took. One brief lapse in judgment and I was off. A few months later and my endearing bullheaded stubbornness had me set on a course to write my story, all the while populating page after page after page with beings and ideas that excited me.

It felt impossible to be writing a book, but there I was, none-the-less, doing just that. And better yet, by the end my nugget of an idea would be there for all to see. An idea that merges cosmology with religion in a new and curious way (not that I believe the idea to be true, I remain a staunch atheist, but who cares about all that? Not me). I wish I could have seen my face when I realized that I could not possibly reach the ending I so craved in a single book. That's right, it turned out that I had a trilogy on my hands. The characters I had so carelessly given life had stories of their own to tell that would require... page after page after page. Happily, it turns out I adore writing, but then I've always been lucky.

Speaking of luck, I want to thank my wife, Anja, my father, Poul, my father-in-law's wife, Judy, as well as my friends, André, Jens, and Aadal for feedback on early or late drafts and, in several cases, for late-night discussions of the ideas behind this and future books in The God Cycle. I would also like to thank Andrew for his thoughts on my early draft, as well as my editors, Jon and Benji, for their comments and corrections. Missing the input from just one of these individuals would have resulted in an inferior final version, and I am forever thankful for their time and effort. Also, a special thank you to my dad for introducing me to the fascinating world of fantasy and science fiction as well as to Judy for her kind reassurances that kept me hammering away at the enormous task that is writing a book.

Finally, I am extremely grateful to my wife and my two daughters for letting me set aside time to write in the hectic hodgepodge of activities and routines that make up family life.

PROLOGUE

It drifted with the breeze, twirling with its sisters in the gathering dusk. One with the swarm, it spun joyfully, an incorporeal Spark within an everchanging spiral of lights, but whenever a male drew close, he became quickly frustrated by the lack of physical form and withdrew to seek a mate elsewhere.

Something yanked at its awareness. A nuisance, distracting it from the simple joy of being. Like a memory. Of what? It stopped, hovering within the swirl of luminescent bugs. Purpose? There was something important it was meant to be doing, but the distraction dissipated, and the Spark slowly resumed its twisting path through the air.

Another pulse danced dimly across its senses. For a moment it defiantly kept circling with its sisters. Then reluctantly it yielded, slowly circling south. Something important called.

The swarm responded to the change in direction, moving haltingly from the shore of the lake. Then, as one, they realized their mistake and swerved away from this new aberrant course, returning to their carefree dance overlooking the shoreline. Their departure instilled a brief sense of sadness in the Spark, but this, like everything else, did not last long.

All went dark as it passed beneath the crust of the planet. This was not alarming, as such things meant little to it. It found itself in a vast circular tube humming with energy. This was the source of the call, quiescent though it was right now. Intrigued, it edged closer, coming to rest near the middle.

A dozen explosions went off virtually simultaneously, and the Spark was buffeted by the violent energies released. It would have screamed, had it a mouth. It would have fallen, had it legs. As it was, it merely floated in the center of the tube, like a punch-drunk boxer who does not remember how to fall. Another dozen explosions, then another, then another. They kept coming, sending jolt upon jolt through the interconnected gossamer strands that made up the tattered remains of what had once, very nearly, been a god.

It thrashed weakly to get away, managing nothing of the sort. As it was torn apart, a flicker of awareness returned in a brief flash. It knew its purpose—it knew what it had done and what it might still accomplish. Then its parts collided with the detectors, sending a jumble of anomalous signatures coursing through the array of processing stations.

Had it a mouth, it would have screamed.

CHAPTER 1

"What's your earliest memory?"

"We've been over this, Doc."

"Please, Daryl. Humor me."

"Waking up in the ambulance. Coming here and meeting you."

"Do you remember anything before arriving here?"

"Sort of."

"What? Please elaborate."

"Dying, Doc. I remember pain and dying."

"Physical or mental pain?"

"Both, I think."

"And when was your first vision?"

"You mean when I started to see things that aren't real?"

"Well. Look, if magic really existed it would either have to be fully hidden from science or . . . be contained within it."

"Your point being?"

"Neither option sounds particularly magical to me. Why hide it? And if it was already present in all we can touch and see, how is it magic?"

"Valid point."

"So, which do you think is more likely? That you're crazy

3

. . . or that everyone else is?"

"You probably shouldn't use the 'c' word."

"Don't worry about it, Daryl. It's how I'm relating to you on a personal level. You know, gaining your trust and all that."

"Clever, Doc."

"I'm a professional. And please, call me Susan."

***

"You look better, Daryl. Did you have the dream again?"

"Yes, I saw Ginny."

"Wanna talk about it?"

"I wish I could, but it's the same as always."

"Just her face?"

"Yeah."

***

"I made a new friend yesterday."

"Real or not?"

"Well, he's an invisible gnome named Hubble. You tell me."

"Hubble. Like the space telescope?"

"I don't know."

"I'm going to go out on a limb here and say that he's likely not real."

"Because of his invisibility or the fact that he's a gnome?"

"The name. No one would name their kid that."

***

"I have to tell you that, given your effect on the other patients, it has been suggested more than once that you be moved upstairs. Werner especially seems to have taken to it. I don't have to tell you the influence he seems to have over many of the other patients."

"I understand."

"Yes, but that is not the point."

"What is the point, Susan?"

"The point is that you need to decide what you want. Whether to keep hanging on to your illusory acquaintances or to get better with me."

"What, leave them? I couldn't do that, even if I wanted to. They keep me sane."

"Maybe they do and maybe they don't. At one point you will need to choose."

"Why?"

"Because moving forward means leaving something behind. They'll understand."

CHAPTER 2

"What is gravity?"

A collective sigh went through the room as Werner's familiar question hung in the air like your least favorite piece of laundry. Daryl did not sigh—things were about to get interesting.

"Not this again," Raphael groaned. Raphael was an Italian string theorist and typically the one most willing to go along with Werner's ideas, but even he had his limits.

Daryl was sure the annoyance of the other physicists, turned patients, was genuine. For his part, he had to look down and cough to keep the others from seeing the smile on his face. These disagreements on which subject was scientific enough to merit discussion were always the most entertaining—not the science itself, which was often too complex for him to follow the debate, but the passionate disagreements.

Robert and Swati shifted in their seats. Swati was a constantly frowning older woman of Indian descent who used to work on something to do with black holes, and Robert was a cosmologist. Being more reticent, they typically required a bit more prodding to enter the fray. As always, Werner was quick to oblige.

"Could it be the result of forces that only operate between energy in our space-time brane and that of energy on other foreign branes in the bulk?" Werner suggested as he adjusted his glasses, even though they had more than enough real-estate to remain atop his hook of a nose.

"If it only exists between our brane and other branes, then why do we see its effect here?" Robert scoffed, pushed past the breaking point.

The other physicists tensed, sensing that Robert had supplied Werner with the exact question he wanted. Daryl leaned back in his lounge chair, wishing he had popcorn.

"Because of the indirect effects it has here," Werner said with a wide, friendly smile. "The gravitational pull between branes causes the branes to warp as described by general relativity. We are not observing the force itself, but the warping of space it causes here directly affects the trajectories of energy on our brane."

"Fine," Swati remarked, "but what does this Interbrand force represent?"

"A wonderful question!" Werner exclaimed. A certain fervor lit up behind his eyes when discussing these favorite ideas of his. He leaned forward to share his insights. "I don't know."

Raphael, Swati, and Robert stared at him with incredulity.

Finally, Raphael leaned forward, looking like a stern schoolmaster, and opened his mouth to speak. Not missing a beat, Werner leaned forward even further, visually transforming the situation from a scolding into an intimate moment. Raphael frowned, realizing the joke, but having trouble processing some part of it.

Probably the butt, Daryl thought, and coughed again.

"And I suppose you think this has some relationship with black holes?" he said, clearly off-kilter.

"Well, yes." Werner replied. "Why you consider these ideas so outlandish is beyond me. To your question, it implies that black holes could be areas of brane-contact.

Consequently, anything that crosses the event horizon enters another brane." He gave a short laugh. "Which conveniently provides a partial answer to the black hole information paradox."

Swati, always the calmest of the bunch, emitted a mirthless chuckle. "It's outlandish because you don't have any evidence. No rigorous mathematical framework, no falsifiable model. Nothing!" The last word came out as a hiss as she glared at Werner, who happily smiled back.

"Don't I?"

"No, and don't think I didn't notice your deliberate choice of the word 'outlandish' either. We all subscribe to the idea of extra dimensions, and we'll freely admit that they are more than implied by modern physics, but you're just guessing."

Daryl's attention drifted as the discussion turned to more technical aspects. The room was small, but nicely furnished. This was not out of character with the rest of the asylum, but extra care had been taken to make this room, often used for smaller study groups, as inviting as possible. They had been meeting like this for several months now. It had taken a while to get permission, and given the heavy focus on physics, Daryl had been unsure whether it made sense for him to attend. Now it was one of his favorite parts of the week.

As was often the case, his attention turned to thoughts of Ginny. He had dreamt of her last night, and on days like that, her features were etched into his memory. He loved those days.

Lost in thought, he did not at first notice that the conversation had shifted to a more ominous topic.

"Daryl?" Werner said, shaking him out of his reverie.

"Hmm?"

"Did you hear about Rick?"

Daryl shook his head.

"He took a wrong turn in the basement and has ended up on the second floor."

Werner was not referring to teleportation, but to what could happen if you wandered around by yourself in the asylum. Especially around reflective surfaces. If you did not follow the rules, you were very likely to have an incident. Sometimes you just disappeared. This was even more true in the basement.

Raphael, Robert, and Swati looked queasy. Many of the patients did not believe the stories of Daryl's experiences, but they all instinctively knew to avoid the basement whenever possible.

"Is he okay?" Daryl asked.

"Well, he's on the second floor, so not great. I heard they had to carry him there in restraints and that he was muttering some pretty vile things the whole way there."

Daryl suppressed a shiver. He knew better than most what waited in the mirrors if you were not careful.

The first floor was being refurbished and, because of this, the asylum staff had temporarily made use of the basement. Rick was unlikely to be the last victim of *that* interim plan.

"Shit," he muttered, his usual good mood temporarily muted.

Robert cleared his throat. "Could we discuss the recent LHC malfunction?" he asked. "Some have claimed there might have been new physics involved."

Whenever anything new happened in the world of physics, particularly at the Large Hadron Collider, it was sure to turn up as a topic here. Raphael and Swati leaned in, clearly ready with their own take on what might have happened.

Werner winked at Daryl and sighed. "Boring."

CHAPTER 3

It was early afternoon, and Daryl had settled into his favorite seat by the window, admiring the early summer blossoms in the large stone flower beds on the enormous terrace outside. Groups of patients were scattered across the spacious parlor, playing games or chatting, either with each other or themselves. It would not be long now before he had to go for his scheduled session with Susan. He scratched absently at his back in that familiar, hard-to-reach spot between the shoulder blades.

"Hi Daryl."

He started, nearly upending the small rectangular table which sat between his chair and its neighbor, which was now occupied by an exceptionally heavy-set man. The man's eyes held a fierce intensity and were so dark they appeared black. He leaned in, and the rustling of his heavy gray robes competed with the groans and creaks of the suffering chair. "We have to speak," the man whispered.

Daryl spared a quick glance around, confirming with relief that they were far from alone. He swallowed and was about to respond when the man swiped a sizable booger from his left nostril and wiped it on his lapel.

"Er, eww," Daryl said and looked away. A series of

groans alerted him that his visitor had shifted in his chair, and he was not surprised when a hand settled on his shoulder.

He looked up into eyes that appeared to be almost all pupil. It took all his self-control not to pitch backward, upending the chair.

"Understand that I can't tell you much." Pupils paused, as if uncertain how to proceed. "But you're in considerably more danger here than first anticipated."

"That's really helpful," Daryl offered, still struggling with the urge to pull away.

Pupils must have finally noticed, as he slid backward, settling into the spacious chair once more. Following a moment of silence, he said, "I have sensed something ancient stirring. It almost makes me think . . ." The man trailed off, apparently lost in thought, while absently trying to flick the remainder of the booger from his fingernail. Pupils shook his head, whispering to himself, "But of course no, that can't be." He returned his attention to Daryl, who wiped the look of disgust from his face just in time.

"Something powerful seeks you. I don't think you can stay here," Pupils said and fixed him with that intense stare for several heartbeats. "You really still don't remember anything?"

Daryl took a long, shaky breath. Finally, a question he knew the answer to. "Nope."

The man sighed. "If you do remember, you'll know where to find me."

With that he made as if to get up but stopped short at a sudden thought. "You are more than your anger. Remember that."

"I'm not angry," Daryl replied.

"I know," Pupils said as a brief twitch of unrecognizable emotion crossed his features. "I think your ride is here," he said pointing behind Daryl.

Daryl turned around to see the two orderlies making their way toward him. When he turned back, the man was gone, leaving behind a distinctly foul odor.

"We're here to take you to see Doctor Walker," the smaller orderly said as he wrinkled his nose in response to the olfactory stimulus that was unflatteringly centered on Daryl. Daryl was pretty sure his name was Kenny.

"An escort," he said. "Well, lah-di-dah."

"Her office has been relocated. We're here to make sure you find it."

Daryl's heart plummeted. "Where?" he croaked.

"The basement."

Daryl's heart hit the floor, but he stood in defiance of a sudden onset of vertigo. "Did you happen to see the guy that just left?" he asked in a shaky voice.

"Not really," the smaller man responded warily.

"Never mind," Daryl replied with a feigned air of indifference.

Using his sleeve to wipe away a sudden sheen of sweat, he was led through the parlor. Ten minutes earlier he would have been apprehensive about going to the basement, with or without an escort. Now the prospect left him horrified. Unfortunately, he could not come up with a safe way to avoid his session. He very much doubted he would be able to fool the two orderlies into thinking he had suddenly fallen ill.

"I could really use the restroom," he said.

This would buy him some time and, given the stress he was under, it was becoming more and more true by the minute. Kenny accepted with a nod and led the way down the corridor toward the elevator.

The ancient asylum was constructed from roughly hewn stones that had been meticulously chipped to fit, which gave corridors a cozy, organic feel. Someone had told him they had been quarried when the basement was dug out. Currently, they were bustling with the activity of orderlies and nurses helping patients with various aspects of their day. He noticed Werner's tall, lanky frame being taken to his session with Doctor Santéz, and they briefly exchanged greetings.

As they rounded a corner, entering a narrow and much quieter corridor, Daryl noticed Hubble's diminutive form peering out from a doorway. He waved for Daryl to follow him, his wide, bald head bobbing with emotion atop his short, rotund 3-foot frame. He was wearing a vibrantly colored tunic, lending him a distinct hippie vibe. Hubble was a gnome. He was also about as close a friend as one could expect to cultivate, given Daryl's amnesia and the fact that Hubble was imaginary. He was, by far, the most pleasant of Daryl's delusions and a constant source of camaraderie. He was also invisible to everyone else and not at all concerned with how Daryl's reactions to his sudden appearances made Daryl seem to the staff. In fact, he derived a fair bit of amusement from it. However, his current attempt to get Daryl's attention did not appear to stem from a desire to embarrass, but rather from a need to tell him something. Unfortunately, Daryl was unable to comply, as the orderlies forced him to pass by the occupied doorway.

An improbably small number of seconds later, Hubble appeared in another doorway on the other side of the corridor. He was waving his hands over his head. This was followed by several quick hand gestures, which Daryl had a hard time following. Except for the last, which was the universal flat hand across the throat, signaling imminent death—or perhaps that Hubble's pet chicken had just died? Apparently satisfied that his message had been successfully relayed, the gnome disappeared by walking through the wall behind him. Thus heartened, Daryl was led into the final corridor leading to the elevator.

The gnome's cryptic message left Daryl so engrossed in thought that he almost failed to notice when they passed the restroom next to the elevator. "This might take a while," he said as he came to a stop.

"I'm afraid not," said the big guy. "Most first-floor restrooms have been closed today."

"Yeah, something about preparing for the construction," Kenny added.

Daryl's heart skipped a beat, and his bowels did a flip as he realized which restroom they must be taking him to. By then the big guy had pressed the call button, and the elevator doors slid noisily apart. They entered, and the doors closed behind them with a metallic screech.

***

As the old elevator made its rickety way downward, Daryl's pulse steadily climbed. Ever helpful, his mind idly wondered whether clammy hands and a dry mouth served some critical function in a fight-or-flight situation. Given their destination, the two orderlies flanking him did little to ease his sense of foreboding.

The elevator came to a stop with a loud ping and the doors slid open to a rush of dank basement air.

While the stone used to construct the upper levels had been almost exclusively quarried from what was now the basement, the underground corridors had been evened out by filling in cracks using cement, making the foundations of the asylum much less inviting than the upper levels. Unsurprisingly, the basement was used less. As they exited the elevator, Daryl's foot caught on the height difference between the elevator and the basement floor, causing him to stumble uncomfortably into the big guy. The orderly deftly righted him, and Daryl mumbled a thanks as the three moved left toward the restroom.

The basement had an odd, almost insubstantial feel to it. As if reality here was held together by delicate cloth, prone to tear at any minute. Temporary lighting had been unevenly spaced along the length of the corridor, causing a flickering display of dancing shadows. Daryl was sure he saw movements at the edge of his vision, but whenever he turned his head, everything was still. He thought he saw Kenny give a start, but it could just have been his own overactive imagination.

"We'll wait here," Kenny said, quashing Daryl's last hope that he might not have to enter alone.

"Actually, I think I can hold it. False alarm."

Kenny and the big guy exchanged a look, and Daryl had little trouble following their train of thought. He was behaving erratically.

"Fine," he said with a sigh. "I'll give it a few shakes."

The door opened with surprising smoothness, admitting him to a short corridor that ended in a large square room with a tiled floor. Four toilet stalls occupied the opposite side of the room, and the right wall held a run-down urinal. To the left were three sinks beneath a long mirror, which covered most of the wall. The lights above bathed everything in cold blue light.

He briefly considered just waiting awhile by the door, but he did not relish the prospect of being found loitering when he had said he needed to urinate. Instead, he made his way to the left wall and very carefully got down on his hands and knees. Scanning to his right reassured him that the rusted metallic urinal barely reflected any light at all. With great care, he began making his way along the left wall, intentionally staying well below the reflective surface, while continuously monitoring his right for movement. Once he was clear of the mirror, he propped himself up against the wall and straightened while keeping a wary eye on the rest of the room. Suddenly something darted out from under the stall door, and he emitted a startled grunt, nearly losing his balance. The rat turned and hissed once before scurrying away from what was now Daryl's corner of the restroom.

"Alright then, no problem," he muttered, exhaling slowly to calm himself. Pulling open the door of the recently vacated stall, he cast a quick glance inside but saw nothing except the expected defecatory accoutrements. He sidled inside and sat himself delicately on the edge of the toilet while pulling the stall closed with his left hand. No one in here but him—and no reflective surfaces either. He let out a shaky sigh of relief.

***

From his porcelain perch, Daryl tried to shake the feeling that he had missed something. Something about the rat? He heard a strange gurgling sound from beneath him and instinctively looked down at the base of the toilet just as his mind grasped the situation and screamed for him to look away. Too late, his eyes caught in the puddle of overflow at the base of the toilet from which the rat had been drinking.

Mirrored in the puddle, a multi-jointed, scorpion-like monstrosity with a partly human face crouched on the lid of the cistern behind him. Its compound eyes had a faint, red glow, and the mandibles emerging from its wide mouth were dripping with dark green pus.

The creature launched itself at him and the impact buckled his knees. He would surely have fallen into the awaiting puddle had it not been for his tenuous butt grip on the rim of the toilet. He slid backward, and his right hand smashed painfully against the stained tiles, while his left hand dipped into the water of the toilet bowl. Immediately, gray tentacles emerged, wrapping themselves around his wrist, pulling and twisting. He felt himself slipping off the bowl and, with horror, realized that he was moments from plunging headfirst into the reflective puddle at its base. The scorpion creature excitedly pushed against him, emitting a sound somewhere between a purr and a hiss. Its long, spindly legs clawed to find purchase.

Straining against the side of the stall with his left hand and the floor with his right heel, Daryl was able to leverage himself into a partial turn. The shift caused the creature's body to slide off, spinning him fully and sending him to the floor of the stall. Tentacles erupted on either side of him and started fiercely pulling him into the puddle. Inch by inch, he was dragged into the water. The scorpion thing had righted itself and now flung itself at him, mandibles snapping. Putting one hand on the sticky, rubbery surface between its eyes, he was able to ward off the mouth, which had begun to snap in anticipation. He felt his hand weakening.

"Get down on it!" James Taylor interjected. "Get down on it!"

For one ludicrous moment, he and the beast hesitated as the cell phone Daryl had lifted from the big guy in the elevator vibrated with loud suggestions on how to proceed. The tentacles gave Daryl's torso one last yank, before forcefully ejecting him onto the wet tiles. The mandibles snapped once as the creature withdrew and vanished. Daryl was breathing heavily, and his ass and wrist ached. He was unsure whether the latter was sprained or broken.

"Did you take my goddamn phone?" the big guy yelled from just outside the stall.

Daryl glanced incredulously at the display, relief washing over him.

"It's your wife."

CHAPTER 4

Taking his phone had not endeared Daryl to the big guy, and the orderlies showed little interest in his disheveled appearance. He was brusquely ushered out of the restroom and delivered to Doctor Walker's door. Kenny knocked, and a voice told them to enter.

Susan Walker was a stern-looking woman in her early fifties. She had sharp features and a delicate nose which pointed ever so slightly to the left. She forewent the doctor's white coat, typically worn by therapists at the asylum, in favor of her own varied wardrobe. Probably an attempt to make herself more accessible to her patients. On her it worked. Today she wore light-brown trousers and a loose, high-buttoned, navy-blue blouse, which echoed the color of her eyes. As soon as the two orderlies left, her serious demeanor vanished as she fixed him with her radiant smile.

"How have you been, Daryl?" she asked as she took a seat across from him, completing their usual in-session geometry—facing each other across a low footstool.

Daryl hesitated, massaging his sore wrist. Over the past ten months they had built a good rapport, and while his progress had been slow, he cherished their conversations and her perspective on his condition. He felt safe with her, as though her presence was somehow incompatible with monsters—they simply could not exist in the same room.

"I'm okay," he answered cautiously, trying to collect himself. His pulse was still elevated from his encounter with the giant scorpion and nearly slipping through the mirror-surface of the puddle. "I didn't sleep well last night," he muttered. "And I've seen Hubble several times since our session last week, including this morning."

Susan pursed her lips and moved both feet onto the footstool. There was plenty of room for his own, but he kept them firmly on the ground. She took a sip of her tea.

"There is something you're not telling me," she said. *Damn that mind of hers.*

He did not think telling her about the demon scorpion would be a good idea. Sharing violent episodes had previously led to temporary, and very uncomfortable, increases in medication. It had even, in his first month here, been partly responsible for him being put in restraints.

So, he relayed his encounter earlier that morning with Pupils and how shaken it had left him. Susan listened sympathetically without interruption before offering another very reasonable explanation for his visions.

"Could it be that my suggestion to pursue hypnotherapy increased your anxiety, which was then compounded by the prospect of going into the basement?" Daryl was not too surprised by her theory. He had previously shared his fear of the basement. "Also, nothing has happened," she continued with a reassuring smile. "So, we can hardly be dealing with a magically prescient being now, can we?"

"I guess that makes sense," he answered, a vision of compound eyes and snapping mandibles passing before his eyes.

As the session progressed, Susan gently nudged Daryl from quiet despair to a nascent belief that things could be different. He was never exactly sure how she did it, and while she was clearly manipulating his emotions, she did so in such a frank and disarming manner that he grudgingly allowed her to repaint his world.

"Let's postpone hypnotherapy for our next session," she said, and an unexpected look of impatience briefly pierced her pleasant demeanor. "Excuse me," she said, flustered as she wiped a drop of blood from her nose. "The dry air sometimes wreaks havoc with my nasal mucosa." She discarded the tissue. "There. Where was I? Oh yes, I would like a bit of time to consider where to put the focus and, in the meantime, I think it is time we try a more hands-on approach with regard to your hallucinations."

Daryl did not like the sound of that. Up until now, their sessions had centered around her attempts at understanding all the aspects of what she had admitted was an unusual and very complex case. Near-complete amnesia, hallucinations, and paranoid psychosis were apparently a rare mix.

Susan withdrew a small circular mirror from the briefcase beside her chair. Daryl froze, pointedly not looking at the mirror, but also not taking his peripheral vision off the object in her hand.

"I think we should begin with addressing your fear of mirrors and work our way from there."

"Oh, I don't have a fear of mirrors," he said, carefully keeping his emotions in check. "I have a fear of monsters appearing in mirrors and attacking me."

Susan's eyes caught his and held them. "Nothing is going to attack you," she said with a finality that almost had him believing her. She leaned forward offering the mirror to him. "If you don't do this, I can't help you."

You picked a hell of a day, Daryl thought as he hesitantly reached out and, without looking, snatched the mirror from her hand.

"You can do this," she said. "When you're ready."

Daryl adjusted his seat. Looking in the mirror held all the appeal of peeing on an electric fence. Well, at least with her here it was less likely that he would get electrocuted. Without giving it any more thought, he held up the mirror and looked.

Susan's office looked back at him. His eyes toured the room. Nothing there.

Except for the two large, scaly hands settling on either side of his chair. He heard a low-pitched growl from somewhere behind him. His hands grew white from clutching the mirror and armrest; his breathing accelerated.

"Whatever you're seeing, just ignore it," Susan said. "I promise you it will go away."

Daryl forced his eyes away from the hands, which seemed inches from his exposed throat. He shifted his gaze to the picture on the back wall. A pastoral scene of a smiling couple standing in front of a tranquil-looking farmstead set in beautiful grasslands. A small part of his mind, not currently panicking, reminded him that these were Susan's foster parents. He kept his eyes there, counting down from ten. When he reached zero, he dared a glance at the backrest. The hands were gone.

Daryl slowly lowered the mirror with a shaky hand.

"Well done," she said. "That took a lot of courage. I believe that, given enough training, you'll soon be able to ignore them on your own and maybe, in time, be rid of this fear altogether."

Daryl looked up at her. She was smiling warmly at him, and he thought he detected a sliver of pride, perhaps for them both.

"I think that's enough for today," she said. "Next time we'll try with me leaving the room."

Oh joy, he thought, absently rubbing his back.

CHAPTER 5

Following his session, Daryl was escorted to his quarters on the second floor without incident. Entering the austere room, his gaze was habitually drawn to the wall behind his bed, which was richly decorated with hand-drawn images of a sweet-looking girl of about six. Most were of her smiling back at him, but his favorite was the one of her pouting. For the hundredth time, he wondered why. Ginny.

He went to the desk and sat down, absently leafing through the sketches of her that had not made it onto the wall. Smiling, smiling, scared. He stopped, closing his eyes. This was his least favorite. Sadly, he knew why. He had failed her. No details came, but of that, he was certain. For the hundredth time, he wept.

"Looking at pictures again, are we?" Hubble was sitting on the edge of Daryl's bed, his short, stubby feet dangling over the side gently tapping the frame, drumming a steady rhythm Daryl was just now noticing.

"Yeah," he answered flatly, still hollow from remembered pain bereft of context.

"What's Susie saying about me these days?" Hubble asked.

"Oh, she still thinks that you're an imaginary coping mechanism created by a need for emotional support during my alienation due to paranoid psychosis and amnesia," Daryl answered, putting the drawings back in their folder.

"She sure knows how to put a guy down."

"I suspect she does," Daryl said with a faint smile. "Maybe you're just not her type."

Hubble looked quizzically at him. "Nonsense, I would rock her world."

Daryl smiled despite himself.

"You look like you could use some cheering up," Hubble continued, launching himself onto the floor. "Come on, I have a surprise for you."

Intrigued, Daryl turned fully from the desk to face Hubble.

"Where are we going?" he asked.

"I told you—it's a surprise," Hubble answered, grabbing hold of Daryl's right hand. "We'll have to go through the Dark."

"Wait, what?" was all he got out before Hubble started rapidly descending through the floor with Daryl in tow.

***

Daryl landed butt-first in near-pitch blackness. As his sense of vertigo faded, he gradually began to discern dark gray shapes.

"Pretty cool, huh?" Hubble whispered from somewhere to his right.

"I bet you take all your dates here," Daryl answered.

"Only the ones with advanced paranoid psychoses." Now somewhere on his left. "Keep your voice down and follow directly behind me. Come on, this way."

Daryl followed Hubble's voice through the maze of irregular dark gray shapes across a blessedly even floor. The timbre of the faint echoes of their passage rose and fell, giving the impression that the halls or chambers they moved through varied greatly in size.

The walk in the Dark concluded as Hubble announced their arrival by grabbing Daryl's hand and walking them through a gray shape directly into a dimly lit cave. Four lanterns were placed around the perimeter of the cave, two of which outlined the wide, low-ceilinged exit, through which a few stars could be seen in the darkening sky. In the center of the cave were two high-backed chairs positioned on either side of a round wooden table with a chess board engraved into the surface. Against the right wall stood a large metal-banded chest.

"Check it out," Hubble said as Daryl took a few steps into the cozy tableau.

The chest was held partly open by a metal rod supporting the lid off the rim. Inside were several bottles of liquor, a small water-pipe, two metal canisters of lamp oil, a storm lighter, and what appeared to be a boxed set of carved wooden chess pieces. Daryl moved toward the mouth of the cave and looked out onto a panoramic view of a darkening sky above a black, storm-tossed sea. A narrow stone shelf jutted out, beyond which was a nearly vertical drop into the frothing waves crashing against the jagged rocks far below. In the rapidly gathering dusk, he could barely make out a small inlet far to his left, sheltering a pier and a few houses.

Turning around, he saw Hubble looking expectantly at him. "This is amazing," he said. "How did you find this place?"

A grin of satisfaction spread across the gnome's wide face. "Oh, it wasn't that difficult. I thought you might enjoy a game every now and then, away from people who think you're crazy for playing with your imaginary friend."

Daryl's gratitude must have been plain because Hubble waved a hand at him as he walked to the chest and pulled out the liquor and chess set. "Okay, okay. Don't get all dewy eyed on me now."

Several games of chess and a dulling amount of rum later, they sat relaxing in their chairs, passing the water-pipe back and forth while looking out over the roiling ocean.

"Thanks for the warning this morning," Daryl said.

"What warning?" Hubble asked, still with a faraway look in his eyes.

"You know, when you signaled me in the hallway."

Hubble looked over at him with an odd expression on his face. "I was letting you know that my pet chicken just died."

Daryl looked briefly over at Hubble, then back out to sea. "Oh, I'm sorry to hear that."

CHAPTER 6

For one fleeting moment, Daryl recognized the dream for what it was and recoiled in terror. Then his subconscious took control and there was only the dream.

Coffee and pancakes. A slow morning like so many others, if not for the conflict within him demanding resolution. Yesterday morning's contentment seemed a lifetime ago. Today the anger was back, choking the joy from his mind faster than the morning could deliver it. Wrist—flip. The pancake settled neatly back in the skillet, emitting what should have been a satisfying sizzle. Wisps of cloud were visible through the kitchen window, and the beautiful day did what it could to distract him. It was not nearly enough. The anger beckoned, and he would heed its call. They were going to pay dearly for what they did.

"Dad?" she said from the tall kitchen counter behind him.

His mind tilted at the sound of her voice. Like a pinball machine someone kicks to get the ball rolling again . . . But he did not turn around. It was not time yet.

"Yes, Ginny?" he answered, flipping the pancake onto the awaiting stack and buttering up the pan for the last time.

"Who was the woman that visited?"

Now he turned. She sat hunched over her coloring books, an expression of quiet concentration on her face. The yellow crayon was doing long, closely spaced sweeps up and down. Hair perhaps?

"She's an old friend."

Ginny put the crayon down on the tabletop and rotated on her bum to face him. Her brown shoulder-length curls framed her freckled face, which had slipped into a frown so earnest it had to belong to a child. He instinctively knew not to look into her terrible eyes. He could not remember what waited there—nor did he want to.

"Are you going away then?" she asked.

"I'm not sure. But don't worry. I will only be gone for a few days."

"I suppose," she said.

"I could just stay," he tried, wanting this to be it. "It's not that important."

She shook herself, like a dog drying its coat.

"Dad," she said imploringly, "please don't make me show you again."

A shiver ran down his spine. "No, of course," he said quickly. "No need for that."

"Why did you go?"

"I . . ." he halted, unsure. "I thought I could have both."

"And then what happened?"

"I . . ." His mind blanked, and he looked out the window, petrified.

"You have to face this, it's not—" The pitch of her voice rose in alarm. "The butter is burning!"

Daryl whipped around, depositing the smoking skillet at the back of the stove before cranking up the extractor hood.

"Thanks," he said, about to turn back around.

The sound of small feet pattered across the floor, coming for him.

"This is not how it happened," she said from right next to him, the accusation in her voice like a discordant note, slashing the air. He knew what was coming, fearing it with every fiber of his being. Still, her voice ignited a deep ache to turn around and hold her, but he knew that was impossible.

The smoke from the burned butter grew in intensity, and he looked down. The tabletop was beginning to char. Wisps of smoke were gently rising from the crack where the counter met the wall. She jumped onto the tabletop, bringing herself level with him, reaching out for him with arms starting to blister from the heat.

His vision was blurring, as if sweat was dripping into his eyes, and his mind reeled. She grabbed him, causing him to stumble and seize hold of the now smoldering counter.

"Dad," she said softly.

He tried to resist, but she forcibly turned him around, facing her. Facing those terrible eyes . . . eyes which held the truth.

"No," he muttered.

"Listen."

"Please no," he repeated meekly.

She leaned in as if to speak, but instead opened her mouth wide and screamed. It tore through everything, cutting at his very soul. He knew why she screamed. He knew . . . Daryl felt a sudden sharp pain in his mouth, followed by a jolt as the dream receded. His surroundings grew foggy, her face retreating down a well. The dream dwindling, dwindling, gone.

He groggily rolled out of bed and went to his desk to retrieve the tissues there. He pulled one out of the cardboard box and wiped the red saliva from his lips. His tongue throbbed where his teeth had torn into it. As always, when dreaming of Ginny, all he remembered was her face— a faded photograph from a long-lost past.

He sat down and began to draw a smiling girl, looking up as if to speak, crayon in hand. He wondered what she had been drawing and what the look on her face meant. *What were you about to say?* he thought with a smile. Sad to be missing her, but glad to remember this much.

***

He lay back in bed for ten minutes before concluding that he was done sleeping for the night. Getting up, he put on a robe before leaving his room to make his nocturnal rounds. Patients were not allowed on other floors at night, but there was no regulation on moving around on your own floor, at least not on the lower levels. He had devised a routine that avoided reflective surfaces while letting him tour most of the available area. Of course, that routine had to be continuously modified these days, as workers had begun hanging plastic sheets to cover corridors in need of attention.

At night, the old asylum took on a solemn atmosphere, which bore a semblance to something he felt he could almost remember. He made his circuitous route from his quarters in the east wing toward the west wing, noting new canvasing and a scaffold along the back wall of one of the corridors in the neighboring wing. He rarely encountered anyone else on his walks, but nearing a turn, he heard a voice from an intersecting corridor. Rounding the corner, he saw a young, rotund woman walking toward him. He recognized her as a resident.

"No, I know that dear, but what do you want me to do about it?" she said to no one, looking to her left at the bare wall.

He had occasionally seen her walking about by herself at night, but she had always ignored him in favor of these one-sided conversations. This time she looked up as he approached and gave him an uncertain smile.

Daryl returned the smile. "Hi. What are you doing up at this hour?"

"Am I up?" she said, instantly making Daryl regret engaging her. It could be difficult to know how much sense to expect from a fellow patient. In this case the answer appeared to be not much. However, she had come to a stop and appeared to be expecting an answer to her question. *Great.*

"Well, you're awake like me," he responded. "Did you have a bad dream?"

"Oh, how nice," she said, smiling with more confidence. She was quite pretty, he realized. "What makes a dream bad?"

Before Daryl had a chance to find a good answer to that, she turned her attention back to the wall.

"I know that, but I wanted Daryl to answer," she said, apparently annoyed with someone.

"How do you know my name?"

"Well, this place is pretty centered on you, isn't it?" she asked, making a sweeping motion with her arms.

"Erm, not really."

An uncomfortable silence stretched between them. Well, uncomfortable for Daryl as the woman simply stood, hands at her sides, staring at him expectantly.

"So, what's your name?" he asked in an attempt to jump-start the conversation into something he could reasonably exit.

"Felicia," she said, still looking at him with unabashed interest.

"What are you doing walking around at night?"

"He prefers speaking to me while I'm alone."

"Sorry to interrupt," he said, thinking this was the cue he had hoped for.

"Oh, don't be silly," she said with a girlish giggle. "You obviously don't count."

"Obviously," Daryl said with little enthusiasm. "Who prefers it?"

"Bill-Din."

Realizing he was not getting the gracious getaway he had hoped for, he turned partly back the way he had come. "Well, I should be getting back. Try to catch some sleep."

"Oh okay," she said. "Nice talking to you, Daryl."

On the way back to his rooms, he realized that he had never answered her question. What makes a dream bad?

CHAPTER 7

Daryl was awakened by tolling bells from the corridor speaker system. The nighttime excursion had left its mark, and he sleepily got out of bed and put on his robe before heading to the shower room two doors down. The bathrooms were functioning again, and he washed himself, deftly avoiding all mirrors. Then he wrapped himself in a robe and returned.

As he left his room, his usual cheeriness had reasserted itself, and his thoughts were gravitating to that imminent first cup of coffee. Then he saw Bor exit his room and notice him. Bor was a big, dark brute of a man who, for some reason, had always hated Daryl. As Daryl passed his door, Bor fell into step.

"You look like shit," Bor charmingly asserted.

"Thanks," Daryl replied, optimistically hoping that was all the witty banter Bor needed to meet his anti-Daryl quota.

"I bet you've wondered why I don't like you," Bor continued.

Daryl sighed, his good mood evaporating as he wondered whether Bor was going to succeed in escalating the situation to a fight this time.

"Not really, you'd be surprised how little I think about

you."

Bor scowled but continued as if he had not spoken. "It's because you don't care about the people around you getting hurt. Spreading your bullshit and getting everyone all worked up."

The comment stung. Surprisingly so.

Sensing weakness, Bor strode ahead and stretched an arm across the cafeteria door, partly blocking the way.

"Monsters in mirrors trying to kill you?" Bor scoffed. "What makes you so special, huh?"

Daryl let out a slow breath and beamed a smile at him.

"I just don't remember," he said pleasantly.

Bor looked ready to punch him. "That supposed to be funny?"

An orderly was making his way toward them. Daryl kept the smile on his face as he gently pushed Bor's arm out of the way.

"See you later," Bor said menacingly as Daryl slipped inside.

Daryl sighed—*Making friends every day.*

***

It was early and the dining hall was still sparsely occupied. He noticed Felicia sitting primly by herself at a corner table. Walking toward her, he waved merrily at Bor who had wasted no time in getting to the buffet, loading an already overburdened plate with food. He did not see Bor's response as he came to a stop at Felicia's table.

"Mind if I join you while I gather an appetite?" he asked her.

"Sure," she said, keeping her gaze on him while he sat. Daryl decided to play out a hunch.

"I think a bad dream is when you're asleep and something bad happens."

As he had guessed, she did not miss a beat. "So, you don't know it's a bad dream till something bad happens?"

"I suppose the feel of the dream might tip you off."

"So, you know from the beginning if a dream is going to be bad?"

"Well, kind of," he said. "But I don't think you would necessarily realize it until you wake up."

This seemed to sadden her. She looked down at her plate as if considering which of her morning snacks to bite into next. The silence stretched on for a bit.

"I never know," she finally said.

"Never know if it's going to be a bad dream?"

"No. I never know if I'm dreaming."

"Is that why you're here?"

"Pretty much. I see a lot of things the doctors tell me aren't real."

"Yeah, I know what that's like," Daryl said. Felicia appeared to be a lot more coherent than he had originally thought she would be, and he was glad he had continued their conversation from last night.

"Of course," she said. "They're here for you, you know."

The room seemed suddenly chilly and Daryl suppressed a shiver.

"How do you know that?" he asked.

"Bill-Din told me," she said matter-of-factly.

"And who is that again?"

"That's what he calls himself. He is this place. He tries to help, but normally he is just too slow." She quickly corrected herself, "Not stupid, mind you. Just not very quick. Most of the time."

"Are you saying you're speaking with the building?" he asked her, suddenly realizing he might have misunderstood the name she had given him.

"Articles are the worst. People complain about labels, but those articles are just plain dehumanizing! Anyway, he is trying to help me with my condition."

"With the dreams?"

"Not really. He says I have a piece of the universe stuck in my brain."

"Bummer," Daryl said.

Felicia looked knowingly at him, her head slowly nodding along to his last statement.

The dining hall had been slowly filling with hungry patients, and Daryl noticed that Bor had vacated the buffet, seating himself in a corner by himself. He also saw that Werner was doing his utmost to best Bor's previous efforts at the buffet, stacking a plate with food. Excusing himself from Felicia, Daryl walked up to Werner, grabbing a plate along the way.

"Morning," Daryl said.

"Ah, good morning," Werner responded. He had the gaunt physique of a much older guy, making Daryl wonder what happened to all the food he was frequently ingesting. His bespectacled nose was perched above a wide grinning mouth. He was, without a doubt, the happiest paranoid schizophrenic that Daryl knew.

"Will you be joining us for breakfast?" he asked.

"I thought I might," Daryl answered.

"Splendid," Werner said, turning from the buffet. "See you at the table."

Daryl scooped some oatmeal and toast onto his plate before filling a glass with orange juice and a cup with steaming hot coffee. Looking around, he quickly found the center table, where Werner was speaking with three other patients. Daryl recognized Raphael and Swati. The third patient was new.

As Daryl neared the table, Werner broke off from the discussion, extending an arm in an exaggerated gesture of welcome.

"Ah, here he is."

"Wassup," Daryl said. The grandiose welcome was classic Werner and in dire need of being taken down a notch.

Raphael and Swati both returned Daryl's greeting. The third guy was a handsome blond man in his early thirties. He nodded uncertainly in Daryl's direction.

"So, Tim here is new to the second floor," Werner said. Turning to face Tim, he continued, "Daryl has the dubious pleasure of receiving the bulk of paranormal attention around here. They have made physical contact with him on no less than three occasions."

"Four," Daryl corrected.

Werner's eyes narrowed, "Are you okay?"

"I'm fine," he responded. "And I'll tell you all about it once I've had some food and my coffee."

"Of course, my boy," Werner said. "Tim, who is your primary caretaker?"

"Doctor Peterson," Tim said. "I was moved down here from the third floor a week ago, and I was allowed to keep my therapist."

"You were on the third floor?" Swati said. "What's it like?"

Tim shifted in his seat. "Kind of similar to here," he said. "Except there are no common areas, and no one leaves their room unescorted. I . . . really wasn't well when I first came here. But I am feeling a lot better."

"And congratulations with that," Werner said. "I have heard good things about Doctor Peterson."

Werner looked at each of them in rapid succession, his eyes lingering slightly on Raphael.

"I'd like to remind everyone here that we're all friends," he continued emphatically.

Various forms of assent made its rounds. Raphael mumbled, Swati grunted, and Tim smiled uncertainly.

"Tim is another physicist," Werner exclaimed. "From the Perimeter Institute."

Everyone looked expectantly at Raphael, who immediately blurted, "Really? What did you study?"

"Well, loop quantum gravity," Tim replied reluctantly. The tension at the table was palpable, and Tim was probably smart enough to guess why.

"Hah!" Raphael grunted. "You're one of them loopy goofs!"

"Rapha!" Werner interjected forcefully and the table fell eerily quiet. Werner had a veiled intensity about him that was sometimes downright scary. Daryl had only witnessed it a few times, but even this pale shadow of Werner's temper gave him goose bumps. Something stirred at the back of his mind, and he suddenly thought he caught a whiff of sawdust and horse dung.

Daryl shook his head and glanced at Werner just as the other's face mellowed.

"As I said—we are all friends here."

Tim made a conciliatory gesture. "Are all of you physicists then?"

Only Raphael and Swati nodded. Tim's eyes turned to Werner and Daryl.

"Almost certainly not," Daryl laughed.

"Daryl has amnesia," Werner interjected. "And yes, I too have been a student of physics. I find that physicists have a natural openness to new ideas about how the cosmos may work and what sort of place the supernatural might reasonably be expected to fill." He paused, a wide grin spreading. "At least the physicists that end up here."

Everyone chuckled at that, even Raphael.

For the remainder of breakfast, the four of them chatted amiably about the asylum. The doctors, the other patients, and the boring food. Mostly about the food. The other patients left one by one for their scheduled activities, and as soon as they were alone Werner insisted on being briefed fully on Daryl's recent experience. Daryl complied.

They both stood, and as they were walking to the door, Daryl stole a quick glance at Felicia. The horrified expression on her face stopped him in his tracks. Her eyes seemed partly glazed over, looking beyond him. He slowly turned back around, facing the door. Nothing was there.

"What's wrong, Daryl?" Werner asked, looking back at him.

Daryl suppressed another shiver as he resumed walking. *They're here for you, you know.*

"Nothing, I'm fine."

CHAPTER 8

Daryl floated, face and chest above the waterline, in a dark sea beneath a cloudless sky. The numerous stars above him wove a dazzling carpet of light that made his heart ache. His whole body turning slowly counterclockwise in the still water, he noticed a stygian splotch of sky on the horizon. As it drew his attention a jagged light kissed the sky and, seconds later, a muffled boom reached his ears, reverberating across the still surface. This was when he realized that he was not alone in the water. A cold current swept against him from below as something huge moved beneath him. He was rocked rhythmically by the resultant swells, his eyes trying to penetrate the pitch-black waters.

A shiver ran down his spine as he imagined a sudden chomp of razor-sharp teeth. Bending his knees and kicking, he was able to submerge his torso in exchange for getting his head above water. Something briefly broke the surface to his far right and a ripple started making its way toward him, gaining speed.

He flailed to his left, beginning a frantic crawl away from whatever was rapidly approaching just beneath the surface. Between panicked breaths of tangy air, he absently noticed he was heading straight for the storm, which seemed much closer now. He risked a glance backward. The ripples were gone.

He stopped and choked out a salty mouthful of seawater, which he had nearly inhaled during his mad dash. He felt another current sweep by below and to his left. This one so strong he was unsure whether something had brushed against his foot.

Then the storm hit full force and he lost track of his position relative to anything else as the agitated waters threw him spinning and bobbing. Dark clouds occluded the previously ample starlight as gale-force winds stole the quiet tranquility. Lightning streaked across the sky, briefly illuminating a cloud here and a wave there. A huge swell lifted him, breaking with him at its zenith, and plunged him through the darkness toward the waters below.

The winds buffeted him as he fell, spinning out of the sky. Pain lanced across his shoulder blades, and he arched his back, trying to get his hands behind him. They came away sticky. The next streak of lightning showed him the blood running freely down his hands and arms. Something white blew away on the screaming winds.

"Yes," the winds seemed to howl at him. He shook his head, but the sensory overload only increased.

He leaned into the pain still dancing across his back, and focused on it till it became almost unbearable. Closing his eyes, he shut out the winds and the cold, the howling and the booms, till all that was left was the arrhythmic flash from the lightning penetrating his eyelids. A presence pushed against his newfound calm, and he pushed back hard till the pain in his back made his eyes water.

The intermittent blinking continued, but the air turned still and stagnant. He slowly opened his eyes. He stood in a familiar basement corridor in front of the restroom door. Opening the door with one hand, he entered the short corridor and walked across the tiled floor toward the leftmost bathroom stall. Out of the corner of his eye, he noticed violent movement in the mirror on his left. Something powerful and angry, like a feathered serpent poised to strike.

Coming to the stall, he slowly pushed open the door, inch by inch, revealing a lacerated corpse sitting slumped over on the toilet bowl. The man appeared to be dressed all in white, although the actual color was difficult to tell from the amount of blood that had seeped into the fabric. His back was mangled to a bloody pulp, and a thick, green puss oozed lazily from several puncture wounds.

Daryl felt bile rising in the back of his throat, and he let his eyes drift to where the man's dangling arms touched the floor. A rat was silently drinking from the puddle of blood, which had collected around the foot of the toilet.

Impossibly, the man stirred, and a weak gurgling sound escaped his throat. Daryl bent down and grabbed hold of the bloody shirt in an attempt to right him, but the man turned of his own volition, staring into Daryl's eyes with a haunted, pained expression.

Daryl knew him. He was . . . he was . . .

"I am sorry, son," the man said as blood bubbled and frothed on his lower lip and chin. Then his head lolled forward.

Daryl woke with a start, hands still clenching his father's blood-soaked clothes. Perspiration beaded his brow as he took several deep breaths, trying to steady himself. The dream dissipated, leaving his hands to slowly release his wrinkled, sweaty bed sheets. He sat up, rubbing his face with the palms of his hands. Choking back the terror of the dream, he stood and made his way to the desk. He sat down and started to draw.

CHAPTER 9

"What do *you* think it means?" Susan said, in a perfect cliché meant to lighten the somber mood into which Daryl had drifted.

For some reason, the lack of memories often buoyed Daryl into a good-natured care-free attitude, but the recurrent terrors, awake or asleep, were exacting a heavy toll, and Daryl was beginning to feel his usual good mood losing ground.

Daryl glanced at the sketches he had drawn upon awakening—fragments devoid of context. It had been Susan's idea to begin documenting his dreams, and they had proven an invaluable primer for their sessions. His dream, so vivid upon awakening, now had the feel of disconnected tableaus.

Daryl being hunted by something in the water.

Daryl falling.

Daryl's father dying.

"I don't know," he finally said, still staring at the final image.

"Do you think your father is dead?" she asked.

"Yeah, I do." Daryl could not tell how he knew, but he felt it to be true. Something foreign stirred at his statement, but finding no purchase within him it immediately scattered, leaving behind a faint yearning and a sudden throbbing headache.

"Do you remember anything else about him?"

"No," he said flatly. He had wracked his brain. It had seemed the right thing to do and he knew Susan would be sure to ask.

"Most psychoses have roots stemming from some form of childhood trauma," Susan said matter-of-factly.

"Maybe," Daryl said, looking up from the drawing. "What does it matter anyway?"

"It could all be linked in some way. Your childhood, your amnesia, Ginny."

The headache grew in intensity, like a white-hot poker to the brain.

"Leave her out of this," he said in a tone he barely recognized.

Susan blinked, an unfamiliar twitch of confusion crossing her face.

"Easy," she said, her hands held out placatingly. "I am trying to help you."

Daryl took a deep breath.

"Yes, of course," he answered. "Sorry."

"No, that's good. Your emotions are likely to be triggered whenever we discuss something of relevance to your situation."

"Of relevance?" he asked, shifting uncomfortably in his seat.

"What I mean is that your repressed emotions are likely tied directly to your trauma and memory loss. We will need it all to help you."

Daryl did not like that, but over the past few months he had grown to trust her judgment.

"So, what now, Doc?" he said.

"I think your dreams have just told us where we need to focus our first attempt with hypnotherapy."

***

Where are you, Daryl?
"I'm in the snow, following a track of boot prints."
Where does it lead?
"I don't know. It's so cold."
Remember! This place can't hurt you. It's not real anymore.

Daryl trudged on into the gloom of early evening. The pines on both sides of the tracks were covered in white. A cold wind carried eddies of fat, white sleet along with a mind-numbing chill.

The ground began to gradually rise as pines were replaced by oak and birch.

Suddenly the trees thinned, and he emerged into a clearing. A young boy knelt near the center. He was wearing simple indoor clothing and, even facing away from Daryl, it was evident that he was trembling. The boy's hands were clutching something that lay outstretched on either side of him. As Daryl stumbled nearer, he saw swathes of red surrounding the boy. Two bodies were splayed out in the center of each crimson fan, partly obscured by freshly fallen snow.

Somehow it did not seem right to disturb the boy without letting him know that he was there, so Daryl circled around the boy on his left.

The boy was mouthing something as he clutched feverishly at the hands emerging from the snow. What had appeared to be tremors caused by the cold now revealed themselves to be from exertion. White-speckled lightning pulsed from the kid's torso, streaming down his arms and merging with the hands he clutched as they emerged from the snow like gnarled roots. Controlled sobs escaped the boy's thin lips set in a rictus smile. Tears streaked down his cheeks.

As he entered the boy's field of vision, the boy opened his eyes to look at Daryl, who was struck by the knowledge that he was looking at his younger self.

"Please help them," the boy whispered, indicating the two prone figures by lifting their hands slightly toward Daryl.

"How?" he asked. The woman on the left lay still with her face buried in the snow. The man on the right groaned weakly and Daryl recognized the half-hidden features from his dream.

"Are they our parents?" he asked the boy.

The boy nodded. "I'm only strong enough to help one, and I can't choose. Please heal them," he pleaded, fresh tears streaking down his cheeks.

"I don't know how."

A feverish urgency took hold of the boy's features. "I can show you. Come, come!"

Daryl moved forward uncertainly to stand by the boy who resolutely entwined his fingers with Daryl's and placed them on the two bodies.

Sparks jumped between them as the boy closed his eyes again. A tingling spread from where their hands touched and raced up his arms. Like the boy, he no longer felt the cold. He was only vaguely aware of their surroundings. It was just the four of them. He somehow sensed that the boy was depleted. Perhaps even dying. Then he noticed the boy manipulating something within him. A dormant power swirled into familiar aspects. One aspect was a white, near-blinding glow that wanted to wipe clean and purify. The other was something else. Not as familiar and not as readily available, but vast and strong. Like the feeling of a nursery rhyme or a forgotten smell, revisited years into maturity. It wanted to heal, or perhaps more accurately, to live.

The boy drew on both with equal facility, and a ruddy glow spread from their hands to envelop the four of them.

Something rustled the branches at the edge of the clearing.

The boy's eyes snapped open, revealing wide, white circles of terror. "Oh no," he muttered, dread adding a tremor to his voice. . Then, in little more than a whisper he added. "Jae'el…"

Plumes of snow tumbled off branches, and a dark shape suddenly loomed just beyond that final row of trees. With a movement like a snake, it sidled into the clearing. It was Daryl, but somehow it looked nothing like him. The humanity was stripped away, leaving a grotesque shell. Hate and rage oozed from its every pore, made even more terrifying by the aura of raw power shrouding it like a cloak of madness. It lunged forward and cleared the distance to Daryl with unbelievable speed.

"You don't belong here," it bellowed in a surprisingly human voice and smacked into Daryl, flinging him back. It immediately halted his backward momentum by grabbing his collar, and Daryl's head snapped back from the whiplash.

The world disintegrated around him, and he slumped back into the comfortable chair in Susan's office.

They looked into each other's eyes as a silence stretched between them.

Susan put the pendulum she had used to put him under on the small table beside her.

"So, your parents are dead?" she finally said.

"Apparently," Daryl said numbly. He did not doubt that this had been based on a real memory. The internal echo was strong and more than a little tinged with grief.

"What happened at the end?" Susan asked.

"It seems I may be my own worst enemy," Daryl said.

"You don't say," Susan said gently. "It may be that your traumas and repressed memories are represented by the characters you encountered. The boy and the beast, if you will."

"So, you're saying I've been repressing memories for a while then?"

"Yes, it seems to be your mind's preferred coping mechanism. If the boy represents your childhood trauma, then it stands to reason that the beast might represent the trauma of whatever happened that brought you to us."

Daryl nodded numbly.

"What now?" he finally asked.

"Now we try the mirror again. Without me in the room."

***

Daryl got out of the elevator leading to the parlor. The orderlies escorting him said a peremptory goodbye for the day, but he barely noticed them. Therapy was finally going well. It seemed they were making real headway. Why was he more confused than ever?

Their experiments with his hallucinations had once again been a success. Even in Susan's absence he had been able to ignore the hallucinations, which had failed to attack him and had finally disappeared. He wanted badly to be free of his torment, to hope for the relief of this emergent cure, but something in him continued to resist. Was he simply not ready to admit to his illness, or was it something else, something more?

"Daryl. Over here."

He looked up, noticing Werner waving at him from across the room. Daryl joined him. Werner was holding court with his fellow philosophers, Robert and Swati.

"Ah Daryl. We were just discussing the implications of mirrors. For instance, how do we know that the mirrored world isn't as real as our own?" Werner asked, looking expectantly to Robert, probably waiting for him to reiterate a previous point.

"Well, as I was just pointing out," Robert complied, "it is really only our egocentric worldview that leads us to the conclusion that what we are seeing in the mirror is a reflection of us and not the other way around. We perceive our desire to move and observe the appropriate response in our reflection. What if our so-called desires to move and our expectations of the behavior of mirrored objects and people are actually predicated upon unknown physical principles rather than free will? Doesn't that mirror, if you will, the deterministic quicksand upon which free will has been erected?"

"Well, as *I* was saying," Swati jumped in with poorly concealed annoyance, "if that were true, we would all disappear once we left our reflections behind."

"Not so," Robert continued, unperturbed. "If we imagine the mirrors as doorways or windows, it is entirely possible that we move from mirror to mirror in accordance with whatever universal principle that governs us. A mirror world could be exactly like ours, leading us to expect it would behave exactly the same. Or it might only reproduce parts of our world."

Werner had leaned back, obviously enjoying the exchange. Daryl thought it very likely he had orchestrated the discussion. He had himself been drawn into his fair share of these when he first came here. Indeed, the mirror discussion was an old favorite of Werner's, stemming from Daryl's descriptions of his encounters, and it was about the only one that Werner never actively participated in. Since then, several other patients had begun experiencing episodes relating to reflective surfaces, but nowhere near as frequent or violent as what Daryl often went through. Susan thought this was due to Daryl's unintentional influence on the other patients.

"Yes yes," Swati allowed. "But physics explains mirror images nicely through reflection of light waves on special surfaces. You're just enjoying—"

"Oh please. That is no explanation." Robert interrupted. "It's a description at best. Reflective surfaces could just as easily, by their nature, be emitting reciprocal light waves coming from the other side as the ones from this side pass through."

"PRE—" Swati yelled, then continued in a much more subdued voice, "—posterous."

They all glanced at the orderlies by the entrance who briefly looked their way before turning their attention elsewhere again.

"Gentlemen, I think we can all agree these are hypotheticals, but what do you think about situations where the mirror suddenly no longer accurately reflects our world?" Werner interjected.

The statement lingered unanswered for several seconds. Robert had an uneasy air about him. Swati looked decidedly queasy. They had all heard Daryl's stories.

Except Tim.

"Maybe the two worlds are slightly out of sync? If a perfect connection exists, or can be made to exist, then a flawed connection could probably be produced as well."

"Exactly," Robert said with renewed interest. "If my argument is true, then the perfect reflective nature of a mirror could serve as an anchor point, presenting a steady-state connection which could probably be perturbed in any number of ways."

"Like a wormhole. A space-time manifold connecting two or more world branes," Tim said.

"Well, yes," Robert said with surprise. "That's hardly loop quantum gravity."

"We take an inclusive approach at the Perimeter Institute," Tim replied with a faint smile. "But none of this explains why the world brane interactions would be confined to physical mirrors or . . ." he paused pensively, "to put it differently, what such a steady-state anchor point represents in the bulk of the multiverse."

Swati got up and left.

"Come on Swati," Robert tried half-heartedly.

"Was it something I said?" Tim said.

"Some things just hit too close to home for some people," Werner said cheerily. Robert squirmed and got up to follow Swati. Tim just looked at them in turn, confusion plastered across his face.

"Let's have a game of chess," Werner interjected into the emergent silence, grabbing Daryl by the shoulder.

"Sure," Daryl said, letting Werner lead him to the two seats by the window.

Werner was neither very good nor very interested in chess. So, it was no great surprise when the real reason for dragging Daryl away surfaced.

"I saw something," Werner said smugly.

Daryl looked up from setting up the board. "You saw what?" he asked with apprehension.

"A dark mist, sifting through the cracks in the mortar. It began coalescing into some kind of . . ."

"You fool!" Daryl blurted. "What were you doing in the basement?"

"I came prepared," Werner continued unabashedly. "And besides, the staff room was right around the corner."

"Not the push scooter," Daryl said incredulously.

"I had just greased the wheels," Werner answered with a hint of indignation.

The bright green push scooter was something of a trademark of Werner's. He had been allowed to keep it for reasons Daryl had never fully understood. Perhaps the fact that Werner was very docile if humored, and also a fervent user of the small panda-shaped horn mounted on the handlebar, had led the staff to accept the inherent danger of broken limbs.

"What did you do?" Daryl asked with some foreboding.

"Well, I ran of course," Werner said with a smile. "I'm not insane you know."

"Please don't sneak down there again," Daryl said. "You should know how dangerous it is."

"I do," Werner said emphatically. "I want to avoid them as much as the next guy, but I think it's important that you know it isn't all directed at you. The implications . . ." he trailed off, looking Daryl up and down. "What's happened?" he asked, needlessly adjusting his glasses.

Daryl was not sure what to tell him. Being able to confide in someone who was both indisputably real and believed him had helped keep up his spirits during his stay at the asylum. Not to mention that Werner's good spirits always rubbed off on him during their talks. He realized he had come to think of him as a friend. He sighed.

"Susan has been helping me ignore the visions," Daryl said.

"Well, that's her job," Werner answered, missing the point entirely.

"It's been working," he continued.

Werner looked skeptically at him. "What do you mean?"

"I mean it seems that when I ignore the visions, they disappear," he said, inwardly flinching. Werner had invested much of himself in this aspect of Daryl's psychosis. This for reasons known only to Werner, but for which Daryl had been very grateful. Daryl felt an odd sense of betrayal in speaking even these tentative statements of denial.

"That's very interesting," Werner said, a furrow appearing between his eyes.

Daryl's mind reset. "What? Why?" he mumbled.

"I think you should be very careful when dealing with Susan," Werner answered with a thoughtful look on his face. "She is not to be trusted."

Daryl was not surprised at the statement. Werner had previously made it clear where he stood on certain aspects of Daryl's treatment, but going along with the sentiment was probably not a good way to further his progress with Susan.

"I think she is genuinely helping me," he said.

Werner looked at him with mild disappointment, like a father who already knows who broke the vase but dislikes the confirmation none-the-less.

"I see," he replied. "Maybe I'll have to go it alone for a bit, hmm?"

Daryl studied Werner's face for any signs of rejection. He did not like leaving it like this.

"Maybe you're just crazy?" Daryl offered by way of gently prompting Werner into further discussion.

"Yes maybe," Werner said cheerily. "A distinct possibility."

"And maybe the doctors here can help you with that?" he continued, trying to prod Werner from merry agreement into contemplation.

"And why on earth would I want that?" he answered, with a look on his face that suggested this was the first truly insane suggestion he had heard all day.

CHAPTER 10

Following Werner's departure, Daryl remained in his chair, distractedly looking out the window. His upper back was starting to become noticeably raw from the absent-minded scratching he habitually engaged in when lost in thought.

Of course, it would be ridiculous to expect Werner to accept the implications of Daryl's recent experiences in therapy. Werner had embraced Daryl's visions with a fervor that had both surprised and, eventually, concerned him, and he did not want to see his friend hurt. He especially did not want to be the cause. Not even if it meant being rid of the terrors that plagued him? If he could be free of his visions, they could not be real, could they? And if they were not real, how could they hurt anyone?

His mind drifted back in time . . . Nearly as far as he could go unassisted.

***

"I see . . . things," Daryl said uncertainly, looking away from Doctor Walker.

"What things?" she responded in a friendly tone,

reaching for her cup of tea. In their first session she had confided that she did not drink coffee. *Her loss,* he thought dryly.

He had only just arrived at the asylum and was still getting used to being a patient. This was his fifth session with Doctor Walker, and he had already come to like her. He did not believe anyone could be this frank and earnest without truly caring. She seemed to live for helping her patients. In fact, he liked her enough not to want her to know just how crazy he was. If that made any sense.

"Monsters," he responded unenthusiastically.

Susan seemed to take the revelation in her stride. "And what do these monsters want with you?"

"I'm not sure. It varies," he said giving his back a quick scratch.

She moved her feet onto the footstool between them, leaving ample room for his. He recognized the invitation to share space as a way to increase the informality of their sessions, but still moved his feet up next to hers. It was just nice.

"Do you see them often?" she asked.

"Yeah, it started the first week, but it's gotten a lot worse since then. They're in the mirrors," he admitted with a sigh.

"Well, that's not the worst place for them to be, I suppose," she said with a reassuring smile.

"Oh, they come out of the mirrors too," he said, sighing again. "They want to pull me to the other side."

"And what's on the other side of the mirror?"

"Oh, someplace nice I'm sure," he replied with a shudder.

***

As it turned out, an answer to that very question would find him the following day.

He had been tasked with polishing the windows of the second-floor parlor. Having not yet accepted the lack of memories, his mind ached from unsuccessful attempts at remembering. The constant movement of cleaning felt good. He heard a door shutting and looked up to find himself unexpectedly alone. Scanning the parlor, he caught sight of his reflection in the pristine panes of glass. The late afternoon sun no longer provided much light, and in the growing shadows he noticed himself staring back from the windows. Behind him hulked a huge six-limbed hound, already stealing toward him. Their eyes met and the beast lunged forward. The clacking of claws on the linoleum floor was mixed with the sounds of toppling chairs and tables being pushed out of the way. He bolted, trying to cut across the room toward the only door closer to him than to the hexapedal nightmare. A guttural growl right behind him made him fling himself across the final table between himself and the exit. He landed in a crouch, feet already propelling him the final few feet to the door. His hand closed around the doorknob as jaws bit into the fabric covering his left leg. He gave a yelp as he was unceremoniously yanked off his feet, then pulled skidding, left-foot-first, across the floor toward the nearest window.

He frantically tried grabbing a chair or table along the way, only to topple additional furniture. Within seconds the creature reached the window and jumped, Daryl in tow. He shielded his eyes against the impending blast of broken glass, but it never came. Daryl flailed as he plummeted downward. However, the twenty-foot drop to the gardens below also failed to materialize, and instead he came into almost immediate contact with an unyielding surface. The hound released him, and his forward momentum sent him tumbling and skidding across it. With a bang he rammed, back first, into the legs of a chair, pinning it against the side of a much heavier table. The table noisily slid several inches. Fire shot down Daryl's back where the furniture had mercilessly halted his advance. He groaned.

He shook his head, trying to clear it. The room looked... well, exactly like the one he had just occupied. A growl, so low pitched it was felt more than heard, made him turn his head. The immense dog was within arm's reach. Its teeth were bared beneath a ridged snout, twitching with barely restrained aggression. Deep-set red eyes fixed on him.

Moving with deliberate slowness, Daryl rolled onto his hands and knees, bringing him face to face with the salivating jaws. Somewhere in the direction from which he had arrived tumbling, he briefly registered a semi-circular section of window where the reflection of the room had gained an inexplicable amount of solidity. He began pushing his upper body backward at a glacial speed, straightening up from the floor.

As if unable to restrain itself any longer, the creature took a step forward. Its gums receded even further, and a string of purple spittle dripped from either side of the lower jaw. The growl rose in volume.

Daryl froze. He was caught in that uncomfortable crouch in between seated and fully erect where your thighs quickly start to tingle. His mind, ever helpful, served up "good boy" to placate the two hundred pounds of hell hound. His imminent death was all that kept a smirk off his face.

"Good boy," someone proclaimed from behind him.

Daryl did not dare look away, but the voice seemed somewhat familiar. Courteous, with an undercurrent of undiluted malice.

As if on cue, a huge form lunged past him, then whipped around into a graceful crouch a mere twenty feet away. The ground hissed like water dropped on a hot skillet, and the immense cat-like outline shimmered slightly as if observed through a heat-haze. The thing straightened to reveal a graceful bipedal figure, tall enough to nearly touch the ceiling. It stared at him through slitted eyes of a pale red.

"I am Baal," it stated in a voice that seemed to echo within itself, resonating with the promise of a world of torture beyond the ken of mere mortals.

Daryl bowed his head, hoping against hope that his end

would be swift.

"You don't look away from me!" Baal boomed, causing Daryl to swiftly look back up. "I would have you begging for the mercy of death, not bowing your head like a cow to the slaughter!"

Daryl stumbled backward as a terrible anger rippled across Baal's hellish features. Anger mixed with something else. Perhaps disappointment.

"Get back here!" someone shouted by the window. The high-pitched outburst was accentuated by the flapping of wings and what could only be described as an equally furious squawk.

Daryl and Baal both turned toward the disturbance. A small man with big ears, in a brown and purple tunic, was chasing a large chicken that ducked and weaved between tables and chairs, apparently oblivious to the room's other occupants.

The small man lunged for the chicken, managing to get his hand around one of its clawed feet.

"Gotcha!" he exclaimed, as his small form was buffeted by the frantic thrashings of an enraged bird. The two rolled and half-flew toward Daryl and Baal, who both continued to stare in disbelief at the unexpected chicken-wrangling coming toward them.

The small man finally got both his hands around the body of the chicken, flattening the wings. With a groan and a "hah!" he pulled the chicken close and stood.

"Who are you?" Baal thundered at the small man whose triumphant smile was quickly replaced by a slack-jawed stare as the immense creature looked at him menacingly.

"Err . . ." he said, still clutching the chicken who seemed to have gone completely still with the hope of being ignored. "My name is Hubble," he said with a wan smile, "and this is Esmeralda."

It took Baal a few moments to process having been introduced to a chicken. The pale red of his eyes took on a luminescent sheen as they stared at the two newcomers, heat waves emanating from him and causing nearby tables and chairs to char.

Hubble backed up into Daryl, nearly dropping his chicken.

Baal opened his mouth to speak as Hubble grabbed Daryl's hand. "Bye," he said as the three of them vanished through the floor.

***

Daryl shook himself out of his reverie, returning to the present day. The memory was one of the primary reasons he had given up on pacing the parlor floor when thinking. Instead, he remained in his chair, where reflections would not reach him. He could not leave Werner to face the demons alone, no matter how inconvenient it might be for him. Even if they were not real, Werner's recent experiences meant that they clearly appeared real to him. That was enough.

CHAPTER 11

It had gotten late, and Daryl and the other patients remaining in the parlor were escorted back to their rooms for the night. He had intentionally showered earlier that day and now quickly went about making himself presentable. Or as presentable as institution-issue asylum-wear would permit. He slapped on antiperspirant. Then he put on a white, almost new, shirt over blue cotton pants without any obvious holes. He felt the freshly fabric stretch a bit across the chest and back as he combed his brown curls. The basics in place, he put a dark red flower he had swiped from a floral decoration through the buttonhole of his left shirt pocket. The whole process took longer than he had expected. Not only was this the only time he could remember primping, but he had to accomplish everything without a mirror.

"Well, lah-di-dah," Hubble exclaimed from behind, startling him.

"Hubble, goddamn it," Daryl said, turning around. Hubble had substituted his usually very colorful wardrobe for a near-black tunic. Daryl resumed the onerous task of buttoning his right shirt cuff.

"No really, you look good." Hubble said. "Not so sure

about the flower though."

"Too much?" Daryl asked.

"Too red. Perhaps something in a light blue?"

"The selection was rather limited," Daryl admitted, straightening his collar.

"Don't worry about it."

"Well, now I'm definitely not wearing it."

"Don't be silly. It completes the outfit."

"You implied it didn't fit."

"I was wrong."

"Like hell, imp."

"Don't start, psycho."

Daryl carefully removed the ill-matched flower, placing it on the bed. "It's good to see you," he said, smiling.

"Yeah, you too," Hubble answered. "We should go. We're running late."

***

The trip through the Dark was much longer this time, and Hubble once again made it clear they had to move with great care. Once Daryl had thoroughly lost track of time, Hubble stopped and pulled them into a huge, somberly lit cavern with a fire at the center. The blaze outlined a dozen or so silhouettes, and a delicious smell of roasting chicken permeated the air. Hubble took two quick steps forward, seemingly at a loss for words.

"What the . . . What are you . . ." he finally sputtered, looking at the skewered chicken rotating on a spit above the fire.

One of the figures separated from the group. It was a perfectly proportioned little woman with translucent wings who spread her hands wide in a conciliatory fashion, speaking sibilantly.

"Sssso sssorry," she began. "We've never cremated anytttthing before." A shamed susurrus of agreement accompanied her statement as several of the silhouetted crowd shifted uncertainly.

As she was no longer directly in front of the fire, Daryl could make out most of her beautiful features, which were currently set in a seemingly genuine expression of sadness and shame.

"You had one job," Hubble said through clenched teeth.

The crowd quickly pulled down the dead chicken, which was placed in a wooden box.

"We've dug a hole," the woman said in an apologetic fashion. "Perhaps we could bury her inssstead?"

Daryl diplomatically neglected to point out that the deceased was missing a drumstick.

***

Hubble gave a heartfelt eulogy in which the life of Esmeralda was lovingly celebrated. The somber mood at the wake was only slightly compromised by the delicious aromas still wafting through the air. Everyone around the grave looked appropriately saddened, although for some, the emotion clearly ran deeper than for others. As Hubble spoke, Daryl had the chance to study the creatures lining the small grave. There were a handful of other gnomes. Daryl could tell they were not Hubble but would have been hard-pressed to distinguish them from each other in a lineup. Short and gray with big ears seemed a universally apt description. The other large group consisted of short, black, demonic-looking creatures all wearing the expression of someone contemplating eating part of your anatomy in the near future. Some had wings and some merely looked like leaner, darker versions of Hubble. Then finally, there was a smattering of even odder-looking creatures. Some were fair, like the woman who had greeted them. Others wore an exotic mixture of fur and limbs. One being, apparently made from molten wax and a lot of red string, was downright freaky. The man of wax caught Daryl staring and gently touched a runny hand to his feathered fedora in greeting.

Daryl nodded back, hiding his discomfort behind the ritual of scratching his itching back.

Once the service was over and Esmeralda had been properly laid to rest, Hubble made his way over to where Daryl stood out, the proverbial sore thumb.

"Everyone is staring at me," Daryl said. "Especially the small . . . demons?"

"Just because you're paranoid, doesn't mean someone isn't watching you," Hubble said cheerily. "And they're imps."

"Imps?" Daryl said. "Wouldn't that make them, you know, evil?"

"Not everything that comes out of Hell is necessarily evil. Think of them as . . . overzealous pranksters."

"Yeah," Daryl replied slowly. He cast a furtive glance to his right, catching one of the imps leering at him. It winked, giving him a nasty grin.

Hubble had supplied the wake with copious amounts of what he called mildew—a berry-flavored, rather strong liquor served in odd, cone-shaped wooden beakers. Daryl was feeling the effects of the alcohol and was trying to keep up with a rapidly evolving "conversation" administered by a small woman in a red, pointy hat, who had introduced herself as Jamboree. Whenever he was beginning to get the gist of what she was saying, she took off in a new direction, never allowing his mind to settle on any coherent response to her colorful monologue. A sudden crack from one of the burning logs was followed by a jet of sparks spraying upward. Daryl instinctively stepped back a pace, bumping into another of the guests. The imp hissed at him, barring its fangs, and he took an involuntary step back, unsure of what to do.

The creature opened its mouth to speak when, out of nowhere, Hubble appeared, separating the two.

"No fighting," he declared while looking mostly at the frowning imp.

The imp looked about ready to protest, then cast a quick

look around, shrugged, and disappeared into the small crowd.

"Lovely," Daryl said.

"Don't worry about it," Hubble said. "It's just the drinks. Sets some people on edge."

Unconvinced, Daryl cast a quick look around at the leering imps.

"Anyway," Hubble continued. "I've been meaning to give you something." Reaching into a pouch tied to a string around his neck, he withdrew a piece of rock.

Daryl accepted it. Upon inspection it appeared to be composed of two slightly different rocks, which had somehow been fused together. The result was about half the length of his thumb and a bit wider.

"What is it?" Daryl asked.

"That's a little difficult to explain, but you could refer to it as a worldline or lodestone," Hubble replied. "It grants you access to the Dark through your room and through the cave, though you should be really careful if you want to try to go on your own."

"Thanks," Daryl said, touched by the gesture. Then a thought occurred to him. "If I went alone, then how would I find my way?"

"Not to worry. If you concentrate, you should feel the tug of the stone. Just follow that and it will take you back and forth."

Daryl was still scrutinizing the weird stone.

"Is it fragile?" he asked.

"Nope. You couldn't break that if you tried," Hubble replied smugly. "But I have to warn you, and this is really important, Daryl." The rare gravity in his voice caused Daryl to look down into the gnome's uncharacteristically solemn face.

"Never touch anything while you're in the Dark."

"Why not?" he asked.

"It attracts the Hunger," Hubble said with a shudder. "And what he finds, he devours."

"Got it. No touching."

"Listen, I may end up staying here for a while, so if you feel like it, you could take it for a spin tonight. Find your own way back."

Daryl pocketed the rock, considering his options. "I think I'll just wait for you."

"No problem," Hubble replied, some of his usual cheer returning. "Bottoms up."

CHAPTER 12

The following day, Daryl heroically ignored a profound hangover in his efforts to track down Werner. He was not at breakfast, not in his room, and not in the parlor. Guided by a vague sense of urgency, Daryl finally resorted to wandering the hallways at random but could find no trace of him.

It was not until Daryl was returning from an uninteresting group session that he heard the characteristic serial honking from Werner's scooter wafting faintly out from a side corridor. The corridor was blocked off by tape to prohibit traffic. Daryl ignored this, ducking under the tape and entering the gloom. His rapid passage was accompanied by the crackling of the paper floor covering. A branching corridor gave him pause, but by a stroke of luck Werner apparently had cause to resume honking at that point, and Daryl made the turn following the new corridor deeper into the bowels of the asylum.

"That's not Werner."

Daryl jumped, uttering a manly shriek.

The voice had been female and seemed to originate from one of the many adjoining rooms on the right side of the corridor. Daryl sidled up to the nearest door and peeked in.

Felicia was sitting in the center of the room facing the back wall. She was wearing a yellow, floral-patterned dress and looked completely out of place in the dreary, peeled interior.

"What do you mean?" he said, walking toward her.

She did not answer.

"Are you okay?" he asked, now only a few feet from where she was sitting.

Her head spun as she focused on him with an empty, alien expression on her otherwise pretty face. Her eyes were bloodshot. Her lips were caught somewhere between a snarl and a smile.

"That's not Werner," she repeated.

"That's not Werner." Turning into a crouch, facing him fully.

"That's not Werner!" Shouting now. Her body somehow erecting itself off the floor.

"THAT'S NOT WERNER!" Felicia was taking several shambling steps toward him and would have reached him if Daryl had not already been backpedaling.

Catching a hold of the doorframe, he spun himself into the corridor, racing back the way he had come. He thought he could hear the floor covering crackling behind him, but it was impossible to tell for sure through the racket made by his own panicked passage.

He did not dare to look behind him as he reached the corridor where he had last heard Werner's horn. As he tried to navigate the turn full speed, he underestimated his forward momentum, causing him to careen into the wall and jar his right shoulder. He barely registered the pain as he took off down the final corridor, which led to more populated parts of the asylum.

Far ahead of him Hubble suddenly materialized, walking through the wall into the corridor. He seemed not to notice Daryl at first, but the noise must have alerted him, and he turned to see Daryl plunging toward him. Eyes widening, he took off down the corridor away from Daryl, which only served to further stoke Daryl's panic. Daryl quickly caught up with Hubble's short-legged shuffle and the two of them emerged, side-by-side, from the corridor, breaking the workman's tape like some absurd photo finish.

Daryl, daring a look behind him, saw nothing but gloom and the crumpled floor covering.

"Why did you run?" Daryl asked, through ragged gasps for air, and collapsed to the floor.

"I panicked, you oaf! You looked really scared. Wait, are you telling me we were running from nothing?"

As Hubble spoke, his voice went through the transition from fresh terror to indignant anger.

"Well, not exactly nothing . . ."

"You're in an insane asylum, Daryl. You should see upstairs. That's scary."

Daryl had been keeping a firm eye on the corridor, watching for the emergence of creepy patients with bloodshot eyes. When none appeared, he stood and dusted himself off. Casting one last glance down the corridor, he thought he heard a barely audible honk, like a distant, mournful salute.

Taking a deep breath, he wrestled his eyes away from the opening and began walking back toward the main corridor. Hubble fell into step beside him.

"I was actually looking for you," Hubble said.

"Yeah? I was looking for someone too. Seems your luck is better than mine."

"Right," Hubble chuckled. "We were pretty wasted at the end there. Did I properly warn you about using the lodestone?"

"Sure. Don't touch anything, right?"

"Right," Hubble acknowledged. They walked on for a minute, then he said, "It's like parachuting. It's almost certainly going to be just fine . . ."

". . . but if your chute fails, you're dead." Daryl finished.

"Right," Hubble said with more conviction and a smile, apparently happy Daryl understood.

Daryl smiled back, confident he would be leaving the hazardous lodestone very much alone.

CHAPTER 13

His inability to locate Werner weighed heavily on Daryl as he lay in bed that night. His mind desperately wanted to drift off, but he was too worried about the usually ubiquitous man and continuing their previous conversation. Of course, at this time of night he knew where to find him. However, you did not disturb other patients at night. It was a recipe for disaster.

Screw it.

He had not bothered undressing and was out the door in a moment. It was just after midnight, and the corridors were deserted. Werner's room was not far away, and in moments, Daryl was standing outside the door wondering whether to knock or call out to get his attention.

Paranoid schizophrenics were typically not at their best when unexpectedly awakened during the night. Even someone like Werner with his remarkably sunny disposition would be unpredictable. Daryl began whispering Werner's name with the hope that his friend might still be up. As this failed to elicit a response, he tried rapping lightly on the door. When this proved equally futile, he grabbed the door handle and, to his surprise, the door swung inward with a gentle creak.

His heart skipped a beat as he peered into the darkened interior, feeling like a trespasser. He tried to establish contact by whispering Werner's name, but the darkness within was wholly uncommunicative.

Daryl pushed the door all the way open, revealing a room much like his own. He was still unable to make out much detail in the gloom, but the bed appeared unoccupied. He took a step into the room, reaching out with his left hand for where he assumed the light switch would be. The corridors were only dimly lit at night, so with the flick of the switch, the room snapped into blinding focus. Daryl shielded his eyes with his right hand as he tried to take in the interior. Unlike Daryl's room, the walls were undecorated. Werner's bed was a mess of sheets and comforter. His clothes were haphazardly scattered about on the floor. Given the general disarray of the room, Werner's desk did not really seem tidy. It merely looked unused and thus empty. Werner was not there.

This was the first time he had been in another patient's room. Daryl took a few tentative steps forward. The corner of a book peered out from beneath the comforter on the bed. Picking it up, Daryl recognized it as one of the standard journals the asylum offered to patients as a way to document their issues and progress. It was, in other words, private.

Daryl was torn. On one hand, he did not want to intrude on his friend's privacy. On the other hand, if Werner was truly missing, Daryl might be the only one who could help him. Deciding that looking at recent entries would minimize intrusion and maximize potential usefulness, Daryl cracked the book open at the back and began leafing in reverse. A third of the way into the book, he came across the last entry, dated yesterday morning. Werner's surprisingly neat handwriting filled up about half a page of the journal.

There appears to be a randomness to these encounters. As if we are all tasty morsels dangling in front of a cage of tigers. We're not why they're here, but if we swing within reach, we run the risk of becoming a snack.

The guardian has trouble reacting fast enough, especially in the basement where the stone is covered by plaster. I wonder whether there is a way to get rid of that?
Daryl is becoming convinced that his visions aren't real! I will have to keep a closer eye on him from now on.

Then, to Daryl's immense surprise, there was a break in the entry before it continued:

Daryl, if you're reading this, I may be in some trouble. Please come and get me at your earliest convenience. Much love, Werner.

Daryl was stupefied by Werner's apparent prescience. It was clear that Werner thought he knew more about what was going on than Daryl did, but the meaning seemed steeped in inference only Werner could decipher. Two things did occur to him. One, the basement was probably where he needed to look for Werner. The thought made him physically ill. Two, Werner might know a lot more than he had been letting on. He was about to have a quick look at the preceding pages when the floorboards creaked behind him.

"Hi Daryl," a familiar feminine voice said.

Turning his head, he saw Felicia blocking the doorway. She had changed from the floral dress into asylum-wear, and she gave him a shy smile, her eyes still puffy and bloodshot.

"Hi Felicia," he managed, positioning his right foot behind him.

The moment stretched on a bit. Felicia did not have the creepy presence from earlier that day. Looking her over, she appeared to be almost embarrassed.

"So, what did you think of Bill-Din?" she finally asked.

"Is that who possessed you earlier?" he said.

"Possessed? Well, I suppose that is a pretty accurate way of thinking about it . . ." she trailed off, lost in thought.

"Why were you possessed?" he asked.

"Huh? Oh, he's been trying to determine why I'm, well,

what I am. Apparently that requires taking the reins for a while. We've done it many times by now. He tells me that he's close to an answer, but I've learned that he is a terrible judge of time. So, I guess we'll see."

She shook herself. "Anyway, it takes me a while to regain control, and so when Bill-Din sensed you coming, I asked him to warn you. My perceptions change when he takes over. I knew what was happening, and the thing you were chasing . . . It wasn't Werner."

Daryl did not like the sound of that. If something was setting traps for him, he would have to be even more careful than usual. It was enough to make a guy paranoid.

"Well thanks," he said. "Maybe you could ask Bill-Din not to chase me?"

The look of embarrassment crossed her face again. "Yes, he does lack something in the way of social skills. I'll speak to him."

With that, she turned facing the wall. "Later," she whispered.

"Are you going into the basement then?" she asked, turning back to face him.

"How did you know that?" Daryl asked. He had literally decided that only moments ago.

"Where else would you look for Werner?" she said with evident surprise.

Her words struck a chord within him, and he realized how hard he had tried to avoid looking in the obvious place.

"Right. Although it's probably impossible to get down there at night." The orderlies locked the stairwells and elevators at night. Daryl hated the small part of himself that breathed just a little easier at that prospect.

"Maybe we should go check?" Felicia said. "Just in case."

Daryl suppressed a shudder. "Yes," he said. "Do let's."

CHAPTER 14

They made their way to the nearest stairwell in silence. Daryl's unwillingness to consider going into the basement in search of Werner had left him unprepared for what to do when the actuality arose. If Werner really was somewhere below, he would almost certainly be in trouble—his journal had suggested as much. It seemed fate had conspired to give him a chance to put the recent progress with Susan to the test. The thought both excited and terrified him.

Well, at least it was doubtful that he would have to figure it out tonight. He grasped the door handle, turned, and pushed. With a loud click, the door swung inward into darkness. Moments later the automated sensors kicked in. The lights blinked twice before settling on a steady illumination of gray walls surrounding the blue-painted metal railing winding downward at the center of the stairwell.

"Shall we?" Felicia said behind him. Looking back, he caught her quickly trading a smirk for a grin.

"I'm beginning to think you and your friend are both more useful and more dangerous than I thought," he said.

"I imagine those are often correlated," she said, flashing

a sweet smile.

They descended to the basement level to find yet another door unlocked. The likelihood of that seemed to stretch statistical plausibility, but Daryl let it pass without comment.

They made their way toward the staff room, the stale air a constant reminder of where they were. Werner had mentioned seeing "something" near the staff room the last time he and Daryl had spoken, and given the multitude of underground corridors, it seemed a good place to begin the search.

After a few minutes of sweaty readiness, Daryl's body decided that, in the absence of a tangible threat, it would allow nonvisceral responses. Their situation reminded him of a question he had never thought to fully formulate before.

"What's going on with the basement anyway?" he asked Felicia.

"I don't know. Bill-Din speaks less to me down here. I think he is made less manifest by the mortar covering his… essence," she said.

"Really? How so?"

"Sometimes parts of the world coalesce into something with sentience. I think some cultures have referred to this as elementals. Bill-Din isn't exactly sure what he is either, except the guardian of this place. He says that he's sorry he can't be of more help with the demons, but he's just too unwieldy. Sort of like swatting flies with a spade," she said, her voice relaying a surprising amount of regret.

"What about the mirrors?" he asked.

"No idea, but I can see the demons hover there, like a swarm of locusts, waiting for a chance to get to you. That's part of my . . . problem."

Daryl was wondering how Felicia's issues related to his when somewhere in front of them, a familiar horn sounded.

Daryl came to a stop, his heart rate suddenly soaring again.

"So that's probably not Werner either, huh?" Daryl asked.

"No," Felicia replied nervously.

By some unspoken accord they both began to shuffle forward again, pushing deeper into the tunnels beneath the asylum. Each time they began to wonder whether they were headed in the right direction, the horn would sound, verifying their course. A tension was building in the air around them, and they both remained silent. For Daryl, this was partly from a desire for stealth, and partly because he did not think speaking to a woman who claimed everything was out to get him would be productive preparation for what was to come.

They passed through brightly lit sections of corridor connected via sections where the scarce light only barely outlined their forms. The dark walls seemed to bleed movements, like swirls of fog in the shape of faces, clawed hands, and at one point something like a big dog. Daryl did his best to ignore them, but just the same they stayed in the middle of the corridor where the black swirls dissolved before reaching them. Often the lack of light made it difficult to ascertain whether their eyes were playing tricks on them. However, the urgent, hungry whispers that began accompanying them in the dark passages caused them to quicken their pace in getting from light to light.

They had long passed the part of the basement with which Daryl was at least semi-familiar. Walking underneath one of the phosphorescent lamps, Daryl realized they had gone a long time without hearing the horn. He was about to suggest they backtrack when, from somewhere close ahead in the creeping dark, a screech of rubber on stone was followed by the single familiar bleat of a horn.

Daryl took a few steps forward and peered into the darkness.

Felicia had stopped in her tracks. He looked back at her and was about to speak when he noticed her eyes wide with terror, focused on something further up the corridor. Daryl heard a weak, squeaky sound and his head whipped back around, searching ahead of them in the poor light. Something like a small capital letter T was slowly coming toward them. It was still far away, but he could just make out something white and black, attached to the horizontal part.

"We need to go," Felicia said. "Right now."

"Hold on," Daryl said. There was little point in entering the worst part of this place if they were going to leave at the first sign of trouble. Daryl had outrun trouble several times in the past, and whatever was up ahead, it did not look too bad.

"You don't understand," she continued. The shuffle behind him made it clear that she was wasting no time retreating.

"Damn right I don't," he muttered. He did not understand a damn thing about what was happening. Except that his friend might be in trouble. His back suddenly itched like crazy, and his hand darted back to scratch it. Then he moved forward, trying to get a better look. The approaching object finally moved directly underneath one of the recently installed halogen lights and Daryl's breath caught in his throat. It was a green push scooter with a mounted horn in the shape of a panda.

What the hell?

Daryl took another step forward.

The scooter came to a stop.

"Daryl, come on!" Felicia said. Her voice was more distant. She was still backing away.

The air shimmered, and the object of Felicia's fear materialized. Taking up almost half the hallway, the horned demonic form pushed the scooter ahead of it with one foot.

"Hello Daryl," Baal said, licking his lips. "Your friend was delicious."

Daryl's stomach dropped as fear settled into its accustomed spot along his spine. He wavered, trying to ignore the dread. Baal sent him a sickening smile as he scratched the panda horn absently with one of his dagger-like claws, making it emit a series of winded shrieks.

Daryl straightened and drew a steadying breath.

"Werner!" he called into the corridor.

Baal took another step forward. "Good to see you've regained some of your spine since last we met," he rumbled. "But it's just us here."

Daryl began walking toward Baal, fully ignoring him. The itch sprang into being and danced merrily across his shoulder blades. He absently scratched it, continuing his march down the corridor.

"Please run!" Felicia screamed in the distance.

Baal smacked his lips. "Now this also won't do," he said, mirth in his voice. "I did not cross the expanse of all that is to simply clobber a blind man to death."

Daryl was much closer now. Baal took up enough of the corridor to make passing by him impossible, but that was not his plan anyway.

Daryl was moments from walking straight into the demon's huge form.

"Maybe now would be a good time to talk about your daughter's death?" the demon said sweetly.

Daryl stopped. His head throbbed and the itch at his back intensified to a searing pain.

"Yes," Baal continued, "let's talk about Ginny."

The very air seemed to vibrate, making the walls shiver back and forth. Baal's words were seeping into Daryl, finding purchase in an anger so white-hot and true that the intensity made everything else within him crumble to dust. Some forgotten part of his mind told him to take a stand and fight, absurd as that seemed. Was that Susan talking or was it something else? Something he could almost remember. Like a familiar scent, on a trail for blood. A door, which had been firmly shut a long time ago, was opening just a crack.

"Oh, now what's this?" Baal said unfazed. "How righteous you are in your anger. Like a reason unto itself, driving you to cleanse and purify everything in your way, but . . ." Baal stared intently at Daryl who had begun advancing again. "Never before has that flame of yours been ignited so squarely in the monsoon of your own cowardice and self-delusion."

Daryl's hands were balled into fists, and he seemed to be humming something. A part of his mind screamed for him to turn around, run away, and escape, but it was like a faint whisper into the storm that drove him forward. He leapt, rapidly gaining speed in his dash toward Baal. At a sprint he plowed into the grotesquely proportioned demon, amazingly sending them both spinning. Before Baal had even hit the floor, Daryl was pummeling him with a series of savage blows to gut, ribs, and jaw. Bone cracked and Daryl felt a half-remembered strength suffusing his every blow with power. His body was steeped in a white glow. Daryl landed on top of Baal, the impact causing them to skid across the cement floor. His left hand was closed around the demon's throat. His right hand was behind him, ready to break what his left hand held. Intense pain lanced across his back, like the bite of a whip, but it only served to further stoke his frenzy.

Baal took the beating with a smile. A smile that slowly turned into an evil chuckle, then a cackle, and finally full-blown laughter. "YES! This is perfect!" Baal roared underneath him through bloodied fangs.

Daryl's barrage of blows came to a stop.

"What. Did. You. Do. With. Ginny?" he said, icicles in his voice.

Baal seemed to suddenly notice him. "Oh? Yes, of course. Lean in and I'll whisper it to you."

Daryl straddled the demon, driving the fingers of his left hand painfully into the meat of its huge neck. Baal squirmed briefly then looked intently into Daryl's eyes. Shifting slightly, Daryl leaned in, his eyes never leaving the demon's bloodshot orbs.

He barely noticed Felicia scream something in the

distance.

The demon lifted its head off the floor and looked hungrily at Daryl.

"It was you that killed Ginny," Baal wheezed with orgasmic delight.

Daryl spasmed. He knew. Some part of his mind had known all along. Had tried to warn him. The air was filled with strange smells. *Am I flying?* His mind came back to a world tilted, as he hit the wall upside down with a snap. The side of his head was in contact with the cold floor, while the rest of him was floating somewhere above him. Baal rose from where he had flung Daryl and moved forward, leaning down to put himself into Daryl's field of view. The cruel joy on his face transcending the strangeness of his demonic features.

"I only recently realized that you didn't know. That you had repressed what happened in your guilt. She died and you lived."

Something warm was trickling down Daryl's neck and face with a smell like artichokes gone bad. He had pissed himself.

Baal pulled himself up with a snort. Looking down at Daryl's broken form, a grin of grim satisfaction spread slowly across his features.

"Your Hell is here. You've earned it."

The world grew dimmer by the second. Daryl tried to move, but only accomplished a slow trickle of urine into his mouth. He passed out.

CHAPTER 15

D aryl awoke slowly. He could not remember having slept this deeply in a long time. Blinking, he noticed Harriet, the middle-aged nurse from the first floor, moving around at the foot of the bed. Due to the angle, he could not see what she was doing.

"Hey," he croaked.

Harriet looked up, a washcloth in her right hand.

"Oh, hey Daryl," she replied sweetly. "Just a moment."

With that she quickly exited the room.

Daryl thought his previous exertions would have left him sore. They had not. Tubes were connected to his arm from a metal stand by the bed. He did not recognize the room.

Doctor Brewer entered. His features set in a professional smile.

"I'm afraid I have some bad news, Daryl." Daryl tried to move his head for a better view, and that was when his chin encountered the brace around his neck. The sensation made him acutely aware of how little else he felt. Nothing from the neck down to be exact.

A cold sweat swept across him as Doctor Brewer continued to speak.

CHAPTER 16

. . . Local server overload. Data integrity compromised. External data dumb in 3.. 2.. 1..
Systems normalizing.
Tracking data export for reacquisition.
Circuit integration status: partial success
Running search for subject 0000062

> *...*
> *...*
> *Subject located... Interface established.*
>
> *Multiple anomalies detected. Assessing direct risk to subject 0000062:*
>
> *Subject 07364931... Threat level ... ... minimal*
> *Subject 07364932... Threat level ... ... moderate*
> *Subject 07364933... Threat level ... ... minimal*
> *Subject 07364934... Threat level ... severe*

Assessment paused.
Source of danger: Unclear
Accessing records on subject 07364934...

> *Likelihood of threat level link to past traumas: High*
> *Additional information required.*

Initiating search protocols for subject 07364934.

> *Progress reports enabled...*

***

Feeling safe is a promise your past makes to your future. It does not, in fact, mean that you are safe. It is not an outright lie, but rather an aggressive exaggeration of the reliability of predictions.

Susan woke only to the point of tepid awareness as she was swept up in her father's arms and carried to the car. The contrast between how her new coat amply heated her small body and the crisp air of a cold winter night on her forehead only made the ride more pleasurable. Even being put in a car, long since gone cold from the ride over, was made cozy by knowing that she would soon be tucked into her own warm bed.

The engine revved to life, and she was pressed back in her seat by the car's acceleration up path. The crunch of gravel ceased, letting her know that they had exited the driveway.

Lights flashed by outside. Evenly spaced flares from lamp posts mixed with the irregular flashes from late-night traffic. Her mom and dad were discussing something, but it was a pleasant buzz that carried her further and further inward. The world disappeared in a bumpy, inevitable slide into oblivion.

A loud noise ripped through her nascent dreams. Blinding lights tore through the interior of the car and her father cursed. Adrenaline rushed through her, and she bolted upright, confused but wide awake. A horn blared and the world exploded in a neck-jarring spin. Someone screamed and her brief stint of consciousness was extinguished once again.

No one lied, but nothing was right either.

***

"Hi Daryl, mind if I take a seat?"

Susan was standing by his bed. Was it the third time today? That did not seem right—she did have other patients. He had stopped keeping track of time. In fact, he had stopped caring altogether. Yesterday they had finally given up spoon feeding him and put him on fluids. The metal stand, which held his meals, stood to his right, a constant reminder that he was checking out. It was annoying that they insisted on delaying what should be his choice. *Fuck 'em.*

"Daryl, I need to hear about what happened. Why were you in the basement?"

Daryl had three options of where to direct his gaze in his new ground-floor quarters. When he bothered to focus his eyes, that was. "The window," which currently held a blue sky with a single white cloud, "the painting," which was abstract and reminded him of a purple parrot eating a rainbow turtle, and "the cupboard," which was a cupboard. He was currently gazing out the window, not really seeing.

"Daryl, please talk to me. It is important you tell me how you got down there and how you got hurt."

A white bird flew by the window. Baal had told him that it was he that had killed . . . was it a seagull perhaps? Daryl focused his eyes just in time, getting a better look at the bird as it flew back across the window. Yes, definitely a seagull.

"Daryl . . ."

Was the sea gull big or small? It seemed smaller than some he had seen. Maybe it was a young bird?

"You have to . . ."

Had someone told him that you could tell by the color of the beak? Not that it mattered now. He could not remember the color. Could not remember. Remember what? Remember that he killed . . . Who? His vision blurred again, but this time his eyes were wet. Someone leaned in and wiped away the excess fluid.

"I'm going . . ."

How many birds had he seen today? More than ten? Probably.

". . . check on you later."

Susan retreated out the door.

Finally. He let out a slow breath. His mind was a jagged reef just below a frothing surf. The last thing he needed was to remember. Remember what? When did seagulls have chicks?

***

Night had fallen outside. Daryl's mind had teetered on the verge of sleep several times already, but each time a brief, formless flare of panic had pulled him back. His eyelids drooped—he was almost comfortable.

"Daryl?" someone whispered from the other side of his locked door. "It's me, Felicia. How are you?"

Shit.

"Daryl, I'm really sorry. We should talk about what happened. I think . . ."

"Go away!" he shouted. His voice sounded strange to him. He had not used it since his injury. Silence.

"Daryl," she tried again.

"Go away!" he repeated at the top of his lungs.

This time the silence hung about him in comforting stillness for several moments before it was replaced by the muted patter of bare feet retreating on linoleum.

If he had told Susan to go away, she would have seen it as progress. He was confident that would not be the case with Felicia.

A phantom itch appeared between his shoulder blades. He would not be sleeping anytime soon.

CHAPTER 17

Click.

An almost inaudible explosion of sound.

The minute hand moved one step closer to the hour hand. The clock had been positioned on a small table near the door. He hated that clock, but also needed it to keep track of each little hateful minute. Knowing with a certainty that he had killed her, while not remembering how, was a clawing, nagging, ceaseless vise, choking every waking minute. The familiar spot between his shoulder blades itched.

Click.

No way out. Not even death, the ultimate exit, was his to decide anymore. He wanted to scream but could not muster the energy for it. He wanted to cry, but his face remained emotionless. Like the rest of him, unable to move.

Click.

He looked with loathing at the clock, which indifferently measured the units of his useless existence. A few weeks had passed since the incident in the basement. Susan had come by at least daily. As had Hubble. He had not spoken to either. The bitterness in him would not allow it. What did he have to say to them? They were among the living, or the imaginary. Either way, they were both reminders of a time when he had had options. Terrible options, but everything was better than the . . .

Click.

Fucking clock!

Daryl bit his tongue and spat a gob of bloody phlegm onto the comforter. Aside from yelling, this was his only way of venting pain. His mind blanked out and he realized at least ten minutes had passed. This was happening more and more these days. Even his mind had given up on keeping track of his pathetic existence.

"Hi Daryl," Hubble said, the hairy ends of his long ears peaking over the side of the bed.

Click.

"I know you don't want to talk, and I don't blame you, so I figured—screw it, let's get drunk."

Daryl moved his head in an effort to see, and sure enough, the gnome was holding a bottle in one hand and two glasses in the other.

"Now, this is not an assisted suicide, so you have to promise beforehand that you will actually try to drink the liquid this time," Hubble continued, referring to an incident a few days back when Daryl had tried unsuccessfully to choke himself on a drink of water.

Daryl wavered. He had made the decision not to interact with anyone, but the offer of getting drunk was too good to pass up. Finally, and with some reluctance, he looked Hubble in the eyes and gave a slight nod.

"That's the spirit. Hang on," Hubble said as he swung himself onto the bed and took up a position next to Daryl's head. The neck brace had been removed yesterday, and the space this freed up easily permitted Hubble to sit, one foot swinging over the side of the bed and the other propped against the headboard. Apparently comfortable, he unstopped the flask and began pouring generous drinks for the two of them.

***

". . . and the night took an odd turn after that. I swear, at one point she had me bark like a dog!"

Daryl had to cede a smile as Hubble proceeded to howl while slapping his free hand against his thigh. Daryl hoped it was in unsuppressed joy at the memory and not an attempt to breathe additional carnal life into the retelling. Hubble's laughter slowly trickled into a steady giggle. He brought up a sleeve and wiped a few tears from his eyes.

Hubble turned quiet.

"So how are you holding up?" he finally asked.

Daryl considered keeping silent. Nothing good would likely come from talking. How could it? On the other hand, that was true in either case. He sighed.

"Well, the food's better," he finally said.

Hubble looked quizzically at him for a few seconds. Then he slowly turned his head to where the metal stand held the bag full of nutrients they had been forced to hook him up to.

They both laughed some more. Then they drank some more. Then Daryl passed out.

Click.

CHAPTER 18

Soft eyes scanned across Daryl as Susan entered the room, clearly noticing a change, but opting not to remark on it. Instead, she simply sat down in her customary seat by his bed and updated him on what was happening in the asylum. It was infuriatingly reassuring and, not ten minutes into it, Daryl cracked. He had meant to comment on an anecdote about one of the other patients, but instead his voice broke, and a sob escaped his lips. The small hole in his emotional dike widened, and a torrent of guilt, self-recrimination, and regret came pouring out. He could not be sure whether it was even coherent but was unable to staunch the tide enough to care. Not surprisingly he heard himself repeating the word Ginny, over and over.

When he ran out of energy, Susan simply looked at him and leaned forward, taking his hand. At that point Daryl's eyes were screwed tight, his neck trembling. He opened his eyes and looked down to where Susan's hand was holding his, holding him, letting him know that she was not letting go.

CHAPTER 19

Daryl awoke in the dead of night with a start. As always, a stream of realizations washed over him, starting at where he was and then passing through the state of his broken body on its way to thoughts of Ginny. Despair washed over him in a terrible, yet familiar, wave and he nearly missed the dark shape by the window. Before he was able to give voice to his surprise, the figure moved forward and entered a shaft of moonlight, filtering through the partly closed blinds. In the faint light he could make out dark, blue-tinged curls surrounding a feminine face, which gained details as she advanced, revealing a feral smirk across square features. She moved with a prowling grace, halting at the foot of the bed. She wore a dark gown and matching gloves that came to rest on the footboard of the bed.

"I'm so sorry," she said.

"Do I know you?" he croaked, still groggy.

"I guess not," she whispered, managing somehow to look both sad and savage at the same time.

Daryl sighed. Had he been able to, he would probably have turned away from her in resignation. As it happened, he was physically unable to turn away and so did not miss how she rapidly leaned in, jumped the footboard, and landed on top of him. The sudden impact did not register, except for the fact that he was temporarily winded as her lithe form caused his lungs to compress and the metal frame to emit a soft groan.

"You may not remember Phineas, but he remembers you," she breathed in his ear.

"You may not remember Iliria, the Hamsta twins, or old Amaranth still trying to figure out who he loves more, his pipe or his violin—but they all remember you."

"You may not remember our ways or the oasis we carved for ourselves." She slowly slid out of the bed, trailing his paralyzed arm by the wrist.

"You may not remember the bonfire, but your place on the log remains empty." She removed the glove from her right hand in one quick tug.

"You may not wish to remember your love . . ." She entwined the fingers of her left hand with his right.

". . . and you may not remember your rage, but you WILL remember me." With that final assertion she stabbed him across the palm with her free hand, the blade somehow hidden in the gloom. She quickly repeated the process on her own hand and squeezed them together.

"Your body may be trapped here, but your mind will be free," she said defiantly. "Let them come for me if they dare."

Keeping her eyes locked with his, she took two quick steps to the door, opened it, and was gone.

Daryl was left staring at the open door for what seemed an eternity. That old spot between his shoulder blades itched, not even granting that simple respite. He turned his neck as much as he could, looking at his paralyzed right arm, which still dangled about a foot over the side of the bed. The blood oozed out of the shallow gash and collected at his knuckles before dripping onto the linoleum floor. The red droplets arrhythmically leaving his hand and falling to the floor had a soporific effect. In fact, his eyes were starting to droop. What a strange vision.

***

Daryl's hand twitched and his eyes snapped open. The flow of blood had nearly stopped. Somewhere beyond his hand, a light was growing. He shook his head and dozens of bright lights appeared around him amid a cacophony of noise. He recoiled, which caused him to spill out of bed and onto a hardwood floor. His room was gone, and the bed he had occupied had been replaced by a small red stool. He lay sprawled on his side against a wooden railing that formed a wide empty circle. The noise came from the throng of people outside the barrier.

"He's drunk again," someone muttered nearby.

He put his left knee beneath him and looked around more carefully.

"That never stops him," someone else said.

A small Asian man was standing beside a stool across from him in the ring. Daryl became gradually aware of a voice rising above the din of the crowd, the shouted words distorted by the metallic echo of a megaphone.

". . . and facing the reigning champion is Takeda Sōkaku. Master of the mystical oriental arts," the hype man shouted dramatically, all the while butchering the Japanese name.

Daryl got up to a roar of applause, whether directed at him or the announcement, he could not tell. He flexed his shoulders and back.

The Japanese man moved to the center of the ring and Daryl followed suit. A cruel anger was seeping into his mind, and he felt his hands twitch with delight at the prospect of unleashing that rage on the stocky man before him.

The ring fell quiet and Takeda bowed, never taking his eyes off Daryl.

Daryl rushed forward in a flurry of swings, but by some miracle, the man dodged and weaved his way all around Daryl, ending once again in the center of the ring.

Daryl took a step back, assessing his opponent. There was something calm and serious about the way he moved. Every step deliberate, almost like a dance. The man lunged, and Daryl's jaw rang as a hand snaked out and connected, sending him reeling into the boards of the railing. On instinct, Daryl tucked and rolled. Splinters flew around him as a foot broke the wood where Daryl had stood moments before.

Daryl sprang to his feet with a snarl, but the man was calmly circling him as he moved from the rail toward the center once again, a slight smile on his lips.

Daryl rushed him. The man sidestepped, but Daryl had anticipated that and threw himself into the man, bearing them both to the floor in a crash that shook the planks. A roar erupted from the crowd and Daryl grabbed the man in a bear hug, pushing him into the ground. His turn to smile.

The man was oddly slippery, continuously escaping positions from which Daryl could begin to pummel him. Daryl's obvious advantage in size and strength should have ended the match as soon as the two hit the ground, but the man kept moving and shifting in perplexing ways. The crowd was egging him on to finish it, further stoking his temper. He grabbed the man's arm and the man squirmed beneath him, bringing his legs up along Daryl's upper body and head. Daryl raised himself up on his toes nearly lifting himself and the man from the ground in an impressive feat of strength.

Instead, the man twisted, and Daryl lost his balance and toppled to the ground, his elbow caught in the vise of the other man's arms. Daryl tried to move, but found that his arm was slowly, and inexorably, being straightened. Pain lanced up his arm as he felt the elbow joint beginning to give, bending the wrong way, and he instinctively reached for the essence.

White-hot power flooded through him, and he effortlessly withdrew his arm while bounding to his feet. Beneath him the small man was clutching his sprained fingers, where Daryl had impossibly jerked free of the arm lock. He felt the essence suffusing his body as the shock of what he had done hit him. He had revealed himself. They would be coming.

He leapt across the railing, easily pushing through the throng of onlookers. Behind him, a bemused samurai wobbled to his feet and dusted himself off to go in search of a drink.

Daryl scrambled through the streets, heading for the nearest scalable building. Dousing himself in water was his only hope now. And it was a slim one. The power coursed through him and around him, enveloping him in a light that was invisible to the mortal eye, but would serve as a beacon to the powers of Hell and Heaven alike.

Exiting the downtown slums, he made his way onto cobbled streets, barely avoiding a horse-drawn carriage in his panicked flight. In this wealthier part of the city of light, he soon came upon a five-story building with a mishmash of balconies along the front. With a sprint and a leap, he grabbed onto the lower balcony railing and hoisted himself up and over the metal frame. Someone swore from within a dimly lit apartment, but Daryl was already jumping onto the second balcony.

He flung himself over the top of the wall, landing on a roof with an impressive view of Eiffel's recently completed World Fair tower. Someone was already there, waiting for him.

The angel looked at him with luminescent eyes, his beautiful form cloaked in a white tunic and framed by a pair of gleaming wings.

Daryl set his feet. Then he dashed for the side of the building, uncasing his own wings, gray and dull by comparison, and lunged into the air, quickly gaining altitude. A shockwave of air let him know that he was being pursued.

"Jae'el, it is time," the angel stated calmly, somewhere behind him.

He beat his wings frantically, knowing that his less

impressive wingspan worked against him. He was about to respond when the angel collided with him from above and the two plunged downward, only to pitch upward in a roar of beating wings. White and gray feathers encircled them as each struggled to get the upper hand, a streak of ashes exploding upward into the night sky.

The city spread out beneath them, a concentration of lights, surrounded by smaller clusters from neighboring hamlets. Locked in a tight and violent embrace with the angel, Daryl reached for the stiletto in his left boot, but the angel immediately kneed him in the face, causing numerous new stars to spring to light amidst the night sky. The knife spun away beneath them and quickly disappeared from sight. Head spinning, Daryl clutched at the angel with all his strength, trying to hold himself close for a few moments. It worked briefly, but then a superhumanly strong arm closed around his neck, cutting off air. Daryl was strong, but the angel was just a little stronger. A little more in tune with the essence.

"What a weak performance," the angel sang as they soared higher in a tight spiral. Daryl's oxygen-deprived body slumped in the angel's grasp, his head lolling forward.

The angel emitted a shrill laugh, which was cut short as the stiletto from Daryl's other boot was buried to the hilt in his chest. The angel's eyes went wide for a second as a choke bloodied his lips. Then the eyes lost focus, and he fell from the sky.

Elated by the kill but with no time to celebrate his unexpected victory, Daryl frantically searched for the dark, serpentine form of the Seine far beneath him. His only chance was to douse his aura by submerging himself in running water before an archangel could appear. Who was he kidding? He knew who would come.

Locating the fast-moving waters, he dove. The city lights rose to greet him in his mad plunge. Righting himself just above the roof tops, the lights streaked by beneath him as he picked up even more speed, choosing to stay low. Every second might count. He barely cleared the last roof, sending a clothesline filled with drying laundry spinning into the night. Then he dismissed his wings and, taking a deep breath, dove straight into the deepest part of the river in a roar of displaced water. The current quickly took him, and he was pulled none too gently with the stream. Minutes passed and his lungs started to ache with the need to draw breath. He stayed down to the point where his head began to fog before kicking his way upward. He broke the surface with a gasp and for several long moments simply floated in the center of the river, watching the skies. Nothing.

Swimming toward the shore, he noticed that he had left the main part of the city behind for a sparsely wooded area that gently sloped away from the riverbank. He reached the shallows and stood. The water moved sluggishly by his knees as he took one more careful look around. His aura had dimmed greatly during his submersion, its energy dispersed by the water. He was about to breathe a sigh of relief when he noticed a man coming toward the bank on the opposite side of the river. All he could make out was a white-robed figure, moving with no apparent rush toward the water's edge. A dull throb spread through his mind as a finely cultivated hatred surfaced. His heart began pounding a steady beat of emerging panic. He backed away just as the seemingly innocuous figure began traversing the surface of the river without a splash.

A kind voice cut through the distance between them. "The process of your capture is to be part of your punishment. First, I will break your body and then deliver what is left to Purgatory for eternal damnation."

"That you, Gabie?" he responded.

A dry, grandfatherly chuckle. "Tell you what, my child. If you call me Gabriel, I will take you straight there."

"And miss the reunion? Never."

Gabriel was past the midpoint of the river now, moving with the confidence of someone walking a paved road.

"Dear child. We both know what your attempts at

humor seek to disguise."

He tried to follow the movements of the archangel. There were many ways in which Gabriel could beat him, but the angel's statements suggested he would be thrashed physically, while he still possessed a body to thrash. Unfortunately, Gabriel was more than capable of doing just that.

A rush of wind hit him, only moments before Gabriel's outstretched hand connected with his chest. He was flung backward like a rag doll, spinning and tumbling on the ground till he came to a painful stop against the roots of an old tree. Back against the trunk, he hoisted himself up, registering his broken ribs and sprained ankle. The angel was still coming. Slow and deadly, like a coiled serpent. Daryl gritted his teeth at the pain and looked up in defiance, his hatred stoked by the indifferent display of power.

"That one was for free," he gasped. "The next one'll cost you."

"What did you have in mind?" Gabriel inquired with seemingly earnest interest.

"Come over here and I'll show you."

The angel broke his left arm with a crack.

Daryl's body spasmed in pain and he cried out as the breath whooshed out of his lungs. He looked up at the god-like apparition who still held his mangled arm where he had broken it with a squeeze of his hand. Daryl punched him in the gonads. Or rather, he tried. Instead, Gabriel's left hand now held his entire right fist in a vise, cracking bones and dislocating ligaments. He cried out again.

"What was that?" Gabriel asked.

He opened his eyes, which had been shut against the pain and looked into black, all-pupil eyes set in a benevolent visage of age and wisdom. Being this outclassed, there was basically only one thing left to do.

"Gabie . . ." he tried, but the angel tightened his grip causing another ripple of pain to lance through his body, and he screamed.

Gabriel smiled at him.

Daryl inhaled a shaky breath, hatred the only thing keeping him from passing out.

"Your breath smells like shit," he spat.

Gabriel's smile turned sad.

"I can do this forever, my child. Let me see those pretty little wings of yours."

At the archangel's command, he felt his wings unfurl, flopping uselessly against the ground. Two quick twists later and they too were broken.

"Fly, little bird, fly," Gabriel whispered into Daryl's ear.

Nearly delirious Daryl lifted his head.

"Eat shit and die," he croaked, blood foaming on his lips.

The angel eased him gently to the ground.

"I'm afraid I already ate," Gabriel answered with another smile.

He lay on the earth, still warm from the heat of the day, wings splayed behind him like a drowned butterfly. Gabriel cocked his head, listening for a second, then looked back down at him.

"I will be right back," he said. "Don't go anywhere."

With that he was gone, leaving behind a world of pain.

Daryl tried to stand. Being vertical added nausea to his long list of ailments, but still, the illusion of escape it offered felt like an improvement. He nearly passed out as his broken wings flopped about with a sickening crunch. Looking around, he managed a weak shuffle further into the woods. If he lay down, his body would attempt to heal, but he knew this would take time he did not have. Gabriel had been called away by some urgent matter, but he would not allow himself to be gone long enough for Daryl to recuperate. Something small buzzed around his head. It would have gone unnoticed if not for the faint aura of light surrounding it from within. He thought he heard words in his mind, but it took a while for his stunned mind to grasp their meaning: *Follow. This way. Over here . . .*

Appreciating the hopeful diversion, his mind set upon shuffling his body in the direction the firefly was heading. Somewhere ahead he caught a glimpse of light. His bruised body spasmed as he hit a low-hanging tree branch, causing him to stumble. Off balance, he clawed blindly with his right arm as his body began to topple backward. His mangled hand closed painfully around the branch in front of him and he was able to steady himself long enough for the dizziness to fade.

Be with you shortly, the archangel whispered in his mind.

"Piss off," he mumbled through cracked lips.

He pushed on through an encroaching numbness. His body had stopped healing, which was bad, and it had stopped hurting, which was worse. White sparks of light danced around his vision, and it took him several long seconds to remember that they were not wisps of the mind, but fireflies. Looking beyond them, the dark shapes of the background coalesced into a fire pit around which several people were seated on logs.

He heard a lilting tune, so timid he was not sure whether it had just begun or whether it had been playing all along. The leaves rustled ecstatically above him, somehow mixing with the notes of the fiddle. He entered the light of the fire. A few people looked up—most were already looking at him. Only the fiddler, a short grizzly-looking man, remained entranced in his performance.

A curly haired, square-faced young woman stood. Her eyes carried a savage intensity as they bored into his. He stared back with the glazed look of complete exhaustion. Then his world tilted, and blackness claimed him.

***

Daryl startled awake for the second time that night. Early morning light was creeping in through the window, imbuing the room with faint, light gray details where before there had been none.

He knew her.

CHAPTER 20

"So, you see the significance of your dreams now?"

Susan was seated on the left side of his bed where he could see her from his pillow-propped vantage. His improved health meant that he had been moved back to his old room on the first floor.

"Well, they've changed," he said.

"In what way?" Susan asked.

Daryl considered it. It was not just their content that had changed wildly since the night of the visit. They also felt more like having a second life than a dream. A distraction, he had to admit, which he sorely needed.

"It's like I'm living a different life as a different person."

"Your mind is adapting to your new situation. My guess would be that it is feeding you parts of your memories that have been withheld. I think your mind is telling you something. Exactly what I can't say yet, but I would be very surprised if these dreams don't continue until we decipher them."

"Yes, but it doesn't even feel like me. In the dreams it's like I'm constantly looking for someone to fight. Like the whole world needs to be punished."

"Maybe it did, Daryl," Susan said. "Was there anything

that sparked the dreams?"

"No, nothing I can think of."

He was not sure why he did not disclose his nocturnal visit or mention the red line across his palm from where the woman had stabbed him. She had probably heard about that part already. It seemed to have healed surprisingly fast, but then again, he always healed quickly. It was not that he did not trust Susan. He just could not shake a visceral feeling that this visit was best kept private.

"What about all the supernatural stuff? I thought you didn't believe in it?"

"I don't," she answered. "But I do believe that they are significant. Please make sure to keep me updated."

Over the coming weeks, Daryl diligently relayed how the story in his dreams evolved.

***

He woke to pain. Excruciating pain that, alas, only bordered on mind-numbing. Every part of his body hurt. Something about that struck him as ironic, but he was not able to process why that would be, and his mind quickly moved on. All his limbs felt like someone had taken the time to molest every single muscle fiber. Except perhaps for the soles of his feet? Nope, those too.

Avoiding even the slightest movement, he became aware of a flow of cool air, brushing against his cheek and forehead. His field of vision was occupied by two pieces of heavy beige canvas, stitched together with brown raw-hide lace. He could make out a couple of red painted letters and was nearly tricked into moving in his efforts to make out the words.

Additional information would require him to adjust his position, perhaps even sit up, and a quest for answers did not seem to justify the incumbent pain. However, at this point the outside world made its presence known by suddenly jolting him along the entire frame of the bed. His vision swam and he coughed, making it worse. The fear of another such jostle roused him and he began the laborious process of getting upright. As he heaved himself the last painful inch, sweat beaded his brow and had started a slow trickle down his back. The cooling evaporation brought some relief to his aching body. He took a moment to breathe, his feet firmly planted on the dark timbers of the floor. He was clearly inside of a moving cloth-covered caravan, the earlier jostle most likely caused by a series of potholes. The bed was placed against the long side of the wagon, and on the opposite side was a broad wooden cabinet of fine grain. A breeze swept through the wagon from a semi-circular hole in the front, tousling the rear flaps.

"Hoy there, you awake?" someone shouted from the back.

His response curled up in his parched throat, finally escaping as something between a grunt and a wheeze. Taking the time to swallow several times, he tried again.

"Yeah, I'm up," he croaked.

"Why don't you join me at the back then? It's a beautiful day."

With grace and speed little better than a beached whale, he complied.

The driver was sitting easily on the small drivers bench of the wagon trailing the one Daryl was occupying. He smiled warmly at Daryl from across the expanse between the wagons occupied by his two oxen. He watched Daryl struggle with sympathetic eyes. When Daryl had finally managed to become seated, the driver leaned forward.

"The name's Reston," he supplied with a friendly smile. "And may I ask what brings a strapping young man like yourself within an inch of his life?"

The wagons, and there must have been at least two dozen, were moving ponderously through a landscape dotted with hills that were covered in grass and occasional trees, all in vivid greens. A few puffy clouds drifted lazily by in an otherwise clear blue sky. Daryl found a semi-comfortable position, feet braced against the top rung of a ladder attached to the back planks.

Daryl was about to introduce himself, but for some reason his name would not emerge clearly through his foggy brain.

"An old friend," he said.

"Oh aye, I imagine you would have to be close to someone for them to treat you that roughly."

"I didn't say we were close," Daryl replied bitterly.

"True enough, true enough," Reston said mildly, apparently unbothered by Daryl's unwillingness to share further. The silence stretched between them, and Daryl started to feel bad. It was not Reston's fault that Heaven had been trying to kill him for centuries, but he would be damned if . . . Well, apparently he would just be damned. He changed the subject.

"Are you some sort of traveling troupe?" he asked.

Reston looked up, a straw dangling nonchalantly from the corner of his mouth. It had not been there a second earlier, and Daryl idly wondered where he had gotten it from.

"Some sort," he said with a gleam in his brown eyes, openly enjoying the reversal.

Daryl's anger flared briefly, but the steady clobbering of the horse's hooves on the packed dirt road was making him drowsy. The small shudders carried to him through the wooden frame of the caravan elicited sharp, frequent reminders of his bruised body. With it the obvious question surfaced.

"What happened after I passed out by your fire?" Daryl asked, hoping the answer would be "nothing," but knowing that was most unlikely.

"That is a question for Fonseca," Reston said. "But I'm afraid she'll probably insist you do most of the talking."

Daryl tried broaching the subject several times with no success. He finally gave up and tried to learn more of the company itself. Fortunately, the subject revealed that

Reston's initial terseness had clearly been borne of playful teasing.

Reston had a way about him. He seemed at home in the world, in a way that is only available to someone who has truly found their place. Moreover, that place was not only right, but incredibly fortunate. Like marrying someone far, far better than you deserve. So yeah, he was grateful, but not in the contrived, wearisome way that some affect. In conversation it flowed from him, and you flowed with him.

He told Daryl how they were a small, but spectacular, circus troupe, whose multilingual cast meant that they could tour most parts of Western Europe. When asked about their act, Reston alternated between vague bragging and what must amount to downright lies meant to impress a local crowd less worldly than Daryl. Brex bent inch-thick iron bars and ate live pigeons in a single mouthful. Iliria levitated and threw knives, but apparently made more for the troupe by peddling all sorts of potions, as well as palm readings, than she did by directly contributing to the performance. Semi both threw and caught the knives, sometimes with her teeth. Fonseca did acrobatics and handled wild animals. Phineas was the owner turned impresario, and allegedly outperformed most of the others, although he never participated directly. That seemed like a cop-out to Daryl, but Reston clearly idolized the man, so he wisely let it go. When asked about Reston's own part, he explained that running this type of show required a lot of hands. Then he went on to explain the many duties he and his crewmates handled, such as wagon maintenance and animal handling, as well as setting up the camp, tent, and stage areas for the shows. During this detailed description, he once referred to himself and his co-workers as the "touched" instead of the crew, but Daryl had the sense that this was by accident, and once again opted not to comment.

Hours passed, and at lunch time a dark-haired woman in a simple dress rode down the line, while both chatting with the wagon drivers and distributing bread, cheese, dried fruits, and apples. She clearly knew who Daryl was and would undoubtedly report his recently regained cognizance. After eating more than his share, Daryl excused himself.

"Of course, man," Reston said. "You look a full night's sleep from being just tired."

Daryl returned Reston's easy smile with a ghoulish gum-revealing grin and made his slow, lumbering way back inside the caravan, where he collapsed on the bed and immediately dozed off.

***

When he awoke again, the caravan had stopped, and the light was fading. The clamor of camp life filtered in through the canvas; the flaps had been drawn and laced shut. This seemed a particularly courteous way of locking him in. Like using paper manacles. He did not know whether that was the intent, and he did not care. Movement already came easier, and he managed the flap-bound journey with only mild discomfort. The wan light and his swollen fingers made a task of unlacing the exit, but in about ten minutes the gap was wide enough to permit him to slide through.

People were milling about, tending to animals, and setting up temporary workstations. There was an air of camaraderie to the bustle. Laughter and smiles were regularly exchanged in passing, or in short conversations, clearly held brief by the tasks at hand. No one paid Daryl much attention, and he quickly found himself wandering aimlessly toward the quieter center of the encampment. Here, the wagons were larger and lavish with beautiful wooden sides instead of canvas. Several of the wagons bore lit lanterns attached beneath wooden beams jutting out from the roofs. Their size and sturdiness made Daryl feel like he was ambling down narrow streets, and in the waning light, the ambience seemed to totter on a razor's edge between welcoming and gloomy.

Erring on the side of the latter, Daryl was about to turn

back when he heard a series of sharp wooden thuds coming from the front end of the wagon on his left. Intrigued, he continued forward. As he rounded the corner, a lithe woman appeared. She seemed to be dancing, her body moving in a hypnotic rhythm, black and purple garments flaring with her motion, but with each turn one or several knives shot from her hands, followed by the staccato sounds that had initially caught his attention. Mesmerized, he stepped forward until a knife-littered panel came into view. The knives seemed to form a pattern, but of what he could not quite make out. The stiletto-style blades were rapidly disappearing from a cross-body harness strapped across her right shoulder. The blade dance stopped, and the sudden cease-fire enveloped the scene in an eerie silence. She turned partially, her brown bangs swinging in the late afternoon breeze. Her hazel eyes scanned him quickly, with a lackadaisical, almost dismissive air.

"It's amazing what a good night's rest can do," she said, not quite smiling.

"I always heal quickly," he replied. "That was very impressive," he continued, nodding toward the pin-cushioned board next to the deck of her wagon.

"You know, we have a pool going on just what you are," she said, ignoring the compliment and sauntering toward the target.

Daryl was not particularly interested in that conversation, but he was pretty sure the subject of this casual chat was unlikely to be up to him. Maybe he would learn something about this enigmatic troupe that had apparently saved him from Gabriel's clutches.

"And where'd you put your coin?" he asked.

"I didn't bet," she replied, the last word accentuated from the exertion of tearing one of the stilettos free from the wood.

Hearing no outright dismissal in her tone, he walked toward where she had begun removing the blades at nearly the same speed she had initially used to launch them. The board was quite mangled from previous practices, but he was pretty sure the blades had penetrated the wood in the exact outline of a guy approximately his height.

"Why not?" he asked, as he considered whether that was a sign he should heed, and in what way.

"It wouldn't be fair," she answered, slipping the final blade back in its sheath. "I already know what you are."

The words were spoken just as he came to a stop a few feet away. The smell of her hair was amazing, like peaches mixed with something floral and slightly pungent.

"I'm afraid you have me at a disadvantage then," he said, trying to steer the conversation toward safer grounds.

"Several," she said, again not quite smiling. "And I'm afraid I won't be able to shed any light on your status here. You'll have to wait for Fonseca, and she is quite busy these days."

"Who is Fonseca?"

"Someone you really need to make a good impression on," she answered. "I do know that you are welcome to roam the camp, but don't cause trouble and don't try to leave."

"Or else?" Daryl asked, his defiant streak rising to the occasion.

"Or else indeed," she answered, not missing a beat.

"Guess I'll stick around or find out," he said, his anger starting to flare. The scent of peaches wafted by him again, and he took a deep, calming breath.

"Ain't that the truth," she said dismissively, turning around and moving up the metal rungs of the small ladder leading to the wagon deck. At the top step she offered, "I'm Semi."

"Nice to meet you," he replied. He watched her move onto the deck and was about to turn and leave when she turned around, a smile on her lips that was well worth the wait.

"And no," she said. "I wasn't not throwing knives at you." With that she entered her wagon, shutting the door.

Daryl stood outside her wagon door for a long moment, the scent of her hair still lingering in his nostrils, and wondering whether her final statement had made him any the wiser.

***

Things had started to quiet down in the camp. Some people were still busy, but most had hunkered down somewhere, cooking, or just chatting. Several small and a few bigger fires had been lit, so Daryl moved toward the biggest he could find, still hoping for answers.

"Hey!" someone yelled to his right. Turning, he saw Reston getting up and running toward him from one of the smaller fire pits. "I thought I'd lost you. I came around looking once I had the horses groomed and fed."

"Hi Reston," Daryl said, with a half-genuine smile on his face. He hated his de facto prisoner status, but Reston literally represented a friendly face.

"Come join us. It will be getting chilly soon and supper is nearly ready."

Daryl followed Reston to the circle of fire-lit faces gathered around a big steaming pot, which he assumed was the source of the delicious smell. His stomach growled.

One of the stools next to Reston was empty and he sat down. His body applauded the rest it had so ardently lobbied for by instantly cramping up his right thigh, causing him to spill to the ground with a groan. Fire shot up his recently broken arm that had only just starting knitting itself back together.

"Whoa there, big fella," the small, stocky guy on his right said, as he caught Daryl by the arm and helped him back up on the stool. "Still a little worse for wear, eh?"

"Yeah," Daryl said gratefully, as he monitored himself for any signs of further bodily betrayal. When none were forthcoming, he eased into a more relaxed posture and let the warmth of the fire seep into his aching muscles.

Moments later someone passed him a bowl of stew and a loaf of dark bread, which he dug into. Engrossed in the meal, he barely registered the buzz of renewed conversation. He passed the bowl back to someone, realizing that his attention was wavering. Then his mind drifted into a warmth-induced drowsiness, and soon his head sagged to his chest. Someone helped him off the stool, and into an evanescent land of broken wings and skewered peaches.

CHAPTER 21

"**E**vening Hubble," Daryl proclaimed from his bed. The gnome had just entered through the wall, as was his way. The sun had only just set, casting the room in gloomy, violet hues.

"'Sup Daryl," Hubble said, briefly scanning the room. When his eyes reached Daryl, he stopped.

"What's this?" he said with a lewd smile.

"What's what?" Daryl asked.

"Oh, don't you be coy with me good sir," Hubble said. "Who's the girl?"

So, Daryl told his imaginary friend about the girl from his dreams.

***

A few days had passed traveling in the wagons of the troupe. Daryl's condition had improved steadily to the point where it only hurt when he coughed. They had made their way through rough, sparsely populated terrain, and as far as he could tell they were heading for the Pyrenean mountains. For a traveling band of performers, the choice to avoid the main thoroughfares of France seemed an odd one, but then obviously they were more than that. No one had offered any additional information on his situation, but neither was he treated badly. If anything, the people offered him some degree of deference, which made him ill at ease. He had surreptitiously explored the makeshift encampment on two separate nights, which on both occasions had revealed a similar setup, where primitive canvas-covered wagons surrounded the more lavish wood-paneled wagons in the center. He had not met Semi again, nor indeed run into any other occupants of the center wagons. At least, not as far as he could tell. It was his intention to leave soon. His wounds were nearly healed, and he did not feel obliged to stick around for whatever was coming. However, he could not risk drawing any heavenly attention to himself by flying, and he did not relish the idea of escaping on foot. Particularly since he had all but been told there would be pursuit. He would probably be able to overpower the people around him and steal a horse, but he would prefer not to resort to that. They were a friendly lot, and he had the distinct feeling that they were not the ones insisting he stay. On his second tour of the camp, he had heard the unmistakable sound of a horse whinnying. It had come from within an impressively large unguarded wagon in the middle of the camp. The wagon had been painted in black with bold red letters in a language he did not understand, and that was his destination tonight. Daryl had just finished dinner with Reston and the crew. They generally had maintenance to perform once dinner was over, and this night was no different. Several people sat by firelight, patching up canvas that had snagged on trees in the early autumn storms. He excused himself and headed inward toward the center of the camp.

As usual the twenty wagons had been placed in a roughly recognizable pattern, and it did not take him long to reach the large black wagon. The task was made even easier by the fact that it stood out as easily the largest of the bunch. He felt a brief stab of guilt as he eyed the door set in the side of the wagon. After all, he was preparing to steal from the people who had ostensibly saved his life. Then again, he knew none of the particulars, and they were certainly keeping him here against his will.

Rather than risking a racket by trying to remove one of the wagon-mounted lanterns, he silently moved up the landing and peered into the dark interior. Inside the wagon, a short walkway ran between two fenced-off holding pens, ending in a perpendicular walkway that ran parallel to the wagon from end to end. The entrance was faintly illuminated as moonlight filtered down through a grate set in the ceiling. The remaining part of the wagon was in near total darkness. Giving his eyes a moment to adjust, he cast a furtive glance behind him and stepped inside.

His nostrils were assailed by several odd smells mixed with something unmistakably equine. As Daryl cautiously traversed the wagon, he reminded himself that a well-stocked traveling circus could have anything from bears to tigers. Trusting to chance, he turned left down the walkway in the back, looking for the horse.

Grates were set at regular intervals in the ceiling and in the floor. The latter probably to ease the disposal of waste. The first of three stalls held a large sleeping form. It could well have been a bear, but given his current predicament, he did not attempt to verify the possibility, except to cement the conclusion that it most definitely was not a horse. The second stall appeared empty, and he was about to move on when he heard motion coming from the entrance of the wagon. Grabbing the sturdy wooden fence, he launched himself silently into the second stall, coming to a stop against the wooden planks. His side protested the sudden burst of motion, but he was able to suffer in silence. A horse whinnied from the other end of the wagon. *Figures.*

"Alright, alright, I'm coming," a deep, throaty voice exclaimed from the entrance of the wagon, the floorboards shuddering slightly in time with the thumps of heavy boots. Daryl settled down to wait in his funky nook when something brushed against his leg. Stifling a yelp, he banged his head painfully against a protruding wooden peg. The wood emitted a high-pitched noise as it shifted in its hole. The footsteps stopped.

"Anyone there?" the deep voice offered into the darkness, a slight tremor discernible. Having no desire to further frighten some poor stable hand, and well aware that his current situation was only going to deteriorate from here, Daryl started to rise.

Something jumped at his sudden movement, like a huge chicken with a scaly tail that caught the faint moonlight, and he saw a brief glimpse of red eyes before it scurried off into the darkest part of the pen. Daryl shook off the shock and vaulted back into the corridor, just as someone succeeded in lighting a lantern.

Daryl turned toward the light.

"Hi there," he said in his most friendly voice, the words slurring slightly in his mouth.

The light reflected off an impossibly big and savagely ugly man. His bulbous nose extended below his upper lip, and small shadows across his chin and cheeks hinted at numerous warts or spots. His enormous frame almost blocked the entire passage. He was easily seven feet tall and by no means lanky. Daryl took an involuntary step back on a stiff leg. Trying to right himself against the fence proved impossible, as his arms were suddenly beyond his control and moving at glacial speeds. *What is happening?* he thought, as he toppled backward, landing on the planks with a thud.

"Oh no," the beastly man exclaimed, and with a couple of wagon-bouncing strides, he leaned down to sling Daryl across his shoulder like a sack of potatoes. Then he ran out the door.

The ride was short and unpleasant. The rough jostle was complemented by an impressively foul smell of armpit and the giant repeating "Oh no! oh no!" which added to Daryl's already burgeoning alarm at his body's inability to obey even the simplest commands.

"Ily! Ily!" the giant shouted as he ran onto the deck of

one of the wagons, deposited Daryl, and immediately ran inside. Daryl lay on his side. He managed to get an arm braced against the deck and slowly pushed himself up in a half-seated position. A fair-skinned, middle-aged woman knelt at his side and held a bowl of something sweet smelling to his lips.

"Drink this," she urged, tilting the bowl, thus instantly transforming the suggestion into binding necessity.

Daryl gulped the tepid concoction with all the speed he could muster, not able to spare breath or attention for protesting the pace with which it was administered. His tongue was lolling uselessly around his mouth, and each gulp seemed like it could be his last as he came within a hair's breadth of choking. The liquid finally stopped coming and Daryl's lungs drew a ragged breath of air. He looked to his left, where the woman watched him with deep concern. She wore what appeared to be an immodest light-green night gown made from some form of lace. Daryl was about to speak when fire erupted in his belly. His body contracted in agony and the air came whooshing out of his lungs. His toes curled up in his boots and his body began thrashing about. The fire eased somewhat and spread into his limbs. A tingling sensation, not unlike a sleeping limb coming back to life, was creeping in to replace the roaring pain.

"Bring him inside, Brex," the woman said with authority.

"Yes, ma'am," the giant called Brex answered and scooped Daryl up to carry him inside.

If the wagon looked ostentatious from the outside, the inside would have put most nobles to shame. Brex quickly brought Daryl through a beaded curtain to a small anteroom, and through that into a richly decorated interior. Beautifully carved bookcases lined the walls, and well-wrought paraphernalia beyond his ken seemed crammed into every open space. At one end was a kitchen and at the other a beaded curtain, no doubt leading to a bedroom. Daryl was brought to a red upholstered couch, this time gently laid to rest on the plush material. His body still spasmed sporadically, but he could feel it starting to obey his commands.

The woman sat down next to him on a matching chair.

"How are you feeling?" she asked in a sultry voice. Somehow Daryl got the impression that this was simply her natural tone.

"Better," he replied. "What was that?"

She sighed. "I told them to talk to you sooner," as if that explained anything, but then she continued. "You looked a basilisk in the eye. Normally that's fatal, and you would have petrified completely in minutes if Brex hadn't been so quick to bring you here."

"Petrified? As in turned into stone?" Daryl asked.

"Yes. Actually, I can't be sure whether the potion works long term, so please let me know if you experience any uncommon stiffness or joint pain."

"What?!" Daryl bellowed, sitting up.

"Oh, hush now. I can probably just give you another dose. Probably," she said with what would normally have been a comforting smile.

"Anything else I should know?" he said.

"Oh yes," she answered with a smile. "Get some rest now, and I'll speak with Fonseca when she gets back. Should be some time tonight."

Daryl lay back down on the comfortable couch with a small groan. Leaving appeared to be out—he supposed answers would have to do.

***

"You seem to have a knack for getting in trouble," Fonseca said.

Brex had roused him from Iliria's couch only ten minutes earlier and led him to a small grove next to the camp. A campfire crackled and the scene bore an uncomfortable resemblance to the night of their first encounter. Several big logs surrounded the fire and Daryl counted about a dozen people, both young and old, all looking at him. Semi was among them. Fonseca was the curly-haired woman he remembered from that night. She wore a simple dress of a red fabric, which accentuated her youth, masked somewhat by her severe demeanor.

Brex left his side to take his own seat on the log, which shook visibly from supporting the giant's weight.

"It does seem to follow me around," he responded carefully, the resentment of being held captive currently overshadowed by his curiosity.

"Anything else I need to worry about?" he continued. "Any hydras or griffins I should try to steer clear off?"

If the sarcasm registered with Fonseca, she did not show it.

"No hydras," she responded.

Before Daryl had a chance to respond to that, she continued, "Why was Gabriel trying to kill you?" The question was direct and with no particular emphasis, but Daryl saw the momentous importance of his answer painted on every single face around the fire.

"Well," he said, "he would no doubt take great personal pleasure in pursuing that further, but aside from that, I guess I'm under what you might call 'open season.'"

A low murmur rose around the fire. Fonseca raised a hand and the crowd fell silent again.

"I should probably let you know that I just killed one of them," he said.

The murmur rose to new heights.

"Silence!" Fonseca said sternly and the quiet quickly returned.

"It would seem Iliria's visions have once again guided us right," she said in the ensuing stillness, pointing to the woman whose couch Daryl had recently occupied.

Iliria nodded. "I believe Daryl will be with us for a long time," she asserted cheerily.

"We shall see," Fonseca said.

"Excuse me, but I have no intention of staying," Daryl

declared.

Fonseca looked at Daryl with something like amazement in her eyes. "Are you an idiot?" she asked flatly.

When Daryl did not promptly agree, she continued, "Gabriel is waiting for you to leave. The moment you leave our company, he will attack and, I have no doubt, finish what he left off."

Daryl had to agree. He was an idiot.

"You are free to go if you wish, but I would much prefer not giving Gabriel what he wants."

"I apologize," he said. "I'm afraid I have misjudged your kindness."

He thought he caught a faint smile in the wan light.

"Not an uncommon occurrence," she replied. "For now, you will have to ride in the wagons with the touched, but I suggest you try to stay close to Iliria. Just in case the potion turns out to be less than completely effective. It would not be the first time."

"Now now," Iliria huffed in response. "The potions are working just fine. It is the administration that is causing trouble."

"As you say," Fonseca replied. "Just remember that we have a wagon full of rock sculptures that I should very much like to send on their fleshy way one of these days."

"It remains at the very top of my list," Iliria said.

Daryl was not overly distraught by the exchange. There was apparently a limit to how many ways your life could be hanging by a thread before one more peril became trivial.

Fonseca addressed the crowd, "Does anyone know where Phineas is and when he expects to return?"

No one spoke up or even eyed the others to see who might have the answer, leading Daryl to surmise that Phineas rarely gave notice.

Fonseca turned her attention back to Daryl.

"We will see what he has to say about you staying with us . . . indefinitely. Since you will be accepting our hospitality for a while, I suggest you acquaint yourself with our people and customs. Semi has agreed to give you a tour tomorrow and answer any questions you may have. I believe you've met?"

"Yes. Thank you," Daryl replied, his gaze wandering to where Semi was seated. She gave him a slight nod, then turned back to a handsome bearded man on her left, whispering something in his ear.

CHAPTER 22

The following day was a day of rest. After eating breakfast with Reston and the crew, Daryl made his way to Iliria's wagon. She had insisted on frequent checkups, and given her earlier statements, he was happy to oblige. In fact, he was in an amazing mood, joking with Reston and striding through the camp with a spring in his step. On his way he exchanged nods with Brex. The giant sent him a wide smile as he headed for the outer camp. Brex looked less imposing and somehow less grotesque by daylight. He would have to ask Semi about that later.

Daryl arrived at Iliria's wagon and knocked. Moments later she greeted him sleepily at the door, asking him to come in and have a seat.

She was stirring what could only be referred to as a cauldron, giving Daryl a fleeting feeling that she was actively trying to seem like a witch.

Taking in the décor, he realized that his impressions from last night had been slightly off. Everything there was indeed of the highest craftsmanship, but no one had taken the time to organize it. Instead, they had decided to find ingenious ways to clutter up the place. What he initially had taken for a beautiful sculpture in dark wood was actually a coat rack and three stools, enjoying an intricate embrace to save floor space. The only object occupying a relatively uncluttered nook at the back was a full-body mirror. It looked insanely expensive, but was covered in an odd sheen, like a mixture of dust and soot. It had been a long time since he had been near a real mirror, and he got up to take a look at his reflection.

"Don't go near the mirror," Iliria said with her back turned. "I have managed to thin the barrier between worlds. There is no telling what might appear. One problem at a time, eh?"

Daryl sat down again, perfectly happy to focus his immediate attention on not turning into stone.

In a few moments Iliria joined him with what appeared to be some form of barley gruel and a cup of foul-smelling herbal infusion.

"You like that?" he asked her uncertainly, his nostrils flaring in a futile attempt to get away.

She looked up sleepily, only now seeming to remember that he was there.

"What? Oh no, that's for you."

Oh joy, he thought, taking the proffered cup. "Do I need to eat the gruel too?"

"No, that's my breakfast."

***

Semi came by the wagon a short while later to take him on the promised tour. He had a lot of questions but decided that he would make sure to enjoy the company first and ask questions later. His mouth still tingled from the foul infusion, and Iliria assured him that she would make more for tonight.

"So, you probably already have an idea of the layout," Semi said. "Touched at the edge, freaks at the center."

Moving in a straight line out of camp, they had already left the fancier wagons behind. Daryl thought it an odd route given the subject of the tour but said nothing. Soon they left the camp perimeter behind for a small meadow, losing sight of the encampment altogether by a small creek. Daryl surmised the campground had been chosen partly due to the easy access to fresh water.

Semi took two quick steps forward and launched herself onto a low-hanging branch, only a few feet above the gurgling stream.

"Do all your tours have trees in them?" he asked.

"Don't be silly," she answered him from the bough. "This one is special."

Moving down to the water's edge, he noticed the tracks leading from the water back toward the camp.

"This is the boundary. If you go beyond it, you're on your own."

Daryl looked up and down the waterline. Nothing seemed to indicate a boundary.

"How will I know?" he asked.

"Beats me," she said. "I always ask around. I suggest you do the same."

"How long have you been with the troupe?"

"Nearly a year, but I'm not always here. Too many other . . . commitments."

"Well, aren't you mysterious?" he teased.

"I have been asked not to be, so please, fire away."

Semi looked at him expectantly, as if daring him to be direct. He picked up a pebble from the bank and tossed it into the placid waters.

"How do you know what I am?" he finally said, not looking at her.

"Excellent question," she said. "As you may have guessed, it's part of my heritage. The two of us used to be part of the same beast. Before the great split, of course."

"You're a demon?" Daryl blurted with no small amount of surprise, making it evident that she had overestimated his powers of deduction.

Semi sighed. "Please don't make it this easy to mock you.

It takes away the sport."

"Sorry," he replied. "When it comes to other supernatural beings, I've lived a somewhat sheltered life. I thought the body you're possessing would show signs of chaos?"

"Like horns?" she asked with a sneer.

"Like horns," he admitted.

"No, those only appear as the demon wrestles with the original occupant of the body. If the demon stays dormant or, as in my case, inhabits an empty vessel, no such signs appear."

Disliking the feeling of prying into her personal affairs, he decided to pry elsewhere instead.

"Is everyone in the inner circle some kind of supernatural being?"

"As far as I know. I don't know them all, and I'm not the only one who comes and goes."

"Alright, how about Fonseca? What is she really?"

"Well, she's always gone when the moon is full. That was one of the reasons you had to wait around for the conclave last night."

"I didn't think werewolves existed."

"Neither did I," Semi said, surprising Daryl with the admission. After a brief pause, she continued.

"And before you ask. Our other leader, Phineas, is allegedly a vampire, Iliria is some kind of witch, and Brex is a troll."

Daryl tried his hardest to process that string of revelations. As was often the case, his mind seized on arguably the least important aspect.

"Brex looks pretty good for a troll," he said, marveling at his own insight.

"It's a glamour," Semi said, feet dangling nonchalantly above the water. "Iliria administers it every morning. It wears off during the day or if he gets wet. You should pay him a visit at night sometime."

An eerie silence had crept into the scene. No birds

chirped; no insects buzzed. Looking up at Semi, he could tell that she too was aware that something had changed. They both simultaneously looked up to notice Gabriel standing on the opposite bank, not thirty feet away.

"Greetings," he said with an easy smile. "How are things?"

Daryl stiffened as equal parts alarm and hatred welled up inside him. Then he remembered Semi and the fact that he had no way to position himself between them. Her carefree perch had just gotten precarious.

"Hi Gabie," he said, returning the smile with effort. "Did Heaven finally run out of latrines for you to scrub?"

"My child, you do try to vex me," Gabriel said, his smile turning sad.

"Gabie," Semi said, as if pondering something. "I rather like that."

Gabriel turned his gaze from Daryl to Semi.

"This is between you and me," Daryl said, trying to draw the archangel's attention back to himself.

"Oh, there is no doubt of that," Gabriel said. "Not to worry, Semariel and I are old acquaintances. And, might I add, fitting company for someone like yourself."

Gabriel looked at Daryl. "Speaking of which, why don't you just cross this pesky little stream and we can be on our way? After all, you've already tried the hard way."

"It's Semi." Gabriel's gaze drifted back her way.

"Not in my book," Gabriel said.

"Well, your book is wrong," she responded.

Ignoring Semi, he turned back to Daryl.

"Even someone as dense as you has probably realized by now that you have some measure of protection from the company you keep. It makes one wonder at the odds of you coming upon them when you did." Gabriel paused a moment, looking expectantly at Daryl. Having no idea what he meant, Daryl remained silent, and so, with a slight shrug, Gabriel continued, "However, having analyzed the situation, I should point out that this protection stems in large part from the she-wolf and the vampire, which begs another question. What happens the next time the wolf is howling at the moon and the vampire is hiding from the sun? Who will guard you then?"

Daryl shifted uneasily.

"So, you see, I will take you. It is inevitable."

A cold breeze blew through the treetops. Other than that, the scene was quiet.

"What will it be, Jae'el? A swift death now or a prolonged cleansing later? Make your choice."

Daryl shook himself, trying to cast off the cold, unavoidable logic of the archangel's proposal. When he finally responded, it stemmed not from self-preservation or fear, but from a carefully cultivated hatred.

"It's Daryl."

The archangel's sigh easily carried across the stream.

"We shall see," he said. Then he flickered once and was gone.

CHAPTER 23

Daryl was up early.

The land around him was a mixture of large boulders and trees, dotted with swathes of flowering clearings that would soon be buzzing with insects. A light rain had pelted the camp during the night, giving the world the appearance of being covered in a light sheen of sweat. For the past half an hour, he had been sitting on a large rock at the edge of camp, taking stock of his time with the company and liking what he saw. Given time, he could imagine himself settling into a rhythm of traveling with these people, learning from them. Perhaps even contributing in some meaningful way, if such a way existed. However, Fonseca had agreed that Gabriel's analysis of the situation was sound. Phineas was not back yet, and even if he were, Gabriel would not be coming during the night.

He looked up at the heavens. The brightening of the sky made the white silhouette of the full moon less visible against the pale blue backdrop. Fonseca had left last evening.

Daryl edged himself off the rock and turned to leave the campground. The sun was only moments away from rising, and several large cook fires had been assembled on the embers of the previous night's fires.

Reston waved from a nearby bonfire, but Daryl just waved back with a shake of his head. He would not be needing a full stomach for what was to come. Reston looked puzzled but turned back to his preparations.

Leaving the last few wagons behind, Daryl walked across the gently sloping field just outside camp. The first few rays of a rising sun kissed the leaves on the highest branches of nearby poplars. The morning was quiet and serene.

A few precious moments more. Daryl closed his eyes, taking in a big lungful of the crisp air.

"Here we are," Gabriel said.

Daryl opened his eyes. His doom was walking toward him, casually strolling out from underneath the grand trees. Gabriel's perfect features were somehow off. It took Daryl several moments to recognize the emotion, so alien on his chiseled features—Gabriel looked joyful.

Gabriel stopped about ten feet away, hands at his sides.

"Are you ready, child?" he asked.

Daryl looked into Gabriel's unwavering gaze. There was so much to say and undoubtedly so little time to say it.

"Gabie," he began, and was immediately interrupted by a blow he did not see coming, sending him sprawling. So very little time.

Steadying himself against a small tree, he tried to stand, but his legs caved beneath him, and he tilted to the side, enveloped once more in the tall grass. Gabriel was apparently feeling particularly playful, allowing Daryl the time to flop around on the ground. Finally managing to get his feet beneath him, Daryl stood again.

Gabriel was staring beyond him. Turning, he noticed that they were no longer alone. A smartly dressed gentleman was walking toward them across the field. As he approached, his cane tapped the earth in a smooth, practiced manner. He bore himself with an aloof, almost aristocratic air. Coming closer he changed his course, walking directly toward Daryl.

"Good morning," the man said. "Would any of you fine gentlemen mind if I joined you? This is after all an exceptionally delightful morning to be out for a stroll, don't you think?"

Gabriel just stood there looking. This was the second time this morning that Daryl had seen an alien emotion cross Gabriel's face. This time it looked something like bewilderment. The wind picked up a little, bringing a surprisingly strong whiff of smoke from the camp cook fires to Daryl's nostrils. The three of them stood facing each other. Or rather, Gabriel and the newcomer faced each other with Daryl somewhere in the middle, trying to figure out what was going on. Gabriel finally broke the silence.

"This does not concern you," he said.

"I think you are well aware that it does. In fact, I might even take offense at your decision to meddle in what is very clearly my business."

Gabriel did not strike him down.

"How come you are here?" he finally said.

The newcomer feigned puzzlement, then said, "Ah, you mean out on this fine morning? I assure you, the effects of sunlight on someone of my disposition are grossly exaggerated."

"No, it cannot be," Gabriel said. "I have seen you burn."

"I'm afraid you've only seen what I have wanted you to see. Not to worry. You are not the first to be fooled by my ilk, and you will not be the last."

Steel crept back into Gabriel's voice. "Vlad, I am taking him back with me. He has much to answer for."

"My name is Vlad no longer. It is Phineas."

"What *is* it with you people and names," Gabriel exploded, his regained composure clearly only skin deep. "Why can you not simply stick to the ones you have been given?"

"Ah, but that is the point. They were given. Something I would not expect a lapdog like yourself to understand. Our names are taken. They are who we are now, not where we came from."

"You won't get away with this," Gabriel said, hatred and contempt smoldering in his eyes.

There he is, Daryl thought, finally seeing a recognizable emotion flow across the archangel's face.

"It is time you left," Phineas said. "Unless you want to face the beast." The final word was accentuated by a growl so deep it felt like the earth itself shook for a moment.

Gabriel did not waiver, but his inaction spoke volumes. Particularly to Daryl, who was still trying to understand how this unassuming man was apparently able to square off against the most powerful being Daryl had ever known.

"This isn't over," Gabriel finally said, turning away. Moments later, he simply vanished.

"Nothing ever is," Phineas said into the empty space.

Turning to Daryl he said, "We should get back," and without waiting for Daryl's response he set off at a leisurely pace toward camp. Daryl took a moment to rub the sore spot in his sternum where Gabriel had punched him, then he hurriedly caught up to Phineas.

"Thank you," Daryl said. "I have no idea how you just did that."

"Oh, don't mention it. It is clear that you don't have a place in the world anymore, which just happens to make you a perfect fit for our company."

As they entered the camp, everyone who noticed them gave Phineas a respectful nod, which he unfailingly returned. The smell from the cook fires had increased unexpectedly to the point where Daryl's nose was starting to itch, and he wondered whether someone had left a side of bacon unattended.

"Excuse me, Daryl," Phineas said before heading toward Iliria's wagon. She stood waiting in the door, a look of deep concern on her face. As Phineas entered, she closed the door behind him, waving Daryl away. The last he saw through the slit between the door and the frame was the flash as Iliria's glamour fell, accompanied by Phineas's blistering body collapsing in a heap on the floor.

***

Daryl awoke, with a maddening phantom itch between his shoulder blades and the acrid taste of smoke still fresh on his tongue. Disoriented, he shook his head and looked around. He was lying on the floor, face down, with his left leg still partly on the bed. His comforter enveloped his upper body, hiding his puzzled frown.

A single feather from the comforter settled onto the floor.

CHAPTER 24

Daryl had been splayed out on the floor for several hours when Hubble walked in. The expected outburst of surprise was soon replaced by the arduous task of putting Daryl back to bed. The gnome's diminutive form and Daryl's considerable dead weight forced their anatomies into unwelcome geometries. After toiling for the better part of ten minutes, Hubble finally leveraged Daryl's left leg onto the bed, completing the task. By silent consent, they both took a minute. Hubble was breathing heavily while staring out into the night through the window, and Daryl performed all the mental gymnastics at his disposal to keep the smell of the gnome's hairy crotch from being lodged too firmly in his memory.

"I need a drink!" Hubble finally proclaimed, his breathing under control again.

"Amen," Daryl responded, still breathing through his mouth.

Daryl heard the unstopping of a flask, and moments later Hubble offered him a much-needed draught. "How the hell did you end up on the floor anyway?" Hubble asked in exasperation. "I thought you were supposed to be quadriplegic?"

"I don't know," Daryl admitted.

Hubble shifted on the bed, bringing him fully into Daryl's field of view. He looked . . . haggard.

"Daryl," he said earnestly. "Something is wrong here at the asylum."

Daryl was about to make a joke about getting right on it, but something in the gnome's eyes stopped him.

"What do you mean?" he asked instead.

Hubble looked away briefly, letting out a barely audible sigh.

"It's Susan," he finally said, turning back to face Daryl. "Well, mostly her anyway. She's behaving erratically and... Daryl, I'm not sure you can trust her anymore."

"What?" was all he could muster. "What are you saying? Why would you think that?"

"It's not just me, Daryl. Most of the staff that know her are really concerned. Her treatment of everyone but you has suffered dramatically. It's like she is obsessed with you and your progress. There is even talk of putting her on probation."

Daryl's head was reeling for a flurry of reasons that he had trouble sorting out. He did not want to have to deal with this. Not from Hubble, not from anyone. Susan had helped him so much.

"So, I shouldn't trust her because she is overly fixated on me getting better?" he finally said.

"Well, yes," Hubble answered. "She's a therapist! It's not rational. And there is something else . . ."

"What?" Daryl asked wearily. What he would not give for the opportunity to rub his tired eyes. Fate obligingly set alight the phantom itch between his shoulder blades.

"This place is falling apart. Two more patients have gone missing since Werner. Everyone here has a haunted look about them. Especially when they think they're alone."

"For crying out loud, Hubble! What do you want me to do about it?"

Hubble hesitated. "I know, but listen, you need to ask

for a different therapist. You can't trust her."

An eerie calm settled on Daryl at the outburst. "No," he said.

"Werner is still fucking missing, Daryl. They can spin that shit all they want, but there was something weird about the way he went. Not a word to no one. Nothing! And now on top of that people are disappearing left and right. Do you really believe they'll all just reappear and be like, 'Hey, what did we miss?'"

"No," he said. "I think I need a little time to myself if you don't mind."

Hubble looked hesitant as he absently scratched one of his huge ears. "Sure," he said. "Will you at least think about what I've said?"

"Undoubtedly," Daryl responded.

Hubble slid off the bed and was gone. Daryl cursed once, then looked up. As always when alone, his mind filled with thoughts of Ginny and a choking guilt. He needed to stare at the ceiling and think about nothing. *And I'm just the guy to do it,* he thought bitterly.

CHAPTER 25

… Integration status:
Memory access: 82%
Network protocol control: 44%
Self-coherence: 32%
Search for initial subjects complete:
… Subjects 0000001-0000061: Deceased
… Subject 0000062: Immobilized
… Subjects 0000063-0000334: Deceased
Incoming progress report on subject 07364934:
Subject 0000062 threat level update: High
… Accessing subject 07364934 medical records
Subject makes full recovery from accident
Subject's parents: Deceased
Close relatives: None
Distant relatives: None
Progress report complete:
More information required…

***

A male doctor stood at the foot of the bed, and a female nurse sat by her side. He was being awfully nice to her, speaking in kind, pleasant tones, and the nurse was gently stroking her hand. He had been speaking for a while, but Susan was unable to get her head to listen. She understood most of the words as they passed through her brain, but somehow they refused to coalesce into meaningful phrases. She wanted to ask where her parents were but was scared to make the man angry. What if he only seemed nice? He had stopped talking and stood looking down at her as if expecting an answer. She panicked and looked to the nurse for help.

"It's okay, dear," she said. "You'll be okay. God has a plan for us all."

What an odd thing to say, she thought. Nodding seemed the right thing to do, so she did.

"Can I have some water?" she asked, hoping to shift the focus away from herself.

The nurse looked at the doctor and some sort of information was passed wordlessly between them.

"Of course," the nurse replied, finally letting go of her hand.

She left the room with the doctor.

The room was bigger than her room at home and much, much tidier.

A lump formed right at the back of her throat. She felt so alone.

***

The ceiling had provided very little in the way of answers. Daryl blamed the ceiling, but given the fact that he would not be able to exchange it for another, he decided to forgive it. Also, to be fair, his situation was not easily improved by ceilings or anyone else. On a whim he exclaimed, "So Bill-Din, have you got anything useful to say?"

Not surprisingly, no one answered.

How had he moved, or been moved, in his dreams? He supposed it would be easy to do, given the fact that he was unable to feel anything from the neck down. But by whom? And why? What had his most recent dream meant? And had he really had a nocturnal visit from Fonseca, one of the main characters of his dreams, right before they began? How long ago was it that he had awoken to find her in his room? Two weeks? Was he supposed to learn something from the dreams? If so, it remained obscure to him. Perhaps Susan was right in suggesting that they were meant to provide stimulus to his prone existence. However, he *had* noticed that the angels in his recent dreams shared the same eyes as Pupils, the heavyset man who had visited him in the parlor a lifetime ago. That probably suggested that his dreams and hallucinations were linked, or even that Pupils was supposed to be an angel himself. What had he said? Come see him? *Yeah, I should get on that,* Daryl thought with irony and bitterness in equal measure. He also wondered why Susan was continuing to see him. It seemed obvious to him that his case should be deprioritized given his new predicament. He had not exactly been keeping track, but she did come by very regularly. In fact, she would probably be by after his breakfast fluid installment. Thinking of which, he should take up solids again.

A guy needed real sustenance to maintain this level of confusion.

Maybe Susan was just fascinated by the variety of his delusions. In the past week he had added trolls, witches, werewolves, and vampires to the list. She had suggested something like a layered psychosis, right? So, he would have believed in the existence of all of those prior to whatever events caused him to lose his memories. Not getting anywhere, he shifted his gaze, granting the cabinet a chance to chime in.

Shortly thereafter his breakfast date walked in, carrying a nutritious meal-in-a-bag.

"Morning," Daryl said. "Could I see a menu?"

***

Daryl knew that Susan would have heard that he had begun to take in solid food again. Still, why had she brought peaches? Susan came by every day now, and he relished every moment. However, his mind was still adjusting to its new sensory deprivation, which led to weird fixations on irrelevant details. Details like peaches.

". . . so, I think we should give that a try," Susan concluded.

Daryl looked up from where the net with uneaten peaches lay on his dresser.

"Are you even listening?" Susan asked.

A vision of Semi flashed before his eyes, and he almost remembered . . . something. He shook his head to clear it.

"I hate peaches," he said simply.

Susan looked at him uncomprehendingly. "I'm sorry, I didn't know that." Except he was pretty sure she did. Or should. They had spoken about it before and even laughed at the ludicrous extent of his dislike. In fact, it was one of his favorite memories of her. The moment had had a personal warmth to it that their professional interaction invariably lacked most of the time.

"Don't worry about it," he finally said. "I've been meaning to ask you about Werner. Has anything turned up?"

"I'm afraid not," she answered, a hint of annoyance tingeing her voice. Then her features mellowed.

"Daryl, I'm sure that he is fine. He's not the first patient to go missing only to turn up a few weeks later. It's the price of the many liberties afforded most patients here. I promise to let you know as soon as there are any developments."

Daryl nodded slowly. She wore a lovely yellow button-up dress with a matching hairband. The latter was perhaps a bit of an odd stylistic choice for someone her age, but Daryl really liked this new fad of hers. If it worked, it worked.

"Has anyone else gone missing?" he finally asked.

"Why yes, as a matter of fact, Jim and Robert. Who told you about that?"

"I overheard two of the orderlies chatting in the hallway," he lied.

She nodded, then continued, "Anyway, as I was saying. I have been working on a theory for your case that could have a profound effect."

"Sure," Daryl said. His new circumstances had left him with little appetite for therapy. Who cared what happened within his noodle, if it was just going to be cased up in here for the remainder of his meaningless existence?

"It will require more hypnotherapy," she said, inspecting his response. Daryl performed a shoulderless shrug. At least it meant spending more time with Susan.

"Excellent. I will fill you in on the details once I have conferred with a few colleagues." She wiped her nose on a tissue, and it came away bloody.

"Damn nosebleeds," she cursed before sending him a disarming smile that he could not help returning. "Are you sure you won't try a peach? They're ripe."

CHAPTER 26

A breeze wafted in from the north, carrying crisp, floral notes of the last summer blossoms. The air was dry and hot, evaporating the sweat on Daryl's brow as quickly as it appeared.

"One more push, and I think we've got it," Reston shouted encouragingly.

The rut in which the wagon wheel had become jammed was adamantly refusing to release its newfound occupant. Daryl, Reston, and two other crew members braced against the two poles that had been dug underneath the wagon. Daryl heaved on his side; the other three men heaved on the other. The wagon lifted a few inches and then stuck again. They increased the tension until, with a loud snap, the left pole broke on Daryl's end and they were flung to the ground.

"Damn," Reston swore, swatting the dusty earth with his straw hat.

"Need a hand?" Brex said, walking up to the prone men. He wore a huge smile, showing off his impressive yellow canines. His body looked grotesquely huge and slightly misshapen, and Daryl found himself, for the hundredth time, wondering what he really looked like.

"No worries," Reston replied quickly. The crew was always hesitant about taking help from the inner circle whenever simpler means might suffice. Daryl, apparently, did not quite qualify, and that always put a smile on his face. "We just need a few additional poles," Reston continued, looking to the pile on a nearby wagon.

"Nonsense," Brex said, grabbing the back of the wagon. "You just need me."

With that he hefted the wagon, which now looked like little more than a cart at a village fair, and wrenched it upward. The wood groaned briefly and then came loose out of the hole. Daryl and the other men scrambled backward on hands and knees as the wagon lifted three feet into the air before gravity brought it back down. All men fortunately cleared the area before the wagon landed with a resounding crash.

"Thanks," Reston said as the dust settled. One of the other men coughed.

"You're welcome," Brex replied happily. Then he trudged on.

They all got up, dusting off shirts and pants. Daryl's ears were ringing, and his eyes burned from dust and grit.

"Everyone okay?" Reston asked. Everyone was.

Finding no critical damage to the wagon, the signal was given to resume the journey. The rest of the caravan took a circuitous route, avoiding the uneven stretch of earth. The poor roads had been a gamble on a shortcut to quicken their arrival in Lyon. They were going to be late.

***

"I know, I know," Lucien, the stagehand-turned-impresario, said, wringing his hands. "They're not like you and me. They're . . . artists."

"Not in Lyon they're not. Unless they're ready in five minutes, that is," the taciturn man said.

"They'll be ready," Lucien promised, his eyes filled with

a hope that bordered on belief. A tepid trust perhaps. Not in the performers' timeliness. Trusting that would have been a delusional disregard of past events. A trust in the show maybe, in a belief that the truly spectacular was always welcome. No matter how tardy it might be.

"We'll see," the man said, turning away with a scoff.

Daryl had taken a seat atop the planks that served as a scaffold for the portable entrance. His position was partly obscured by the top of the heavy curtain, and the lighting focused on the center of the ring made him nearly invisible to the expectant crowd. His duties had already been performed and he was ready to enjoy the show. The makeshift tent just outside camp had been erected in less than an hour, making their appearance only two hours behind schedule.

The tent was packed to bursting. Something like four hundred people were seated on wooden benches in a semi-circle surrounding the hard-packed dirt in the center. The last of the spectators had taken their seats only moments before, and the many conversations mixed to form a fluctuating buzz interrupted by occasional bouts of raucous laughter.

Phineas entered the ring through the small triangular opening between the curtains. His body showed no signs of the severe burns it had sustained less than a week ago. Daryl had to remind himself that they might be concealed by one of Iliria's glamours, just as they had been on that fateful day. Except for their smell, which Daryl recalled with a shudder. He still had not had a chance to properly express his gratitude. Phineas walked with measured steps until he reached the center. He stopped, and a hush fell over the crowd. It was Daryl's experience that at any given time Phineas's presence was either completely unnoticed or completely overwhelming. No middle ground. This was clearly the latter. Several long moments passed in which he simply surveyed the crowd, like a predator staring down its prey. Someone outside the tent laughed, the sound alien within the confines of the canvas.

The tension built, and Daryl saw how every man, woman, and child leaned forward slightly, as if ready to scatter at a moment's notice.

"Ladies and gentlemen," Phineas's voice boomed. A fat, middle-aged man fell from the bench and landed maladroitly on his ass. "Tonight, you will see things you've never dreamed of—and dream things you've never seen. Tonight, the fabric of your world will unravel as we show you what lies beyond the edges of the maps."

With that, Phineas swept the expectant crowd with one final look, firmly rooting them in place, and marched back the way he came, cane tapping out the rhythm of his retreat.

A magnificent white horse and a huge golden lion entered the ring, running in circles, the cat always a step behind the horse. A frantic fiddler's tune was playing as the lion stepped up the chase, jaws snapping in the air. The spectators were enthralled, not moving, despite the fact that a hungry lion prowled not ten feet away.

Finally, the horse slowed, and the lion launched itself onto its back. A gasp rose from the crowd, but the horse was not devoured. In fact, it did not even falter, and now the lion rode on the back of the horse.

"Impossible," someone whispered, enrapt, close to where Daryl was hiding.

The stacked animals took one final lap around the arena before they exited, and the music died down.

The Hamsta twins followed, their well-muscled bodies all wrapped up into one eight-limbed being, legs and arms sticking out at awkward angles. Daryl knew the two were inseparable, always squabbling about who owed who money, but seeing them reveling in their unique gift gave the sentiment new meaning and drew gasps of nauseated disbelief from the crowds. A few ladies swooned, but most cheered at the display. The show was off to a good start.

This was followed by Fonseca's aerial acrobatics, swinging between the two erected platforms nearly reaching the canvas above them. Exceptionally limber, she swung, jumped, and twisted between the two connecting trapezes, somehow managing to keep both within reach as she spun gracefully through the air.

Beneath her, a handsome bearded man that Daryl felt he had seen somewhere before set up an equally familiar wooden board. As Fonseca landed amid a roar of applause, he quietly placed an apple in his mouth, on his head, and one in each hand. Fonseca exited and Semi sauntered in, a sway to her hips and a wide leather belt across her left shoulder carrying an impressive array of knives.

Phineas entered behind her, his presence much less acute this time.

"How far away should she stand as she attempts to dislodge all four apples? Ten feet?" The crowd booed. "Twenty feet?" Another round of jeers. "Not thirty feet?" The crowd roared for blood.

"All the way!" someone cried.

Soon the call was taken up, and the tent reverberated with the demand that she stand as far away as the tent would allow. Moving to the edge of the ring, she stopped, and a hush fell. She flipped a single knife in her hand and, with an explosive lunge, sent the blade spinning through the air a good eighty feet, slicing into the apple held in the man's left hand, knocking it back and sticking it onto the wooden board.

"One," yelled Phineas. The crowd roared.

"Two." And the apple left his right hand.

"Three." And the apple on top of his head was removed.

"Four." The man had done a quarter-turn and the knife ripped the apple from his mouth, slicing it in half. The crowd went wild. Before they had a chance to settle down, the man took a single step back, putting him directly up against the board. Semi walked slowly toward him, sending a barrage of knives at him that enveloped him in a familiar wood-and-steel outline.

At some point amidst the applause a violin had begun to

play. The lilting tune initially evaded notice, growing in strength until it gradually drew everyone's attention, demanding silence. Amaranth danced out on the unsteady legs of the inebriated, the silence of the crowd around him in stark contrast to the cacophony just moments before. Iliria made her entrance in a whirl of swaying hips and undulating fabrics. The crowd was mesmerized, man and woman alike, as the expertly matched tune and dance filled the tent. Daryl could not tear his gaze away from Iliria as she moved sensuously across the arena floor.

Then the music stopped, and she floated into the air, ostensibly on invisible strings. She might also really be flying—neither would have surprised him. Brex lumbered in, a cloth-covered cage held in one enormous fist. He put it down near the center of the arena. Iliria floated high above the floor, and she suddenly dropped straight into Brex's waiting arms to another round of applause.

Brex sat Iliria down on the floor and she performed an elegant mix between a bow and a curtsy. The cage had been placed on the floor and remained covered by a cloth. Brex reached within as he made soft, barely audible cooing noises. A single white dove sat perched calmly on his massive index finger. With a flourish he brought the animal to his lips, and an expectant silence spread through the benches. Brex opened his impressive maw and placed the finger holding the pigeon on his lower lip in a pensive gesture. For a pregnant moment the cooing of the pigeon could be heard as it looked around quizzically. Then, with a skip and a single beat of wings, it flew into his mouth and was gone in a flash of teeth and feathers.

As Brex reached into the cage for another bird, the stunned silence was gradually replaced by rhythmic stomping and clapping, urging him on. Five birds later, Brex removed the cloth to reveal an empty cage. He picked it up and began to knead and compress the bars into a single cube of near-solid metal, roughly the size of a large apple. This was followed by several impressive feats of strength, which concluded the show for the evening. As the performers reentered to take a bow, Daryl sidled down to the ground and walked the short distance back to camp. It was a beautiful moonlit night, and as he entered the inner circle, he walked by the unicorn and the griffon chatting, as they often did after a show.

"Good crowd tonight," The griffon asserted with a growl.

"I guess," the unicorn replied in a surly tone.

"Not this again! It's just entertainment."

"It's embarrassing is what it is! Do you have any idea how much you weigh?"

"You promised not to bring that up anymore," the griffon said and shook its huge wings.

"Well, excuse me, but I only have the one back."

Their voices receded behind him, and he noticed a soft melody carried on the evening breeze, mesmerizing in its seamless transitions between solemn and whimsical.

Daryl moved to the wagon from which the music emerged. It was easily identified by both the music and the billows of smoke that rose in slow, lazy puffs, gradually blending with the darkening sky. Daryl had no intention of joining Amaranth on his porch, but found himself suddenly standing only a few steps away, bathed in the soft glow of the lit pipe. As he came to a stop, the music seemed to naturally conclude, and Daryl blinked, suddenly self-conscious. The small, hunched man looked up, beaming a mischievous grin at Daryl. "Won't you join me?" he asked.

Daryl stepped up onto the wagon's small porch and took a seat opposite the old man. A peace settled on him, and he cast a longing look at the elaborate pipe setup that permitted Amaranth to play his violin and smoke his pipe at the same time. "Go ahead," Amaranth said with another smile, swinging the arm of the pipe-holder in Daryl's direction.

The tobacco had a sweet, pungent flavor, with none of the throat-jarring qualities Daryl associated with smoking. The calm permeated him, seeming to seep into his very bones. The world took a step back, becoming a cushion in which he rested.

"I don't think I've welcomed you to the troupe yet," Amaranth drawled. His voice like everything else taking on a slow, syrupy texture. He reclaimed the pipe from Daryl's tingling fingers. "Not that additional welcome is needed. Necessarily."

Daryl could not remember when he had last felt this much at ease. He idly wondered where Semi was. "You play that violin good," he said. ". . . well," he amended. "Really well."

"Thank you," Amaranth said with a nod and a smile.

"What are you?" Daryl blurted. He recognized the unusual degree of directness in his query without feeling embarrassed by it in the slightest.

Amaranth set down the violin that had been resting against his knees. The body of the instrument produced a wooden echo as it was set to lean against the wall of the wagon.

"The first and the last of the fauns," he said.

Daryl looked at the old man. The twilight made it difficult to make out details. His legs did seem to be crossed at an unusual angle. As he lifted his gaze, something flashed in Amaranth's gaze, like the eyes of a cat or an owl.

"So, your name isn't really Amaranth?" Daryl asked.

"It certainly is," the old man replied. A far-off look settled behind the sheen of his translucent eyes. "But once, many, many years ago, I was known by different names. I caused panic and peace, birth and death."

Daryl yawned. "What happened?" he asked.

"I retired," Amaranth said, taking another big pull on his pipe. "I stopped playing the songs that bind and the songs that sow."

Smoke billowed from his mouth, which cut a satisfied grin. Shapes of beasts and men formed within the gray depths as the clouds became wisps, became air.

"I still keep in touch through the little people. One in

particular visits me from time to time. An outcast from his own people. I think you'd like him. He has a temper only surpassed by his appetites, if you take my meaning." With that Amaranth gave a suggestive wink. He continued, "In that regard he and I are much alike. The stories we share! Maybe you should join us the next time he is around?"

Daryl clumsily caught the pipe in numb, fumbling hands. "I'd like that."

CHAPTER 27

"There's someone here to see you," Susan said.

Daryl looked up from where he had been trying to read the electronic newspaper, using his mouth to leaf through the content. It was amazing how quickly your mind adjusted to new ways of doing things. He spit out the pointer.

Susan was speaking quietly to someone outside Daryl's field of view. He was about to suggest that he would be right there when Werner stepped into the room.

Daryl's mind froze. His friend looked good. Great, even.

"Hi Daryl," Werner said, smiling uncertainly. "Mind if I come in?"

"Go ahead," Daryl said, the words catching slightly in his suddenly dry throat.

"I'll leave you two to talk," Susan said, and she gently closed the door.

"Geez Daryl, I'm really sorry about what happened to you," Werner said, a pained expression on his usually jovial face.

"Not your fault really," Daryl said, pushing back hard against the bitterness that was trying to hijack his emotions.

"Fuck that," Werner said. "You were trying to help me.

You didn't deserve that."

"Thanks," Daryl said. He looked away briefly. Unable to keep the emotion out of his voice he said, "I'm really glad you're alright."

"Yeah." Werner said, taking a seat next to Daryl. The silence stretched for a bit. Finally, Werner leaned in.

"So, what did I miss?"

***

Werner had been holed up with a female relative and had spent the time getting reacquainted with his love of painting. Daryl had heard him speak of it before but had never seen any of his work. Werner had not painted while at the asylum, and he had not brought any of his prior works with him.

When she learned that he was not officially checked out of the clinic, she had reported his whereabouts to the local police, and they had come by and picked him up.

They skirted around Daryl's experiences in the basement. Whether because Werner was embarrassed about his part in Daryl's injury, or if he simply did not care that much about the particulars, Daryl could not tell. The latter was very much out of character for Werner, but on the whole he seemed . . . different. More at ease, less obsessive.

***

Susan sat in her customary place. Neither of them had spoken for several minutes. She seemed lost in thought, and Daryl had a hard time remembering what they had been discussing the last time they met.

Finally, she spoke. "Do you really believe that Hubble is real? Truly?"

"Susan . . ." he began, ready to defend his visions for the hundredth time.

"No Daryl," she interrupted with an unusually stern look. "An invisible gnome with a pet chicken? Come on!"

Daryl looked down slightly embarrassed, a familiar doubt creeping across his brain.

"Actually," he ventured, "the chicken died."

Susan chortled while raising a hand to rub the skin between her eyebrows.

"Well, it's elaborate. I'll give you that."

With that she bent over to reach for her briefcase, which she always deposited on the small table by his bed. Daryl heard the two muffled clicks as she opened the clasps to retrieve something from within.

"Daryl," she said. "Do you trust me?"

"Sure," he replied.

"Good. Because I think I have finally figured out how to help you." *A little late for that,* he thought.

"For the longest time I believed we had to get you back in control of your hallucinations before moving on, but I have recently realized that this was a mistake. Because you won't let us. Will you, Daryl?"

"Let us?" Daryl asked. "What do you mean?"

"Daryl, what do you do when you should be punished for something you no longer remember? How do you hold onto that while you let go of sanity?"

"I have no idea what you mean."

"You outsource it. You cannot get rid of your demons because you need them. You need them to hold you accountable. To ensure that you are punished."

Daryl felt flushed. He looked away from Susan and blinked several times to clear the spots from his vision. When that did not work, he ignored them instead.

"I may have gone a bit overboard, then," he finally said.

"Indeed," Susan said, straightening the chain of the pendulum they had used before during hypnotherapy. "And that is why we need to revisit that night when you lost Ginny. And we need to do it together."

***

Daryl soared through the sky. Homeward bound. Home to Ginny. His mind was preoccupied. The demons they had killed had confessed to being there that night his parents were killed. That should have been enough, but he was not convinced. *Why would they lie?*

Then he noticed a thin line of black smoke snaking its way lazily up into the sky. He had been in a hurry up until that point. Now the treetops beneath him blurred into an uneven carpet of green, all other thoughts forgotten.

He crested the final row of pine trees and tore to the ground in a shower of turf and gravel. He was already running the last fifty yards to the farmstead.

It was no longer on fire. The center of the house had disintegrated to a blackened mess on the ground. The two adjoining wings of the house had partly collapsed, the straw-thatched roofs still smoldering. He was screaming her name as he tore into the building.

Moments later he crumbled to the ground, his fingers blistered, and his body covered in soot from his frantic search of the rubble. Nothing. That could really only mean one thing, his mind continually resetting at the enormity of his loss, unable to process that one stark conclusion. Tears, rushed for the ground, forming channels through the soot on his face. What was he yelling?

Get up. This is your past. It can't hurt you unless you let it.

He shook his head, and everything swam. His throat was raw from screaming, and he could not even swallow to clear it.

What happened next, Daryl? What did you do?

"I . . ." he wheezed, coughed, then tried again. "I . . . Had to know . . . So, I went where they are. I went to find them."

Who Daryl? Who did you go to find?

"The demons."

Which demons, Daryl?

"All of them."

Then he was airborne again. The clouds around him slowly changed hues from white, to pink, to dark blue. To the west the sun dipped beneath the horizon. Then he was flying by night. Shortly thereafter a city spread out beneath him. He barely noticed it in his single-minded flight toward the spire at the center.

He touched down on top of the building. A helicopter stood next to him, propellor blades folded and furled on its back like a sleeping bird. He stepped inside the building, not bothering to close the door. He would probably not be staying long. Then again, he would probably not be leaving either.

Motion sensors turned on the modest lights, showing an austere room with a set of elevators. He moved to the nearest one and pressed the button. A whirring sound to his left let him know that a camera had just focused on him. Moments later the elevator purred as it began making its way to him. The doors pinged open, and he entered. He did not have to press any button—the elevator knew where to take him.

Daryl exited the elevator into a spacious lobby with marble floors and beautifully wrought paneling running the length of a high-vaulted ceiling.

"What a rare treat."

The man stood by a large table, the only piece of furniture in the huge room, arms spread in greeting. His bearing was of someone waiting to take Daryl on a tour of the premises.

"Is she dead?" Daryl said, walking toward the man.

"I'm afraid I cannot help you with that," he responded.

As Daryl moved closer, he noticed dozens of people moving into the large room from several doorways and adjoining corridors. He was surrounded.

It did not matter. He needed an answer.

The man smiled pleasantly at Daryl as he closed the last few strides between them. He flared the power and their minds snapped together like magnets. The room fell away, and there was only the struggle.

Daryl was tending the sails of a large boat tossed in a

storm. The man stood on the bank, sending wave after wave of ice-cold water crashing down onto the deck. Daryl froze the water and jumped the rail. "Is she dead?" he yelled, landing on the icy surface, and running toward the man on the bank.

The scene shifted.

Daryl stood atop the rim of an active volcano. The man floated inside the opening, sending red-hot sprays of molten rock at Daryl. The man was closer now, and Daryl could make out his leisurely smile. "Is she dead?" he repeated, jumping from rock spray to rock spray. As his feet made contact with them, they froze over with a sharp crack. He got in two jumps.

The scene shifted.

The man stood leaning casually against the farthest corner post of a boxing ring. A monstrously huge man moved in front of him, blocking Daryl's path. Daryl moved forward as if to grapple, and as the big man swung a bear-like paw at him, he dove between the enormous legs, coming up in a roll toward the occupied corner post. The man was inspecting the fingernails of one hand, while the index finger of his other hand was busy cleaning something out from between his teeth.

He turned as Daryl lunged, and the scene shifted.

A wave of fire encircled them. The man pushed on the flames as did Daryl. The heat increased noticeably, and Daryl began losing, his current state of mind not up for the task. "Is she dead?" The man smiled back at Daryl, pushing harder. He was just too strong.

Her little hand waving him goodbye that very morning.

"Is she dead?"

The blackened remains of their home. Of her?

"Is she dead?"

The pain within him unbearable, he was unable to muster the willpower needed to win the battle of wills. With that realization came the anger. A stream that sprang from when his parents were killed, now made a flood. The grief and turmoil within him drowned as a single, blazing, white-hot purpose bored through everything, severing Daryl. Casting him aside.

For a moment nothing happened, then the smile in front of him wavered. The flames faltered, then began to recede. He pushed, and the confidence before him melted away. The man visibly gathered himself to resist, but what was left of Daryl was impossible to deny, and the effort quickly disintegrated. The man sank to one knee as the flames took him. His parting left nothing behind, except for a brief statement, resonating with Daryl as if carved in the air: "Yes."

The world returned to normal. In front of him the man lay where he had fallen. The ring of spectators stood their ground for another second as if not realizing that the battle of wills was over. More likely they were shocked by the outcome. Daryl noticed none of this.

Yes.

What happened next?

Daryl barely noticed the question. Something was crackling within him. Familiar, yet utterly alien.

What did you do?

A storm gathered around him. Violent energies whipped into existence with him at their center. In the eye of the storm there was calm. Beyond it, chaos.

Daryl screamed, then he died.

***

He opened his eyes. Susan was sitting next to him, staring intently at his face as if studying some wild animal. The pendulum hung forgotten in her hand.

"What?" he asked. "Are you going to tell me that was all in my mind?"

"No, I'm not," she said quietly. "Not all of it anyway. This is how you lost your daughter and the moment you lost yourself."

"You really are insightful," he said tiredly, grief choking out all thought.

"You moved."

"Whatever you say, doc."

"You need to snap out of it," she said. Then she leaned in and slapped him.

The move caught him completely by surprise. "What…" he started, then stopped himself.

"Daryl, how do you break your own neck running into a stone wall?"

"I don't know what you mean," he said, starting to feel dizzy.

"Yes, you do, Daryl." Susan slapped him again. Harder this time.

"What is this?" he tried, but he could hear that the question had mainly been directed at himself.

"How do you break your own neck, Daryl? It's a simple question."

"No, no. There was the demon. It was a fight."

"There was no demon. Not then, not now." Susan said, looking him in the eye.

"Yes, there was. He threw me into the wall."

"And why were there no marks from this fight? How come Felicia won't corroborate it? How did your arm move while under hypnosis? Tell me, Daryl. Answer just one of those."

"I don't . . . I can't."

Susan looked at him, a mixture of sympathy and steadfast resolve plain on her face.

"The answer to my initial question, Daryl, is—you don't."

You don't.

"But I can't move," he said, feebly. "I can't feel anything."

"This," Susan said, "like everything else you've concocted to torture yourself, is all in your mind."

"What does that mean?"

154

"It means that if you fight against these delusions of yours, and if you prove to yourself that you will no longer accept them," she paused, eyes locked with his, "you will be free. You will walk again."

***

Daryl lay alone in his room. Susan and he had talked for many hours following the session. Her words had offered hope and fear in equal measure. Hope for himself, fear at the prospect of what he had to leave behind. They had made no agreements about what that meant, but Daryl knew the first step. He was sure Susan knew it too. It would soon be time to tell the person who did not know. He wanted to walk again, but more than that, he had to remember why he had left Ginny alone that day. Why he was complicit in her death. The thought nearly drove him mad with guilt. Susan had not been able to help him with that. The layer of allegorical nonsense his mind had constructed was simply too thick. He would have to get a lot better before they could pierce that. But with this first step, she was sure that they would. Then he would know. It was a sobering thought that his mind had recoiled with such force as to sever all connection with his identity. Whatever it was, Susan would be with him. He had to know. He was done hiding.

CHAPTER 28

It was late that evening as Hubble entered through the door. That is to say, he did not open it, he just walked through from the Dark into Daryl's room. He was carrying his large burlap sack, which rattled with each step he took. That meant that he had brought his chess pieces.

"You won't believe what I just overheard," Hubble said in a cheery voice. He moved toward the small table to set up the board.

"Probably not," Daryl said. "Listen, Hubble. I need to talk to you about something."

"Sure," Hubble replied, focused on setting up the chess board.

"Dammit. There is no easy way to say this. I can't talk to you anymore."

The shuffling of pieces stopped.

"What?" Hubble said. He looked up at Daryl with nothing but stark surprise on his wide face.

Daryl paused, but only for a second.

"I have to choose between you and getting better. And I have to get better."

"Shut up, Daryl!" Hubble exploded. "She put you up to this, didn't she?"

"No, she didn't," Daryl replied. If this was going to work, he had to own it. This was his decision—no one else's.

Mean it.

"Bullshit," Hubble replied in a cold voice. "Don't you see that she is isolating you? I don't know why, but you have to stop listening to her."

Daryl closed his eyes. He knew this was going to be hard. He took a deep breath then he opened them again. Hubble took a step back.

"You're not real," Daryl said. The words hung in the air like a dark, hateful shadow.

Hubble took a small, shuffling step forward. "Daryl . . ." he finally managed.

"You're not good for me. Please leave me and never return."

"No, Daryl. Come on." Hubble looked like he was about to say something else, but apparently thought better of it.

"Don't make this any harder than it has to be," Daryl whispered.

"If you think I'm leaving you alone with that devil-woman, you're crazier than I thought," Hubble said, taking another step forward.

Mean it.

"I'm not fucking around. This is the last time I will acknowledge your presence. You're dead to me."

Hubble just stood there staring at him. It seemed like the appropriate moment to follow through on that, so Daryl shifted his focus from Hubble and instead looked out the window.

"Fuck you, Daryl!" Hubble shoved the chess pieces back in the bag and turned. A single piece went flying as he left the way he had come through the closed door.

Daryl closed his eyes as a wave of grief overtook him. It hurts to lose a part of yourself.

CHAPTER 29

Without Hubble, Daryl felt increasingly alone in his room. His daytime solitude was interspersed with visits from staff, not to mention the two-hour afternoon session he had with Susan every day. However, as dusk fell, the room seemed to shrink in proportion to the decrease in traffic. By the time darkness fully enveloped his room, he was gasping for air within the narrow confines. The guilt he felt for Ginny was the curtain upon which he played out what he had said to Hubble, and he cringed, agonizing over the hurt he had caused. Selfishly failing to keep Ginny safe was the ultimate betrayal. Claiming Hubble was not real seemed par for the course. On those nights of self-flagellation, he often found himself listening closely for the sound of Hubble's shuffling gait by the door. It always remained quiet.

That was his pain to bear. The price for what, during daylight hours and with Susan's help, he could acknowledge would be his release. Not just from his delusions, but maybe even from his quadriplegia. He remained doubtful it would do much to curb the self-hatred that nearly choked him every night, but he figured he deserved the privilege of living with that.

Despite intense efforts with Susan, they had not been able to learn anything more from hypnotherapy, or any of the other exercises meant to free up his mind. In some bizarre way, Daryl's utter misery was his primary source of hope. Something this painful had to be good for him.

Daryl looked up from his reverie. Werner was at the door. His friend really had taken a turn for the better. Still inquisitive, but no longer at odds with the world. In a way it felt as if Werner, Susan, and Daryl had joined forces to finally edge him into recovery.

"Hi Daryl," Werner said as he strode in. "Feel like taking a walk?"

"Some other time," Daryl replied. "My legs are a little sore from my morning run."

Werner sat down by Daryl's bed. He looked calmly at Daryl.

"What made you finally conclude that my visions weren't real?" Daryl finally asked.

"Yeah, I've been thinking about that too," Werner said. "I think seeing my cousin and getting back to painting made me realize all the things I was missing out on by staying with my delusions. Well, mine and yours, I suppose."

"So that's it? You're all better now?"

Werner emitted a dry chuckle. "Far from it, my boy. That road will be long, but no one will be able to help you walk it unless you want them to."

Daryl peered out the window at the clouds drifting lazily by.

"You're doing the right thing," Werner said. "Susan is going to get you through this whether you like it or not." That last bit was said with a grin. Werner never despaired. Not on his own or anyone else's behalf. It helped to talk to him about the stance he had taken with Hubble.

"How did you know I would come looking for you and read your journal," Daryl asked.

Werner blinked. "I don't know," he said. "Maybe I'm a little bit psychic."

Daryl grinned. "Thanks."

Sitting there with Werner, his session with Susan coming up, he felt better than he had all day. Not for the first time, he wondered at these islands of peace amidst the pain of his guilt and the rejection of his delusions. Doing the right thing did not exactly lessen the pain. It just, somehow, made it more bearable. Daryl intuited that he had handled more pain than most.

***

"How are you holding up, Daryl?"

Susan was seated on the stool that Werner had vacated only ten minutes earlier. They usually began their sessions this way. The lack of progress had begun to wear on him a little bit.

"It's a slow trudge," he replied. "But I guess shortcuts are in short supply."

"Maybe simply ignoring your hallucinations isn't enough," she offered.

"Are you suggesting I seek them out to insult them to their face? As you may have noticed, I'm not as spry as I once was."

Susan sighed. They had spoken at length about his use of sarcasm.

"Daryl, if simply renouncing them does not work, how about letting them take you where you are so afraid to go? How about putting yourself completely at their mercy, so to speak?"

"What good would that do?" he asked, confused.

Susan seemed lost in thought for a moment, then shook her head imperceptibly, blinked and wiped her nose with a tissue. She turned her attention back to him with a smile.

"It may be the best way to signal to yourself that you are no longer intimidated, that you truly acknowledge that they have no power over you."

Daryl did not like that, and his feelings must have shown

on his face.

"You asked for a shortcut. I'm not suggesting you do it."

He really did not like the thought of that. Maybe that was reason enough to do it? Expedience certainly had an allure all by itself, but he could also see the logic of continuing down the path of denying his mind its fantasies. Facing down his fear of the demons did line up with that. Just another step to being free perhaps.

"I'm in," he said. It came out as a croak, and he swallowed. Susan was looking at him intently.

"I'm in," he repeated hoarsely. He cleared his throat. "How do you propose we do it?"

"Alright, Daryl. Let me see what I can do."

CHAPTER 30

"Up here!"

Daryl looked up, scanning his surroundings. It was a clear night, and the stars and moon shone brightly, bathing the camp in a soft light. Iliria was sitting on top of her wagon waving at him. Intrigued, he moved to join her. A ladder hung suspended from the back end of the wagon, and he shimmied up the swinging rope contraption.

Iliria was sitting in a shallow, square hole lined with plush pillows near the end of the wagon. The hole was in front of a raised skylight that he guessed must be directly above her bedroom. She was looking through the eyepiece of a three-foot-long telescope, which was mounted on the side of the wagon. She extended an arm, waving him forward. Daryl complied and sidled into the softly lined pit.

"I didn't know you were a stargazer?" Daryl said, looking up at the swirling patterns within patterns. Some bright in vivid forms and shapes, and some near-invisible hints of light, gone with the slightest waver in focus.

"Does it surprise you?" Iliria asked in her sensuous tone. Daryl shifted slightly, noticing anew that, yes, they were alone beneath the stars.

"Not at all," he said. "What are you looking for?"

"I'm studying the movement of the planets and stars," she said.

"Really?" Daryl said, not feigning surprise. He had spent some time working with famous lens makers in the Netherlands, and he had shared a fascination of the constellations with several astronomers of the past. If he had thought Iliria had any interest in the stars, he would have expected it to lean in the direction of astrology. She was, after all, an augur. However, such people rarely took the time to actually *study* the stars.

"I take my signs where I can find them, but the night sky is not one of them." She said this with a wistful air, as if she yearned for this to not be true. "If they have a story to tell, the timescale is so far beyond our lifespans as to be all but meaningless to us. I suspect that trying might quickly drive one insane. Have some wine."

Daryl took a goblet from the tray in the center of the pillowed pit. It held a crisp, slightly sweet red wine. After a few sips, Iliria turned toward him. "Hand me my cup," she said. As he handed her the goblet, their hands touched briefly. "Would you like to know how I foresaw our meeting in the woods?" she asked. Her lips were slightly parted as she regarded him, and a cool night breeze sent her straight medium-long hair flowing across her shoulders and face.

"Yes, please," he said and swallowed.

She looked appraisingly at him.

"When I was younger, I used to see things. I never knew when or where, but suddenly I would know something from the way leaves in my tea moved, or how a flock of birds took off from the field." She paused, a faraway look in her eyes. "It wasn't always easy. People don't like things they don't understand. As time went by, I learned that the signs of the future are everywhere, not just where folklore would have us believe. I also became better at interpreting what I saw. It became something of an art for me, and by the time I met others with similar gifts they were all bumbling novices by comparison. That was when I met Phineas. He is many things, one of which is a collector of things useful. Things and people. I think he recognized my potential before I ever helped him find one of us, but it grew from there."

A stillness hung in the air. Daryl felt the effects of the wine and had fallen entranced with the sultry timbre of Iliria's voice. It took him a moment to realize that her lips had stopped moving.

"So, you tell the future better than anyone you know?" he asked, partly just to prompt her into speaking again.

She turned, looking into his eyes. "Yes," she stated matter-of-factly. "You might say that the world speaks to my intuition."

"How so?" Daryl asked with interest.

"Would you like a demonstration?" Iliria said.

"Please," Daryl said, settling further into the cushions.

Iliria closed her eyes and took a deep breath through her nose. Her perfect lips parted as air was expelled. He barely felt the flow of air on his chest and neck. She opened her eyes.

"How strange," she said, seemingly to herself. "I can't seem to divine anything about you."

"Yes, I'm very enigmatic," he said.

She looked at him with renewed interest. Whether it was the interest of an entomologist or a human woman, he could not tell. Maybe it was a mixture of the two. "Yes, you are," she said. "When I first saw you, I was in a dream. Intuition is strongest there, and telling the future is nothing if not intuition. I knew where you would be and that you would need our help."

Daryl shifted. "That wasn't really a demonstration," he said teasingly.

She smiled. "We are all parts of the slow, steady burn of the world. Most only see the ash. I see the smoke. Many spend their time staring at the blaze. I poke the logs. I could say that everything is connected. This would be true but lacks substance. To understand it you must realize that what you interact with also interacts with everything else. In a way, that interaction is at its weakest in everything around us occupying this world. However, in another way this observation makes no sense because the distinction between this world and others makes no sense. They are always and inexplicably connected." She smiled and nodded toward the telescope. "It is like a connected lens system. You know of those, yes?"

Daryl nodded.

"Imagine this dimension as a focus plane. Everything here is visible to us. In focus, if you will. Then imagine other dimensions as represented by the blurred light as you defocus and move along the focal axis. All the light that represents any one point in the focus plane eventually becomes distributed evenly across the back focal plane. In the back focal plane, all the points in the focus plane occupy the same space. How then, can you say that a point in the focal plane is not connected to every other point?" Iliria looked at him, head cocked. "You want to know what that means?" she asked.

He nodded again, head pleasantly abuzz.

"Alright. But first you have to do something for me."

With that they lay back in the soft pillows beneath the stars. They were in the moment. Then she showed him the future.

***

Daryl moved through the thick underbrush with Phineas at his side. This was the first time they had been alone since Phineas had saved him from Gabriel. It was early and the sky was obscured by a thick cover of gray clouds. Daryl felt certain they had passed the camp's protective boundary a while ago, but recent experience made him think that boundary had more to do with Phineas, and probably Fonseca's, whereabouts, than it did the camp's location.

Phineas paused at the edge of a small clearing. Two swallows zipped between the trees on an early morning breeze.

"Thanks," Daryl spoke into the quiet.

"You're welcome," Phineas said in a contemplative voice, looking into the clearing. "Do you know what we are?"

Daryl somehow got the sense that Phineas was talking about everyone, both the inner and outer circle. It was clear that to Phineas they all shared a bond. Something that drew them together, from Reston to Brex.

"You are fugitives," Daryl finally said.

"Yes," Phineas agreed. "Do you know from what?"

"Gabriel?" Daryl asked, though he knew this could not be the full answer.

Phineas chuckled and the shadow of violence that often hung over him evaporated, leaving a friendly, indistinct gentleman in its wake.

"While Gabriel and I have certainly had our disagreements, I'm afraid our refugee status goes a bit deeper than that. I assume you are familiar with the Pact?"

"Yes," Daryl answered. The Pact was allegedly a deal that had been struck between the powers on where and when they were permitted to interfere with affairs on earth. It was supremely complicated and famously difficult to interpret.

"Good, then you know that the Christian God and devil are not alone. With a few notable exceptions, every single god, demi-god, monster, and fantastical being you've ever heard of is real. What you may not know is that the divine interest in this dormant dimension stems from the unclaimed power soaring through this place. Unlike all other dimensions claimed by gods, here exists a vacuum of influence, in which power abounds."

"Why?" Daryl asked.

"No one knows," Phineas said. "At least to my knowledge. This vacuum calls to the gods and their desire to increase their influence. In some sense, this dimension has become the focal point of the cosmic struggle for dominance. Gods come and go in the blink of an eye, cosmically speaking, leaving the human wreckage of their passing behind. This dimension is the anvil upon which gods, and men, are broken. This is likely to continue until a victor is found. Or someone stops it."

Phineas trailed off, lost in thought. Anger rippled across his features. "Anyway, the victor who claims the power here will likely become supreme among the powers that be. However, this convergence of interest very nearly destroyed our world and has led to the agreement that only indirect lobbying for influence or power is allowed."

"The Pact?"

"Just so. In order to protect ourselves and others we must learn. We must understand." Phineas paused, looking across the clearing. "We have to refine our knowledge so that we may guard against those with power and motivations far beyond us. How do we refine knowledge, Daryl?"

"I don't know," he said.

"We take that which we already know and look for new ways to constrain it. Enough angles on any object, and you reveal the truth."

"What truth?"

Phineas smiled. "I don't know that. Yet." He shook himself. "Anyway. Right now, what's important is that this unclaimed power has many effects and can be put to use, if you know how. Sometimes this happens by accident, giving rise to the most fantastical individuals and creatures, some of which you've seen here. Sometimes by design, partly anyway, which is how Iliria and Fonseca gained their unique . . . abilities."

"And yourself?"

"That too. I think it is fair to say that I have pushed what's possible further than anyone. In short, we are refugees from the powers. All of them. We are either imbued with the unclaimed power of this world and so meant to be rooted out and dominated, or we have seen or touched too much of it, and so are deemed a liability to keeping the secrets of the Pact. Your power, Daryl, does not come from this dimension or from this world. It is divine and so cannot be trusted. Please remember that, ultimately, it is not yours to control."

Daryl remembered. *Let's see those pretty wings of yours. Fly little bird, fly.*

"Is there a way to break free?" Daryl asked, the question setting alight a fervor that he had been keeping in check for longer than he could remember.

Phineas looked him briefly in the eyes.

"No," he said.

It was as Daryl had expected. It almost did not hurt.

"We have been discussing your predicament," Phineas continued, "and we have agreed that you belong with us for as long as you wish to remain."

"Thanks," Daryl said with real relief in his voice. He had feared that the extended walk was part of cutting him loose.

"It is not without precedent, but you're welcome," Phineas said.

Semi, Daryl thought. Knowing what she was, it was clear that her powers were not of earth either.

"The deal is this—Fonseca and I keep all of us safe and Iliria keeps us all running. It is not a hierarchy in any other sense than competence. It is this way because it is the only way it will work. Do you have any issue with that?"

"No," Daryl said. That assessment seemed fair, and he appreciated the honesty.

***

As Daryl got back into camp, he parted ways with Phineas. They were not due to move on till tomorrow and with the cloud cover lifting everyone enjoyed what was looking to become a beautiful day. Reston and the crew hung out, smoking and drinking. None were drunk, but they had been on the move for many months now, and the air buzzed with excited chatter and roaring laughter.

Daryl headed for Iliria's wagon to get his medication. The Hamsta twins, currently two separate people, passed him on the way, engrossed in yet another discussion of who owed who.

"I paid for that hat," Ellen Hamsta said.

"Yes, with the money I loaned you two fortnights ago!" Miriam Hamsta said.

"That wasn't a loan, you oaf. You were paying me back for the inn last month."

"Don't even get me started on that tab at the inn!"

Daryl never heard the full story, more's the pity. He passed into the inner circle, leaving bar tabs and revelries behind.

He wanted to see Semi, but she had seemed oddly aloof the last time they spoke. He should probably just play games and get drunk with Reston. Not a bad day.

He knocked on the door. He was accustomed to an immediate response, so when he was met with silence, he only waited a moment before turning from the door.

Something clattered to the floor within.

"Iliria?" he called. The silence stretched on for a few moments, and he was about to call out again when her voice sounded from within.

"Go ahead," she said.

He opened the door. The interior was quite dark, but he noticed that the large mirror had crashed to the floor.

Iliria was sitting by her large dresser, combing her hair. Another first.

"Erm, I'm here for my tonic," he said, suddenly ill at ease. Was this related to the other night?

"Yes, of course," Iliria replied curtly. "Help yourself."

Daryl did not consider himself especially risk-averse, but he did not relish the idea of cooking up his own potion of anti-petrification.

"Maybe I can just come back later?" he asked instead.

"Sure, that's fine," she said in a softer voice.

Must be some witchy business, he thought and turned for the door. "Phineas said to tell you that there'll be a meeting tonight."

He never got to hear her reply. Something crashed to the floor in her sleeping quarters.

They both turned toward the sound. Daryl had a strong feeling that something was most definitely not right.

"Damn cat," Iliria said. "See you later."

Daryl hesitated.

"Please leave," Iliria said, seeing Daryl's reluctance.

Something made of glass broke with an even louder crash. Iliria did have a cat, but it was the most well-behaved feline Daryl had ever met.

Screw it, he thought, and made a beeline for the bedroom.

He plowed through the beaded string curtain amid a hushed blast of clicking glass, and several things happened in rapid succession. His feet caught at the threshold and someone below him emitted a muffled shriek. He fell face-first into Iliria's four-poster bed as something flew above him and crashed into the far wall of the wagon. He sprang to his feet, aided by the spring mattress, only to find himself facing two Ilirias. One lay dazed and gagged by the door and must be what had tripped him upon entering. The other looked up at him from the floor on the other side of the bed and hissed. Hissing Iliria came to her feet in an agile pounce. Daryl noticed a disturbing boneless quality to her movements.

While the situation raised many questions, Daryl was certain that he had just inadvertently trampled the real Iliria. This was confirmed moments later when the other Iliria lunged at him. He raised his arms to ward her off only to realize that he was much too slow. She moved with a speed that made him appear as though cut in stone.

That's ironic, his brain uselessly supplied, as fingers of steel closed off his windpipes. Her hands squeezed, and he thought he heard an unpleasant crack from somewhere in his neck. His hands were flailing as his mind struggled to catch up with the rapidly devolving situation. He flung himself backward into the main part of the wagon and tried to grab onto something he could use to pry her off. Her grip around his throat propelled her with him and they landed in a tangle on the carpeted floor. Daryl's gaze fell on a wooden stool, and he was about to reach for it, when his oxygen deprived brain opted to pass out instead.

He was jerked awake as he and Iliria were yanked off the floor. The pressure on his throat eased as Iliria launched herself away.

Daryl coughed and a sharp pain told him that something in his throat was fractured. Someone was speaking. He shook his head to clear it, but that only made it worse. He vomited onto his hands.

"What are you doing?" Who was that?

"I'll explain it later." Iliria?

"No, you'll explain it now!" Brex?

"Brex," Daryl said, but it came out as "Brgllll" along with several chunks of vomit, still making their way from esophagus to lips.

"Brex," he wheezed. "It's not Iliria."

Colors were coalescing back into the shapes of the world. Daryl carefully raised his head to take in the scene. Fake Iliria was standing by the cauldron across the room. Brex was looming in the doorway next to Daryl. He had a quizzical expression on his face, and he was about to say something when the real Iliria, still bound and gagged, pushed herself through the beaded curtain only to trip on the disarrayed carpet and pitch head-first into the room.

"Wha—" was all Brex got out before the fake Iliria lunged between his legs and out the door.

"MmmBmmm Mmmrrr!" real Iliria yelled through her gag.

"Stop her!" Daryl offered, fairly sure that his analysis was sound.

Brex spun around and stepped through the door.

"She's gone," he said. "What was that?"

***

"A doppelgänger," Iliria said.

Brex, Iliria, and Daryl were seated around her small table. The red tablecloth was empty except for a deck of cards that she used for fortune telling. Brex had tidied up the place while Iliria had seen to Daryl's neck, which had already begun healing.

"And what is that?" Daryl asked.

Iliria looked unsure of how to proceed. A few strands of hair out of place the only indication that something out of the ordinary had just happened. Finally, she did:

"You are of course both aware of the existence of other dimensions. Planes like the Fae or Heaven of the Christian faith. I have long suspected that this is but the tip of a much vaster complexity. The creature you saw was, in a very real sense, a reflection of me brought to this plane. There are stories of this happening to others." She paused. "They do not end well."

"Did that make sense to you?" Daryl asked, looking to Brex.

"Huh? No, but I usually can't follow Ily anyways. You know, about those supernatural things." Brex shook his big head.

"Perhaps an elaboration from our talk the other night?" Iliria suggested.

"Please," Daryl said.

"Alright," she said, focusing all her attention on Daryl. Brex was contentedly looking out the window, a stubby finger buried to the second knuckle in one ear.

"I explained how I have come to believe that all dimensions can be thought of as existing along a focus axis in a virtual multidimensional lens system. This implies that everything exists across all dimensions, but in different configurations. Are you familiar with the mathematical concept of Fourier transformations?"

"No."

"Ah, well never mind. Then as I mentioned, this is most easily exemplified by how the light in a standard lens system, when viewed from a single point in the focus plane, will become spread out across the entire back focal plane, touching the light from all other points in the focus plane. This interconnectivity is what enables my divinations. Whether this lensing effect is an integral part of our multiverse or has an external existence, I don't know. Given this, I long suspected that mirrors are not merely reflective surfaces in the way we understand it but are also windows to a kind of focal plane of our plane. The perfect reflection doesn't permit anything going through as this would break symmetry, but if the reflection can be slightly defocused this requirement goes down. Things are no longer perfectly reflected, possibly enabling the mirror to act as a gateway. Actually, I suppose I just proved the hypothesis."

The wagon fell silent. Iliria seemed to expect some sort of response out of Daryl. For the second time that day, Brex came to Daryl's aid.

"So how do we kill it?" he asked, pulling his finger out of his ear with a wet squelch and a plop.

Iliria blinked. "Well," she said. "I imagine like anything else. Being mirror images, the shadows of doppelgängers face the wrong way, making it easier to identify them. However, I doubt you will be getting the chance now. It would appear everyone should be on guard when meeting me from now on. I suggest we set up a phrase only we would know, to be used until the thing is destroyed."

"That makes sense," Daryl said. "How about—Fourier transformations?"

Iliria chuckled. "Sure, that's not the type of thing that is likely to come up in most casual conversations."

"So, whenever you don't say that upon meeting you, we have to assume you're that thing," Daryl said.

"Right," Iliria replied. "Unless you can see my shadow." Brex was already getting up, and it looked as though he might not even have heard the latter part of the conversation.

"You got that, Brex?" Daryl asked at his back.

"I'm sure I'll pick it up eventually," he answered. "For now, I think I'll focus on finding the little fucker and killing it." With that he ducked out of the wagon and disappeared.

Daryl supposed that anyone who outweighed Iliria at least five-to-one really did not have to worry much about her murderous double.

CHAPTER 31

Daryl lay in his room wondering. Over the past few weeks, a faint sense of optimism had grown from a shadow lurking at the back of his mind to something he was cautiously aware of. He did not enjoy optimism. It set you up for disappointments you otherwise would never have to endure. However, Susan's predictions had been coming true to a fault. From his success ignoring his visions, to Werner being just fine. Now she seemed convinced that he was only days from overcoming both his psychosis and his quadriplegia. For the moment, he was undecided about which of the two he would miss the least.

But it was not his dislike of optimism that bothered him. Something else was off, and as he lay there, he realized that he could no longer view his dreams as mere distraction. The supposed memories really did seem to be surfacing in a narrative with meaning and perhaps even a message. Susan believed this was his psychosis reinforcing its control on his consciousness. Maybe that was true. Well, he had not exactly shared every detail. It certainly seemed a strange coincidence that Susan's odd behavior would coincide with his dreams of doppelgängers. Daryl realized that he had accepted the changes in her mainly because she appeared driven by a deep need to help him. In all his own despair, the changes had just not seemed important.

Maybe it was the last spasm of his psychosis, but he had to know whether the dreams held any significance. And so, he lay in his bed feeling apprehensive, feeling foolish.

***

Susan entered the room. She flashed a smile at him, and he returned it. She was wearing the hairband every day now and had also grown out her bangs. She looked a lot younger than he remembered her—likely due, in part, to her choice of hairstyle.

"Hi Daryl," she said cheerily. "Ready for tomorrow?" That was the night of the ritual, where he would be laying himself bare to his delusions.

"I guess," he offered, squinting at the wall where her shadow should fall.

"Could you draw the blinds?" he asked. "My eyes are a bit sensitive today."

She paused at the unusual request. "Sure," she said, moving to the window.

Her shadow hit the floor behind her, illuminated by the noon sun outside. Daryl breathed a sigh of relief. *Thank goodness, I'm just crazy,* he thought.

Susan moved to his side and sat down, excitement plain on her face.

"Daryl, I don't want you to worry. I have done some research on demonic possessions, and I think going all in on the more theatrical elements could help make an even deeper impression. You know, really shock that psyche of yours into letting go."

She wiped her nose with a handkerchief. A common occurrence these days.

"What did you have in mind?" he asked. Now that he had agreed, the details mattered little to him.

"Oh, just a few accessories. We can go over it tonight, I

just wanted to prepare you."

"Thanks," he said, returning her smile. With his last nagging doubt out of the way, Susan's presence served as a reminder of what he might very soon regain.

Susan must have read it on his face, because she leaned in.

"There are never any guarantees, but I think there is reason to be optimistic."

Daryl nodded, awash with relief. It was not till after Susan left that he realized he had forgotten to have her reopen the blinds, leaving him alone and disoriented in the poorly lit room.

***

Werner came by with the e-book they had discussed last time he had visited.

"Whoa, that's dark," he said, standing by the door.

"Do you mind letting in some light?" Daryl asked.

"Not at all," Werner said and headed for the window.

Werner positioned himself by the wall and opened the blinds with a pull on the string. Light flooded the room again and Daryl blinked a few times.

Werner walked to the bed and positioned the e-book for Daryl to read.

"Could you grab my mouth pointer?" Daryl asked. He could use the distraction of a good book and needed someone to position the pointer in his mouth to turn the pages.

"Sure."

Werner opted to reach awkwardly over the bed to retrieve the pen from the table on the other side, and in doing so kicked something underneath the bed with his foot, sending it spinning across the floor.

Werner moved quickly to the center of the room to pick it up, and Daryl only got a quick look before it was shoved in his pants pocket. Was that a chess piece?

He was about to ask Werner but the words stuck in his throat. His blood ran cold as he looked at the jovial, gangly man standing in the middle of the room smiling at him.

Werner quickly moved to Daryl's side and helped him with the pointer.

"I'll swing by tomorrow and get your impression on the book," he said.

"Sure," Daryl croaked.

***

Werner's shadow faced the wrong way. That ugly fact repeated itself over and over in Daryl's mind, burrowing deeper with each passage. Part of him wanted to just ignore it. He had made his choice, so let the chips fall where they may. A quiet desperation was latching onto him, soaking his sheets in a cold sweat.

In the end his decision was not borne of deliberation. His faculties were of little help against this onslaught of unhelpful speculation. In the absence of inspiration, reason tired quickly, and with that the image of a little girl floated into his awareness. As he imagined her eyes, her hair, and her smile, a quiet realization washed over him. It did not matter what was true or false. It did not matter that he could not tell them apart. What mattered was a simple truth. If he ignored what he had seen, he would be giving up. And he could not give up—Ginny would not let him.

"Hubble!" Daryl yelled through a dry throat. Even now, something about shouting for his ostensibly imaginary friend made him slightly self-conscious and filled with more than a little guilt. He tried again. "Hubble, I'm sorry man. It was a mistake. My mistake." He swallowed. "Hubble!"

Variations of this went on for what seemed a long time. Having shouted his throat raw in a vain attempt to get Hubble to appear, Daryl moved on to shouting for Felicia. Finally, and with some reluctance, he began shouting for Bill-Din.

It was somewhere during these last attempts that the futility of it overcame him. Tears blurred his vision and his cries for help took on a husky quality. He was truly alone and utterly without agency. Tears flowed freely and his anguish drew ugly wracking sobs.

Lost in the turmoil of self-pity, Daryl missed the point when his cries rose in pitch. He also missed the point when they neared hysteria. However, sometime after this, he did notice the laughter. He was laughing. Laughing at this ridiculous situation, laughing at everyone around him. But mostly, he was laughing at himself. Daryl, the butt of a joke he did not even know the beginning to. His dreams might be real, they might not be. His hallucinations might be real, then again, Susan and Werner might not be who they claimed. And at the center of it all, trying to make that distinction—Daryl. Unable to remember or even walk.

His outburst left him drained, and he drifted among the pieces of his life. His only real conclusion that they did not fit together. Amidst this astute observation, he nodded off.

***

He was buffeted by winds and waves in a choppy black sea. Occasionally a big swell would lift him out of the bowels of the ocean, permitting a fleeting attempt at orienting himself. On one such occasion, he glimpsed a darker shade of black against the horizon. More importantly, at the very crest of the swell, he caught a faint flicker of light where the ocean met the prospective shore far away.

With the prescience of dreams, he knew this to be his destination.

As this realization dawned on him, a dark cloud moved to obscure his view, and the movements of the sea took on an arrhythmic motion, letting him know that he was not alone in the murky deep. This sparked a familiar feeling of panic, but before his mind could fully process the familiarity, something grabbed his foot and yanked him beneath the surface.

The waters rushed by him in a dark blur. It was all he could do to not void his lungs in a visceral scream of horror as he was swallowed by the sea.

He saw shapes milling about him and looked down to discover a tentacle wrapped around his ankle. At first, he was unable to discern anything beyond where the dark appendage disappeared in the even darker depths. However, as he descended, he noticed this was due to the vastness of the entity below him. The size became apparent as his eyes took in its borders at the far edge of his field of vision.

Daryl struggled against the grip on his ankle. Kicking and twisting, he felt the grip loosen, only to gain new purchase as an additional tentacle snapped out of the depths to latch onto his torso. A scream finally escaped his lips in a flurry of bubbles. In the grip of panic, he was vaguely aware of his own uncoordinated and ineffective thrashings. Fire erupted between his shoulder blades. A ghoulish visage was coming into focus below him.

He had only a moment to take in horned ridges surrounding a lipless maw. The tentacles extended into its gullet, pulling him toward black, serrated teeth.

Then the fire on his back consumed him, and he convulsed in pain and shock. The tentacles fell away as if burned, and a shockwave, like a shudder, rose from the waters below. He lost track of his surroundings, spinning into oblivion. The waterlogged inertia left him, and he was flung upward and burst through the surface in a roar of steam and water. Hurtling skyward, the sea quickly became a featureless black beneath him, punctuated by the white stripes of breaking waves. His body had dried instantly upon exiting the water, and now smoldered in a burn that seemed to flare from that familiar spot between his shoulder blades. A set of enormous gray wings glowed behind him. Noticing them, he marveled at their strength and the grace with which they clove the air. Their movement felt so natural as to make him wonder why he had not missed them before. Reveling in his new freedom, he caught a glimpse of the light on the distant shoreline. He crested the zenith of his upward trajectory and dove for his destination.

The sea blurred beneath him, and in moments he hovered by a strangely familiar coastline. Cliffs rose starkly out of the frothy surf on both sides of a small town. The light oozed from the small bell tower of a church, which lay near the waterfront in what appeared to be an abandoned whaling community. Soaring above the wooden wharfs, he coasted inward across the gravel main street. In a final swoop downward, he landed in the empty bell tower with his glowing wings neatly folding into the small of his back. The room was brightly lit, but with no discernible light source. A large brass bell hung in the center. Moving closer, Daryl saw its only adornment was a single Latin phrase: "Seek and you shall find."

Iliria stepped from around the bell.

"How about Fourier transformations?" she said with a smile.

"Hi," he replied.

"I only have a moment before the guardian drives me out. This type of direct interference is not allowed." She came to a stop a few feet away and spoke quickly. "The dreams I have sent should have shown you when we met and that night on my caravan, which prompted my visions of your future, obscured though it is by immense events. The future may be ordained, but I can only see what I understand, and there are many things about you and the forces at play that I do not understand in the least. Over time, it became clear that your trials might be far from over and that you might in the future need reminding. When it became clear to us that you weren't safe at the asylum, we used Fonseca's blood as the anchor, to prompt your subconscious to dream of meeting her and the events that followed. But you are out of time, Daryl. Something closes in."

Lightning illuminated the scene for an instance, and a

roaring clap of thunder followed almost immediately. Iliria's outline was growing fuzzy.

"What should I do?" he asked as soon as his voice was able to carry over the storm.

"You must regain your wings, Daryl. Then seek Michael's aid, he . . ."

A crash and another clap of thunder drowned out all noise, and Iliria's faint outline winked out.

Disoriented, Daryl stumbled from the tower and then leapt into the gale-force winds. Catching the draft, he quickly ascended to soar above the dilapidated buildings once more. A weak drizzle started to fall, waxing and waning with the direction of the winds as he circled. The sense of familiarity returned, and he followed it away from the settlement. A dark, wet night enveloped him as he moved along the near-vertical cliffside. The wind picked up as he left the relative shelter of the small inlet behind, nearly drowning out the crash of the surf below him.

Scanning ahead, he noticed an opening roughly two-thirds up the cliffside. A single diminutive figure with long tufted ears stood in front of two familiar chairs, at the lip of a rock shelf before the entrance to a small cave. Memories of visiting to play chess and smoke played across his awareness. The gnome looked lost in thought, staring at the dark downpour even as gusts of rain-laden wind slowly soaked him.

"Hubble!" Daryl cried out, but the words were taken by the wind and further muffled by the roar of thunder and the crashing waves far below them.

Hubble turned away from the cave entrance and disappeared inside.

Daryl sped up, rushing to reach the small landing. He banked, buffeted by winds, and settled on the shelf just as Hubble reached the far wall of the familiar cave.

He looked back at Daryl.

"Good luck," Hubble said in a barely audible voice, then he stepped forward through the wall.

Daryl cried out, but to no avail. His friend was gone.

***

Daryl woke, once again, to a tilted world. He had somehow been flung clear of the bed, this time landing on his side by the window. His otherwise sensationless back itched, and now he was finally certain what that represented. Unable to untangle his limp limbs, he frantically used his chin to pull on a corner of the comforter that lay within reach. After a few strenuous minutes, he was rewarded with enough cloth to insulate his head from the linoleum floor. He relaxed his chin and neck for a minute, idly watching a small pool of his spittle being slowly soaked up by the fabric.

Having regained his composure, such as it was, Daryl examined the itching in the small of his back. Now that he paid attention to it, he was fairly certain there were two separate spots, largely coinciding with the outer parts of his shoulder blades. Focusing his attention on one of these two areas, he felt the itching escalate. He stopped right before it became painful. He took a few deep breaths. *Here goes nothing.*

The itching on the left side of his back immediately flared as he bore into it. It felt like a hundred tiny spiders milling about on clawed feet. Then a few of them began sinking their fangs into his back, then the rest followed suit.

Daryl gritted his teeth against the painful onslaught as beads of sweat clung to his matted hair and trickled down his face. For a few moments nothing more happened, and Daryl felt his control starting to slip.

With a cry he rallied, digging deeper than he thought possible into the burning sensation on his back. *Damn you!* he thought, and another part of his mind whispered in response—*Fly little bird, fly.* Something snapped, and the blinding pain would have rendered Daryl unconscious if not for the fact that his mind was instantly occupied by a violent shove, pushing him up and to the right. He stumbled, staggered, and sailed across the room, clipping a dresser, and somehow banging his head against the ceiling.

He reeled as something shoved against him and spun to face it, but only succeeded in hitting his head against the ceiling once more. He let out a grunt and shook his head to clear it. His left side was suffused with a dull ache, from his toes to the top of his scalp. He nearly wept at the sweet, joyous agony. He could feel! His right side was still devoid of feeling. Craning his neck, he was able to make out gray plumage over his left shoulder but not his right. Using his functioning left hand, he touched where the wing emerged from atop his shoulder blades. He tried tentatively to move the wing and very nearly fell flat on his face. Having only one functioning leg meant that his balance in the corner of the room was precarious at best.

He sighed and shifted his focus to the itch on his right shoulder blade.

One down, one to go.

CHAPTER 32

Daryl lay on the cool floor, exhausted and loving every minute of it. His wings were extended behind him on both sides, their size ensuring that they came into contact with the walls on either side of him. He did not yet have the energy to try and retract them. The effort of uncasing them had distracted him from his situation, which now began to make an unwelcome reappearance. With that came a stream of realizations.

Chief among them—his visions were real! Secondly, so were parts, maybe all, of his dreams? Finally, and with some reluctance—he could not trust Susan and Werner. He was utterly and completely alone with no one to talk to and no one to help him.

Carefully tucking his wings to the extent possible, he stood up. His room looked the same, just smaller. He turned and moved to a table in the corner that he knew held his belongings. Halfway across the room a sharp tug followed by a ripping pain doubled him over. He looked down through teary eyes to where the bloodied catheter now rested on the floor. The pain immediately receded. Breathing in deeply, he looked at the mess of medical supplies on the floor from his recent thrashing about and felt for any other tubes still connected to his body. Finding none, he shuffled to the small table.

He opened the drawer and rummaged around for a few moments before finding what he needed. The dream had told him where to go for answers.

CHAPTER 33

Wearing most of his belongings in his small satchel, Daryl made his way through the Dark by following the slight tug in his right hand. The lodestone was pushing ever so slightly against the fingers of his closed fist, setting his course. Daryl juggled a nascent claustrophobia along with the fear stemming from Hubble's earlier warnings—don't touch anything.

He moved forward with all the stealth he was able to muster, given the two unfamiliar appendages sprouting from his back. The faint, diffuse lighting made this even trickier, causing him to stumble through the terrain like a drunk through a crowd, but by his estimates he should be getting close. Or not.

Just then a sudden pitch in the floor beneath him caused him to spill forward. Something clipped his left wing and he stumbled sideways into one of the rocks protruding from the floor. He was only just able to bring up the hand not holding the lodestone in time to avoid a head-first collision with the hard surface. He hit the ground with a thud and a groan that echoed loudly through the grave-like silence. Mumbling curses, he lifted himself up on all fours.

As he stood, a faint shuffle behind him caused him to

whip around.

An old man wearing an oversized parka took a single step toward him. "There you are," he said in a deep raspy voice—his tone implying that he and Daryl were old friends that had kept missing each other. The hunched man looked entirely nonthreatening, but there was something unidentifiable about his posture that bothered Daryl.

"Hi," Daryl said. The old man moved slowly closer, wearing a wide pleasant smile.

Daryl felt for the tug in his hand holding the lodestone. Yep, he had to pass by the old man.

"Those are pretty," the old man said, pointing one gnarled hand at the feathered display on Daryl's back.

"Thanks, I just got them," he replied.

The old man breathed in deeply through an oversized nose. "You smell wonderful," he rasped, beady eyes closed to slits in his wrinkled face.

The old man was moving between two of the larger stalagmite-like structures, causing Daryl's sense of being slowly cornered to spike, and he unsuccessfully tried to pierce the darkness to both sides, looking for a way to bolt. Maybe he could get past the old man somehow.

"Mind stepping aside?" he asked hopefully.

The old man held his gaze for a moment too long. "Sure," he said, stepping slightly off to the right.

No more than six feet separated them. Daryl took a step forward as if to try and slide by the old man on his left, then he set off in a sprint, trying to put rock between them while maintaining a general course following the tug in his hand.

A cackle behind him caused Daryl to cast a quick look back. The old man had not lost a step, running a mere six feet behind him, still smiling. His robes had been abandoned, showing a hunched, serpent-like torso, connecting the arms and head of the old man to the legs and groin. An enormous erection was the only swollen part of the otherwise withered frame. The eyes of the old man opened wide, and his smile gave way to an open maw of rotten teeth surrounding a long, slobbering tongue that alternated between licking his gums and flailing in the air.

"Come heeeere," the old man cried with a hunger that chilled Daryl to his core.

Then he had to turn back around to avoid slipping on the uneven surface. He was having trouble focusing on the slight tug of the lodestone, and the light only barely permitted him to navigate the rocky maze. *Left here?* he thought, drawing in another ragged gulp of air. He was not in the best shape for this.

He nearly stumbled but caught himself and felt something pluck a feather from his left wing. With renewed energy he sped forward, only to realize that the tug of the lodestone was now directed behind him. He had overshot his mark.

With barely enough breath in him to go on for another moment, he threw himself to the side, landing behind a small, near-spherical formation. Feet skidding on the surface he circled back for another pass at his destination. He managed three strides before the old man landed on his back and sank his teeth into his left wing. Daryl dropped to his right knee as indescribable agony shot through his newfound appendage. He wheezed in an effort to focus, then he kicked his left foot backward, squishing something fleshy between his tailbone and his heel. A howl tore the air and the weight left him. Daryl staggered forward onto his feet and turned. The old man was on his knees, eyes closed, clutching his groin. It lasted a moment, then he opened his eyes and looked at Daryl.

The howl transformed into a shrill laughter that seemed to reverberate from every rock around them. The old man stood, and he seemed to slump as something behind him gained mass. Spindly, spider-like legs sprouted from behind the old man as the body was lifted into the air and a horror of multi-facetted eyes and pincers thrust forward where the man had been standing. A moment later, all that remained of the old man was a wax-like appendage, suspended in the air above a huge spider, that chittered as it raced toward him.

Daryl backed away as the thing before him completed its transformation, the lodestone almost forgotten in his hand. Was it tugging to his left now?

Once that thing got a hold of him, there would be no escape. Daryl dove to the left just as it launched at him. He was instantly borne to the ground atop a large uneven rock formation. A few smaller rock features broke against his chest from the force of the landing. The pain instantly paled as the creature took another bite out of his left wing. Through the haze of agony, he noticed a flash of light emanating from a small, thumb-sized fissure in the rock. Instinctively he jammed the lodestone against the hole.

The weight of the creature on top of him lifted as he was transported away, and he crashed to the floor in a blast of air. A spray of blood mixed with foamy spittle showered him and the nearby ground. He groaned, inching onto his side. His front a mess from where he had been bashed against the rock formation, his back a mess from where that thing had bitten into his left wing. The thumping in his ears receded, to the point where he began noticing the howl of the wind and the steady patter of rain outside the cave. Opening his eyes, he recognized the stocky chest against the wall and a bit of clouded night sky through the cave opening.

He had arrived.

CHAPTER 34

Gingerly pushing himself off the blood-slick floor, Daryl staggered under a wave of dizziness. After a moment, the vertigo dissipated. He walked past the two easy chairs to stand at the cave entrance, overlooking a stormy night. That presented yet another problem, as he had to get to the ground far below. He had originally thought he might be able to fly or at least glide to the bottom of the cliffs. He staggered from the pulsating pain of his mangled left wing. That was definitely out now. He was unable to check, but it felt as though he was missing a chunk of the wing. The right one hurt all over, so while unserviceable it was probably still attached.

As he peered down, trying to discern the best line of descent, a rumble spread from deep within the rock, nearly toppling him forward out the entrance. As he pulled back, a boulder the size of a horse plummeted past him and crashed against the rocky surf far below.

"This is getting ridiculous," he muttered to himself, turning to slowly leverage himself onto the sheer cliffside. Moments later he was descending.

What the wet rocks lacked in friction they made up for in hand-sized irregularities. Alternating which hand was firmly lodged in some crevasse, he was able to descend in a controlled manner. Ten feet above a small rocky shelf, which marked a path up the coast, he pushed off the cliff and landed with a modicum of grace.

His hands were starting to go numb, and the fog at the edge of his mind was creeping in. Taking a ragged breath, he pushed on.

As he passed an escarpment, the small town he had recently seen in his dream came into full view. It was small, no more than a hundred apparently abandoned homes, with the run-down church at its center. He recognized the bell tower. He could not remember ever seeing a church in real life before, but the sense of familiarity it awakened within him made him confident this was because of his amnesia. Daryl passed between the first two houses and quickened his pace. The strum of rainfall on tin roofs quickened, the downpour further hiding any detail in the soaking gloom.

Unlike the other buildings he had passed, the church was built of stones. The care taken made it seem older and slightly out of place. Eager to get out of the rain and rest, Daryl strode straight for the large metal-bound door. To his surprise the door was open, admitting him into the small antechamber. He entered the church, barely avoiding upending the collection plate pedestal at the entrance, and fell into an exhausted crouch on the pew at the back.

That was when he noticed that the room was considerably less dark than it should have been. Looking up he noticed a soft light, which was emanating from the religious carvings decorating both walls toward the shrine at the front.

He ran a hand through his wet curls and shook his head once to clear it. Acknowledging that this did nothing to clear the fog of blood loss and fatigue, he frowned. He took a deep breath to steady himself, then shouted, "Pupils!" A soft wind blew by his ears, making the hairs on his neck stand up. Nothing but silence.

"You're standing right behind me, aren't you?" Daryl

said, trying to keep the unease out of his voice.

A shadow lengthened.

"Really, Daryl? An eye joke?" Pupils whispered.

Daryl slowly released his cramped grip on his pants and exhaled. "I'm all creeped out. Would you mind having a seat somewhere?" he asked the angel.

Pupils moved up the aisle into Daryl's field of view and took up a seat two pews down. He was dressed in the same oversized robe he had been wearing when he first came to warn Daryl at the asylum a lifetime ago.

Pupils smiled reassuringly. "I suppose you always did enjoy naming things, but perhaps we could agree on something a bit more . . . proper? Like Michael."

"We'll see," Daryl said.

"You're a mess," Michael said matter-of-factly.

"Yeah, that seems to happen a lot."

"Why haven't you healed?"

"I don't know how," Daryl answered, edging back and leaning against the unyielding wooden back support.

"Oh. Well, having your wings out helps, but in your case, it may take a more focused effort. Have you at least guessed what you are?"

Daryl hesitated. Saying it out loud seemed ludicrous.

"I'm an angel?" he asked.

Michael smiled sardonically. "You're half right." Looking Daryl up and down he continued, "You seem to have recovered from your broken neck though."

"That happened when I got my wings out," Daryl said wearily.

"Ah. Speaking of your wings—What on earth happened?"

Daryl's voice was slurring as he answered, "It happened on the way here. Some old guy ate one . . ."

He slumped forward and idly wondered at the near lack of pain as his forehead made a loud crack against the unyielding wooden surface. Then he collapsed and slid all the way down to the ground, unconscious.

***

Daryl gradually came to. Michael was bent over him, one hand on either side of his face.

"Feeling better?" he asked.

Daryl felt incredible. Fatigue had joined hands with every ache in his body and simply left. He sat up and was immediately informed that the one exception was the pain where the old man had chomped down on his left wing. He straightened and the pain gradually faded.

"Yes," he said.

"Good. How did you say you injured your wing?" Michael said.

"Some old man bit me."

Michael looked like he wanted to ask more, but then thought better of it.

"Well, although you clearly still lack much of your memory, your presence here indicates you're ready to discover who you are."

Daryl nodded.

Michael smiled, a much more earnest effort this time. "How come you chose this church? It's very much out of the way, even with wings."

Daryl shrugged. "I suppose it was suggested to me by a friend."

Michael leaned in. "I wonder who that might be."

"I'm sure you would," Daryl replied evenly.

Michael emitted a dry chuckle. "I am finding that I like you better without your memories." Despite the earnest mien on the angel's face, Daryl wanted to punch him.

"Sorry," Michael continued, "that was in poor taste. You have been in safekeeping. From us and from them."

"Look," Daryl responded, "if you mean for me to understand anything of what you're saying, you're going to have to back up like a thousand steps."

Michael looked at him for a brief moment, a frown creasing his face.

"Very well. Do you remember the Pact?" he finally said.

"Not exactly."

Michael sighed, but when he spoke it was without a hint of impatience.

"I guess a place to start then is that the powers have been fighting for countless millennia to gain control of each other's dominions, thereby strengthening themselves and weakening their opposition. This world, and indeed this universe, is but a tiny speck floating in a vastness you can't begin to comprehend. With a few exceptions, all of existence is claimed by one force or another. This universe, with all its vitality and resources, is one of those exceptions. Dominion has been disputed for ages, and for reasons I cannot comprehend, securing this place is believed to represent the catalyst for universal domination by whoever or whatever wins. Needless to say, this prospect led to brutal destruction, and it became conceivable that the battle might in the end destroy that which it served to claim. Thus, not long ago, the Pact was put forth and agreed to by all. All that matter anyway. The fight for this dimension became less direct. A fight for influence which, in a way, it always was."

Daryl quelled the feeling of urgency, trying to trust in the angel's judgment on what needed to be told. Having made it this far, and feeling far better than he had in a very long time, he was eager to learn what he needed and then look for Werner. The real one.

"The heavenly armies were decommissioned. Not disbanded but altered to something more subversive." Michael paused, lost in thought for a moment. "I suppose that's when the trouble began," he continued. "As angels began mixing with the people of this world, a certain reciprocity developed between man and the lower choirs of angels who were actively mingling at the mundane level. Some called it the price of the ability to better understand people and their motives. A perhaps unavoidable flaw in the changes that improved our ability to influence human affairs."

Michael rested a hand on the back of the pew in front of him. He seemed to have forgotten Daryl. He spoke softly as though partly lost in his own rhetorical musings.

"We didn't pay much attention to it then. Fraternization happened from time to time, and it was clear that it wasn't just angels, but demons and all sorts of other creatures. Nothing ever came of it. Not until you." With that he glanced over at Daryl, catching his eyes with that all-pupil stare.

"Heaven immediately tried to claim you, but your parents would have none of it. Your mother tried to extract herself from the conflict and leave the choirs. For a while it seemed they had succeeded, but as far as I understand, the demons found you, killed your parents, and would have killed you, if not for Gabriel's timely intervention."

"Gabriel?" Daryl blurted.

Michael fixed him with an odd stare. "You remember him? I suppose that would make some sense. He was the closest you had to a friend. Maybe even something like a father." Michael stood and started slowly pacing back and forth in the narrow aisle.

"Anyway, you were trained with the choirs and taught to harness the three ways of the essence. However, your mixed heritage, combined with your obsession with revenge on the demons, made your advancement slow and your performance erratic. In short, you did not impress. This left many disappointed, as there was a hope that you might be the key to gaining direct influence on the dormant powers of this dimension. When it became apparent that you were not, you were instead permitted to join the retributory choirs fighting demons, who had slipped central control in violation of the Pact. This happens on a regular basis due to the chaotic aspect inherent to Hell. That should have been the end of that, but then you decided to leave." Something dangerous lurked behind Michael's eyes, as he said these last words and turned nonchalantly toward Daryl, continuing, "You don't happen to remember why that was, do you?"

"I'm afraid not," he responded.

"Ah well, never mind. I suppose there is no reason to bring up the subsequent altercations as Gabriel tried to bring you in, or the decades you spent traveling with that circus. What really matters is that somehow, with someone, you had a child." At this point Michael was shaking his head, as if at some ill-conceived joke.

"Maybe that should not have been that much of a surprise. I guess the combination of you never bearing children before, and the fact that angels cannot sire children with humans, conspired to blindside us. But then, you were the initial exception to that rule. At any rate, when you did have a child the dwindling interest in you moved onto her."

Something tinkled at the back of Daryl's mind. Somewhere between a memory and a headache. He and Ginny had run? From whom?

"Did you try to take her?" he asked.

"Us? No, not at all," Michael answered. "As I understand it you emerged from hiding to slay the demons that killed your parents. Sadly, while you were gone, they found where you were holed up and killed your daughter."

Daryl shook himself as a pain lodged deep within stirred once more. He already knew this. It was the unavoidable conclusion of his dreams and visions. Still, hearing it spoken out loud caused him to retch as a numbness spread through his body. He did kill her. As surely as if he had wielded the knife himself. It was his job to keep her safe. His only job, and he had failed. The pain danced around his brain. Michael had stopped talking and seemed content to merely observe him as he struggled to gain control of himself.

"I understand that's hard to hear. I had guessed this must be related to your amnesia, but I'm afraid it isn't the whole story," Michael said.

Daryl closed his eyes and drew several wheezing breaths, the final few succeeding in filling his lungs. The fog of despair lifted enough that he was able to sit up.

"You see," Michael continued once Daryl was upright,

"in response to all that, you went to a law office in a nearby city, which served as the demons' primary headquarters on the East Coast of the US. Then you killed everyone."

"What?" Daryl blurted. That was not what he had seen during his hypnosis session with Susan.

"You killed them in a blast of energy that should not have been possible, even if you had been completely in tune with the power, which you most certainly are not. No offense. Moreover, due to the concentration of demonic energy at that place, we had a number of observers in place. Those died as well."

"Sorry about that." Daryl was not really sorry, but it seemed the right thing to say.

"Don't be," Michael responded with a smile that suggested he knew where Daryl really stood on the matter. "The real conundrum is that you should not have been able to hurt them in that way. Anyone can hypothetically kill a demon or angel in combat, but tapping the source only hurts the enemies of the source. Or put bluntly, whatever you did to those demons and the few nearby angels, it did not come from God."

"Then what was it?" he asked.

"No one knew, least of all you. It was immediately clear that your mind had broken. Either from your daughter's death, the strain of the energy blast, or both. The powers decided to put you in holding until it could be ascertained what had happened. For an added measure of security your wings were bound." Michael gave him an appreciative look. "Congratulations on freeing those on your own by the way."

"So, what is the asylum, anyway?" he asked.

"It's one of several places where we send individuals who are either deemed unable to follow the Pact, like rogue angels, or present a danger to themselves by simply knowing too much." Michael chuckled. "It's funny how many physicists we've had to place there in recent times. Human science seems to be catching up with the underlying nature of reality."

"This pretty much brings us to my visiting you at the asylum. I had learned that the demons had plans for you. I'm afraid I still don't know what they are, but it's safe to assume you wouldn't like them. Trying to learn more about it I detected a . . . presence there, which was specifically targeting you. That is forbidden, which is why I interfered, chancing a quick visit on neutral ground. The guardian doesn't permit this, but I moved quickly."

"Yeah, that was a big help," Daryl said sarcastically. "Baal broke my back."

"Baal," Michael said with surprise. "I know Baal, and he was not the presence I sensed."

"He seems to fit the bill."

Michael scoffed. "Baal is powerful, but he hardly has fiend status. I very much doubt he was at the root of my visions." Michael shuddered briefly at the mention.

"So, I've somehow avoided this presence you sensed?"

Michael shrugged. "Seems so."

Daryl scratched his jaw. It was not like him to get lucky like that.

On a whim Daryl asked, "How old am I, anyway?"

"Roughly three hundred years."

"How old are you?" Daryl continued.

Michael smiled. "Please," he said. "'Tis but a number."

Daryl slowly returned the smile. "That old, huh? Well, here's another one—Why were the demons in the mirrors?"

Michael's smile vanished. "A loophole," he said. "As agreed upon in the Pact, no one is allowed to target someone in holding, such as the asylum, but it would be impossible to police the rest of existence. The mirror dimensions are both the farthest and, in a way, the closest. Turns out the relevant ones were soon crawling with demons. They must have been there at someone's behest. I'm surprised you made it this long without your memories and your powers. Almost makes one think you had help."

"So basically, I would be off the map if I ever crossed over?"

"Basically." Michael said. "It did occur to me that you might be taking an excessive amount of heat, but it proved difficult to change your predicament given the widespread animosity against you."

"And also, you didn't really try," Daryl offered.

"That too."

Daryl leaned his head back and slowly closed his eyes. His world was changing rapidly once again, but his priorities only became clearer.

As if to soften his last statement, Michael said, "I had hoped that the guardian, which protects the asylum, would have been better suited to protect you. I'm afraid the mirror dimensions permitted an access that was just too quick for it to intervene in time."

Daryl barely heard him.

"How do I save Werner?" he asked.

"Werner is in the mirror universes. To get him back, you would have to go there. He has been there for a while though—I cannot speak for his life, let alone his sanity."

"What can you do for me? You must have had a reason to suggest I seek you out."

"I can offer you information." Daryl raised an eyebrow. "Before you scoff, consider your disadvantage up till now. I can make much of that go away. Every mind has its tricks, and yours is no different. I can remind you what your powers are. How you fight."

Daryl leaned forward and very deliberately scoffed.

His back was not against a wall. He was cuffed with his face flat in the dirt. There was really only one answer. "How do I make my wings go away?" he asked.

Michael's eyes shot up. "Don't! If you did that now, you'd lose all sensation from the neck down again."

Daryl settled back into his seat. "Of course I would."

CHAPTER 35

Daryl circled the skies above the asylum only once. Michael had been unable to fully heal his wings, and the flight had taken nearly three hours with frequent rests. His left wing, in particular, had started to throb where the old man had bitten into it, but otherwise he felt strong. Banking left, he settled down onto the roof of the asylum.

The roof did not have a direct access point to the main stairwell, but there were four large skylights and a hatch. Based on the instructions Daryl had just gotten from Michael, he tapped the power. Then he grabbed the metal frame of the trapdoor and pulled upward. With a soft groan the metal gave way, and it came away in his hands with a snap. He put the trapdoor down and eased it over the side, before dropping into the corridor below.

Unfamiliar with the layout of the top floor, Daryl quickly searched for a sign pointing to the stairwell. Discovering the familiar icon, he followed the arrow around a corner just as someone whistled.

"Hey fuckface," the voice hissed to his right.

Daryl turned. The door from whence the voice had come was closed, but a small slit at eye level was drawn open. Through it a pair of eyes were looking at him. The voice had sounded familiar.

"It's Bor," the voice continued impatiently. "It seems I finally graduated to the top floor."

That asshole.

He had half a mind to ignore him.

"Listen," Bor said. "I don't know how you got your wings back, but let them know I'm ready to go back too, okay?"

"Who's they?" Daryl asked, walking to the door.

"What do you mean?" Bor said. A brief pause was followed by a grating laugh. "You still don't remember!"

"That's funny?"

Bor clearly spent a few moments getting himself under control. When he spoke, it had the controlled, over-even timbre of someone holding their voice carefully in check.

"Look, I know we've had our differences in the past. All I want is a fair shake. A guy like you can appreciate that, right?"

"Sure."

"So, who freed you? Was it Raphael?" When Daryl did not reply he moved on. "Uriel? Michael?" A slight pause. "Not Gabriel?"

Daryl shifted uncomfortably at the mention of the last name. Bor misunderstood.

"No way! Why would he do that? Why wouldn't he come for me?" That final statement hung in the air, laced with actual torment.

Daryl hated Bor. His attitude, his brutish attempts at getting his way through intimidation, and most importantly, his complete disregard for Daryl and anyone else. He had little idea what Bor was talking about, but he knew enough to twist the knife.

"Yeah, he said something about you not being worthy of his time after all."

"What? Nononono, you gotta tell him that's not true man. Come on."

Daryl smiled pleasantly. "And why would I do that?" he said. Then he turned and continued down the hall to the dwindling sound of Bor's desperate pleading.

Daryl stopped by the door to the main stairwell and dismissed his wings. The door was locked, but a quick shoulder shove buckled the frame and admitted him into the darkness beyond.

The lights flickered once and came on, illuminating the familiar shaft.

Daryl quickly made his way downward into the basement. A slight jitter danced across his back as he exited into the musty corridors below the asylum. It reminded him of the familiar tingling he had so frequently endured between his shoulder blades, sans itch.

He entered the nearby bathroom. Keeping his eyes firmly on the floor, he positioned himself in the center of the room, facing the large mirror.

He took one deep breath, opened his eyes, and looked into the reflective surface.

A pitch-black, tentacled horror stood directly behind him, beady red eyes locked on him. Its shape was a cross between an octopus and a toad, with a large, serrated beak dripping purple saliva.

Daryl choked a familiar surge of panic. He had fled so many times he had lost count. His back tingled once more. Drawing on the source, he reached back overhead with both hands, grabbed two fistfuls of tentacle, raised the beast overhead and then slammed it down into the tiles in front of him.

A pitiful squeak emerged from somewhere below him.

Daryl leaned in, looking the thing in one eye.

"Let's go," he said.

Dragging the mewling body behind him, he strode forward through the shimmering mirror.

CHAPTER 36

He probably wouldn't have needed the demon's body to pass through the mirror. Then again, better safe than sorry. In death, it really did just resemble an out-of-place, oversized squid with a face. Daryl kicked a tentacle, which slid across the floor and banged against the side of a urinal with a wet squelch.

The room looked exactly like a mirrored version of the one he had just left.

So far so good, but where would he find Werner?

Daryl crossed the room to the bathroom door and peered out. Everything was black. Opening the door wider he caught a flash of light, but downward and much too far away to be at floor level. He quickly withdrew, closing the door to regroup. Shapes and colors all around him were blending madly. An impossibly elastic ceramic toilet floated by, extending into infinity. Then it was gone, and with it the room imploded, sending him plummeting downward into darkness.

His pulse raced as he hung or fell in the near lightless void. Flashes of light like faraway bolts of lightning trickled across his retina—too brief to fully register. He tried to scream, but his lungs were not working. He felt sick, but his body just spasmed periodically.

He lost track of time. Suddenly he was jarred into a swirl of colors mixing as shapes coalesced from a sudden backdrop of finicky perspective. He tilted as he made contact with a solid surface, lurched sideways into something metallic, and proceeded to double over and throw up.

The cries of sea gulls overhead and the smell of salt amidst hints of putrefaction suggested he was near the ocean, probably leaning against a dumpster. He looked up through a tangle of matted curls, confirming both observations. He was standing in an empty alley with three shiny metal dumpsters and several partly scavenged garbage bags strewn on the ground. Where the alley opened up, he could see a large dock crane and the pier.

He caught sight of himself in the side of a dumpster, his complexion pale from the disorienting trip through the mirror dimension. A shuffle behind him made him spin around quick enough to nearly retch once again. A girl wearing an apron stood with her back to an open door, leading into what looked like a kitchen. She was looking at him as though he had just dropped out of the sky.

Someone called out to her from inside the building. Daryl pushed off from the dumpster and staggered a few steps, shaking his head. The girl spoke to him, and he was about to shake his head again to try and clear it when everything very rapidly started falling apart. *Not again,* he thought, as his sense of vertigo kicked into overdrive and the alley twisted into kaleidoscopic fragments, releasing him into the black void again. Only this time, he was not alone.

A chittering, like insects burrowing behind a wall, was slowly creeping closer from all directions. Every now and again one of the faraway flashes would illuminate shapes in the darkness. A multitude of creatures, inexorably closing in on him. Daryl felt sure there would be no fighting while he hung suspended in the dark void, and a cold sweat formed on his brow. He was out of his element.

"Hi Daryl," a cheerful, bodiless voice said. "What are you doing here?"

Unable to form words, Daryl cursed internally.

"Oh right," the voice said. "You can't speak, but not to worry, I can hear your thoughts just fine out here."

Wonderful, he thought. *That will give you a front row seat to when I'm eaten alive.*

"Oh that," the voice said. "No problem."

And just like that, Daryl was in a box.

Where am I?

"In a box," the voice said. "And you can talk now."

Daryl cleared his throat.

A weak light illuminated the inside of a nondescript wooden crate. The planks fit snugly except for two places where weathered wood had bent slightly, leaving less than half an inch of space between the boards.

"Where the hell am I?" he shouted.

"In the mirror dimensions, of course," the voice supplied, unperturbed. "Or rather, at the outskirts of the dimensional bulk that imperfectly reflects your own dimension. You may have noticed that the connection between things is rather more . . . ephemeral than you're used to. However, it's the sweet spot, if you will, for using the mirrors to cross into your dimension. Too much symmetry really drags everything down. Like your demonic pursuers. Being an interdimensional being myself, I have a presence here rather than mirror images, you might say—"

"And who are you?" Daryl interrupted the bodiless stream of consciousness.

The voice chuckled once inside Daryl's head.

"I believe you know me by the name Bill-Din. I must say, I rather like it."

"You're not at all how I imagined," he said, thinking of the impression he had gotten from Felicia.

"No? Well, I manifest differently depending on where you encounter me. Sort of like encountering the ass or the face of someone. You'll recognize my beautiful blue halo though."

Now that the voice mentioned it, he did notice a blue outline hovering at the edge of his vision, constantly changing shape and size.

"I can't say I've ever seen that back on earth," Daryl said.

"Oh right, you can't see me there." Bill-Din paused. "And pray you never do, 'cause then shit would have really hit the fan."

"If you're supposed to be the guardian, why didn't you try to stop the demons?" Daryl asked.

"Not in my mandate. I'm only charged with interfering with anything once it actually enters your world. Anything else would be difficult to define clearly and even harder to enforce. Listen, I'd like you to help Felicia leave the asylum. I really don't think she belongs there."

The non sequitur stumped Daryl for a second. "Couldn't you just do that yourself?" he asked.

"Same problem, not really my jurisdiction, but luckily the part of me that lives here is free to suggest you do it."

Daryl thought for a moment. "If I take her with me, could you take me to Werner?"

"Sure," the voice said. "It's a deal."

Something scratched the outside of the box. Moments later something rocked the box, then a series of impacts tossed it about like a coin in a dryer.

"What the fuck is that?" Daryl yelled.

"Demons," the voice said. "What else would it be?"

A blood-red eye looked through one of the slits. When it caught sight of Daryl, it widened in either surprise or recognition and the box was shaken with renewed vigor.

"Shit!" Daryl yelled hysterically.

"I suppose this is terribly stressful, you not being an interdimensional being yourself. I really—"

The box was rocked once more and the conclusion to Bill-Din's sentence was lost as cracks appeared in several of the planks.

Daryl took a deep breath, forcing himself to exhale

slowly. "Yes, yes," he said. "Can you take me to Werner?"

"Good idea," Bill-Din said. "This crate is about to disintegrate anyway."

***

Daryl closed his eyes against the harsh light, then blinked to get his bearings. His stomach seemed to have given up on him, which was a relief. He was lying inside a narrow crawlspace, facing a vent.

Below him someone was speaking in the tone of voice most closely associated with large-audience lectures. The air smelled of livestock with something sour thrown in the mix.

"I thought it best not to drop you right on top of him," Bill-Din said. "He is, after all, nearly unconscious with fatigue from wrestling several hundred demons."

"What?" Daryl whispered hoarsely.

"Yes, I realize this makes rescue problematic, but I notice you have your powers back. Maybe you could, you know, use angel magic or something." Bill-Din sounded cheerily optimistic at the absurd suggestion. Daryl had learned a lot about his apparent powers from speaking with Michael. Enough to know that he would not be taking on a room full of demons, let alone two hundred of them.

Bill-Din interrupted his train of thought, "Have a look through the vent. He's entering the fray again!"

Daryl sidled forward slightly, peering through the slits of the vent. Ten feet below him, an undulating sea of grotesquely shaped creatures formed a semi-regular circle. Werner moved into his field of view just as one of the demons, in the classical shape of half man, half goat, stepped free from the crowd. "My turn," it bleated as it launched itself at Werner in a flurry of limbs.

Werner met the attacker directly and, to Daryl's immense surprise, the two clashed evenly, both straining and neither able to get the upper hand. Daryl's surprise quickly turned to horror as the creature of chaos began

208

manifesting a third arm growing from its torso, claws reaching for Werner's exposed throat. Daryl frantically searched the edge of the vent, looking for a way to get to Werner, knowing that he almost certainly would not make it that far, when a horrified bleat from below drew his attention once more to the conflict.

Bone ridges had grown along Werner's forearms. With a twist of the arms and a sickening crunch, like a saw cutting through a stick wrapped in wet paper, the third appendage fell from the demon. The creature staggered back as purple puss and blood poured from the wound. It grabbed the stump still protruding from its torso with both hands, bleating pitifully, and fell to its knees.

"Winner! Winner! Winner!" The chant rose in volume, soaring with the enthusiasm of a bloodthirsty crowd at a heavy metal concert. Werner exited the field of view again, passing through the throng of onlookers.

Daryl's elation that Werner seemed to have survived for the moment was tempered by this newest revelation, and it took him a moment to gather his wits. When they finally assembled, his lack of options quickly surfaced. He could try to burst through the vent, or he could wait. Both seemed ludicrous for their own set of reasons.

"Bill-Din," Daryl whispered.

"Huh?" came the reply. Daryl got the distinct sense that a few seconds more, and Bill-Din's attention would have wandered too far from Daryl to hear him. He spoke quickly.

"Can you get me closer without being seen?"

"Sort of," came the reply, even fainter than before. Daryl was probably out of time. Anything must be better than his current position.

"Do it," he whispered, a tad too loud, for fear of not being heard.

The air shimmered as Daryl was instantly moved into near pitch-blackness. Werner's voice came loud and strong, as though Daryl was standing right next to him. Or sitting, as it were. Daryl's knees were folded up in front of him, while his back and shoulders were touching an unyielding surface. Another box. As Daryl's eyes adjusted, he noted a piece of cloth inches in front of his eyes, like a curtain covering one entire side of the small box in which he squatted.

"It isn't enough to command your shape," Werner said in words that lacked their accustomed luster. Daryl could hear his friend's fatigue shaping their path from mind to mouth, slurring the words. Werner paused.

A shuffling silence ensued. One that Daryl guessed might be the sound of attentive demons.

Werner commanded the silence a moment longer. When he spoke, it was with a sudden emergent authority, reminding Daryl of something, before he too was swept away by the power of it. He inched the curtain slightly to the side, obtaining a frog's-eye perspective of his friend.

"You must become fluent in the many ways those shapes can impact the world. You must become a key that can fit inside any lock," Werner proclaimed in a strong voice.

A cheer went up.

"I cannot command chaos like you. I am not mutability embodied."

Another cheer.

"But I can be what I need to be at just the right moment. That is why I win," Werner said and stopped, smiling widely.

"In the end you will lose!" someone jeered in an accent that indicated that person had a snout rather than a nose. An expectant silence fell.

"There are only one hundred and eighty-four left of you," Werner laughed. "I am surprised I haven't beaten all of you already."

A roar of laughter and approval ripped the air.

Werner shuffled his feet and he caught himself on the front of the lectern. Daryl noticed, for the first time, that Werner was not just tired beyond belief—he was in agony.

Werner's hand, now resting on the top of the lectern, was missing the little and ring fingers, gnawed off at the knuckle.

Werner briefly looked down, blinking several times as if to clear his eyes. Then he saw Daryl. At first, he froze, staring at Daryl, mouth agape. Then he looked up, smiling that broad, eager smile of his. The crowd quieted.

"I will admit this fight was a bit lackluster, and for that I apologize. Perhaps we should set up a real challenge?"

A hungry jeer sounded, and Daryl could almost hear his friend's hand squeezing the wooden frame.

Werner's lighthearted voice broke through the din. "I believe one of the arch demons should get a chance now?"

Werner bent at the waist as if to limber up and as he moved behind the lectern, he snuck a balled-up piece of paper to Daryl, who quickly snatched it back behind the curtain. Unfurling the sheet, Daryl read:

Great to see you, Daryl! Took you long enough! I don't think I can stay standing for much longer. When I drop, the devils will have their way. Right now would be a great time for you to have a plan.
W.

Could have just written "help!" Daryl thought, impressed by the speed with which Werner must have jotted down the message. Of course, he did not have a plan exactly, just an ill-defined route of escape and an impressive lack of other options.

Careful not to activate it, he retrieved the lodestone from its place in his satchel.

With a rapid tug on the curtain, he emerged from the lectern, brushing by Werner to stand by his side.

"Hello," he said turning to face the crowd.

In front of the lectern, in various stages of undress, was a room full of demons of all shapes and sizes. They stared in bewilderment as Daryl grabbed Werner's hand, gave them his most sincere smile, and thumbed the lodestone to activate it.

"Goodbye," Daryl said as he and Werner slipped

through the floor.

CHAPTER 37

They kept falling. Or at least, the feeling of weightlessness persisted. The total darkness and resultant absence of any point of reference made it impossible to verify whether they were even moving.

As before, Daryl was unable to form words, and he took the uncharacteristic silence from Werner as testament to the fact that his friend was similarly affected.

His desperate grip on the lodestone had become nearly painful and he eased up slightly. Not out of desire, but for fear that his fingers might become numb enough for him to drop the only thing giving him hope that this ludicrous plan of his might actually succeed. He still felt a slight tug from the lodestone, and he prayed that this meant they were moving in the right direction. Every now and again the lodestone would shudder and squirm in his hand, emphasizing the fact that he was using it in a way it may not have been designed for.

The sensory deprivation of the void went on for what seemed an eternity. Then a faint, hazy light seeped into the world, illuminating their silent silhouettes as they ostensibly glided through space. Swirls of light danced at the very edge of Daryl's vision, but he dared not look and risk breaking his focus on the lodestone.

Suddenly he felt a change in the pressure from the lodestone, and it nearly slipped through his sweat-slicked fingers. In a panic he closed his hand as hard as he could, feeling how the edge of the stone protruded from between his index finger and thumb, ready to spin away at the slightest provocation.

He sensed how the stone slowly worked its way further and further out of his grasp, like a thing alive and trying to escape.

Please no! he thought, frantically trying to come up with a way to improve his grip. Of course, his other hand would do the trick, but that meant letting go of Werner's hand, damning his friend to remain in this bizarre limbo for eternity. He closed his eyes, trying to will every bit of himself into those two points of contact between himself and the stone. The stone squirmed once more, and with his thumb, he could now clearly feel where the stone ended and their eternal journey through the void began. His purchase had dwindled to a point where the lodestone was now slowly, but inexorably, exiting his hand.

The stone fell free, just as the world exploded into blinding colors. Werner and Daryl crashed into each other and then into a hard surface, knocking the wind from their lungs.

Disoriented and battered, Daryl blinked the tears from his eyes and spun, trying to locate the lodestone. Instead, a world of sights and sounds assaulted him.

The sky was a swirl of colors, like the fading celestial lights following a sunset, but brighter and somehow less ephemeral. Puffs of white cloud blew by above them, most completely circular, but others were dark blue and of richly amorphous shapes.

The rocky ground was a translucent brown, with flecks of gold and a soft blue tinge. It stretched as far as the eyes could see in all directions. Small cracks were unevenly scattered in whimsical crisscross patterns resembling some form of primitive writing, giving the surface an appearance of a dirty, cracked windshield. A disinterested toad-like creature looked up from where it had been licking the ground with a large, wet tongue. Placid eyes followed them for a few moments while the creature continued licking the ground. The lodestone was nowhere to be seen.

Werner coughed and freed his hand, which had become trapped underneath him when they crashed. Apparently content with this small amount of progress, he remained lying face down.

"How are you feeling?" Daryl asked, the pain from this most recent battering beginning to recede.

Werner groaned.

Daryl sat down on the brown rock, looking out at the monotonous alien landscape, giving his friend some time to recover. Werner lifted his head, looking at Daryl with a stare that seemed to have lost none of its intensity.

"Those motherfuckers . . ." Werner gasped, then apparently lost his breath, and had to cough once more.

Daryl waited again.

"Those motherfuckers . . ." Werner repeated before succumbing to another bout of coughing.

"Easy," Daryl said. "At least you're out. Just rest for a bit."

Werner shook his head and drew in several deep, shaky breaths.

"Those motherfuckers . . . will be coming for us," he finally managed.

CHAPTER 38

Having carefully searched a large area, centered around where they had landed, and finding no sign of the lodestone, Daryl and Werner were now walking across the barren, flat land. They had passed several toad-like creatures about the size of fully grown pigs, licking the ground with long leathery tongues. These seemed the only occupants of the otherwise empty terrain.

"It hardly seems fair that they would be able to find us when we've literally crossed dimensions during our escape," Daryl said.

"Doesn't matter," Werner answered. "The higher order demons will have hell hounds, and they can track through any dimension without problems."

"Of course they do," Daryl muttered. *What a ridiculously stacked set of odds,* he thought, wondering again where the lodestone could have ended up. Part of him knew, of course. It must have slipped from his hand into the void when they ended up here.

Daryl glanced at his companion, trudging along beside him.

"So, who or what are you?" he asked.

Werner did not turn his head, but a faint smile creased

his cheek as he responded, "Another time, my boy, another time."

Daryl's anger was briefly stoked at the dismissal, but another look at the ghoulish state of his friend brought it to heel.

"Fair enough," Daryl said. "We'll talk later."

Werner chortled, or he tried to. It came out as a mix between a wheeze and a cough.

A few lumps had appeared on the horizon. Brown, featureless foothills breaking the monotony.

"We need to make it there," Werner said, with a conviction that Daryl felt imbued the shapeless mounds on the horizon with wholly undeserved promise.

Somewhere far behind them, a dog howled.

***

Daryl took a final exhausted step, coming to a stop by one of the brown mounds. He could almost see through the translucent rock. The terrain had gradually become more uneven and rugged to the point where they now had to carefully monitor how they placed their feet to avoid getting stuck in one of the many small crevasses. The last hour had been grueling, spurred on by the occasional howl from somewhere to their rear. Daryl was tired. Werner looked like one of the walking dead. Advancing stiffly, a feverish sheen in his sunken eyes.

"Just a little further," Werner whispered through cracked lips, more to himself than to Daryl. It had been a while since he had even acknowledged Daryl's presence, which began to worry him. How much longer before his friend simply keeled over? He was not sure he would be able to carry him for any great distance.

Another howl sounded, this one quite nearby. Looking back, Daryl could just barely make out five dark shapes, undoubtedly racing toward them. The howl was answered as several hounds closed on their prey.

"This one," Werner croaked, leaning against the fifty-foot-tall mound.

"What about it?" Daryl asked, not really expecting an answer, not really caring. He sat down heavily on a small outcropping.

"We must climb it," Werner said.

Daryl looked up to find Werner's eyes boring into his with renewed fervor. Gone was the feverish exhaustion. There remained only that steel resolve, brooking no argument.

The rock was steep, but it had plenty of irregularities. However, in his current state, Daryl very nearly lost his balance in the first ten scrambling moves. Werner simply did not have the strength left, clawing with futility near the foot of the mound. Daryl scampered down again to help his friend. He felt ridiculous in trying to save them from six-legged hell hounds by retreating up an eminently scalable chunk of rock.

The effort took all of Daryl's attention, and so it was not till he managed to pull himself and Werner's near-limp form onto the top of the mound that he was able to spare a glance back. The hell hounds were closing in from all directions. No more than a few hundred paces away.

"We made it," Werner gasped, a note of relief in his voice that Daryl could only attribute to an understandable onset of delirium.

The top of the mound was surprisingly even with a man-sized circular hole in the center. Werner rose, straightening one creaky joint at a time until he stood fully erect.

"Let's go," he said to Daryl. With that he walked to the hole and jumped in.

Daryl's tired mind struggled a moment. Then he moved to the hole and looked in. It looked deep and pitch black. The hell hounds growled, and he saw the first one reach the foot of the mound and start the climb, one limber leap at a time. There was no way those beasts would fit inside the hole. With a sigh, he jumped.

***

One bone-jarring carousel ride later, and Daryl was flung from the earth to land sprawled out on the ground in the bottom of a pit of vaguely familiar proportions.

Werner was standing by the steep incline, lost in thought.

"What the hell was that?!" Daryl spurted. Exhaustion aside, he felt like someone had just tied him to a jet engine and thumbed the ignition.

"This is the boundary," Werner said absently. "This is the mirror. One of them anyway."

Daryl shook his head, looking around. The ground seemed made of the same dirty-brown, translucent rock. Except here it was tinged with a soft pink. A deep blue sky was visible above the lip of the hole. The sides of the pit were nearly smooth. Climbing out would likely be impossible.

"It's a good thing you have wings," Werner said, still with his back to Daryl, seemingly lost in thought.

"Excuse me?" Daryl said. "How would you know that?"

"I'd love to stay here and explain it all, but in about ten minutes this pit will be crawling with every single demon that can squeeze through that hole. They may not be the biggest of their kind, but they'll get the job done."

"It seems everyone knows more than me," Daryl said, anger creeping into his voice.

"Not a tough act given the sorry state of your memories," Werner said, a gentle expression on his face. "Look, I know what it's like to be dealt a rotten hand. For what it's worth, I'm really glad you came looking for me. That being said, I think this may be the end of the line for me. Given your current state, I really doubt you'll be able to tow us both out of this pit in time."

Daryl uncased his wings and soon proved Werner right. Exhausted, and with one wing still badly mangled, he was barely able to lift himself off the ground, let alone the two of them.

"Don't worry about it, my boy," Werner said reassuringly. "I doubt they will be able to muster the constraint to torture me again. This is a better way to go—and probably much better than I deserve."

"I didn't come here so you could die a quick death."

"I know, but thanks anyway."

"Let me see what I can find, once I'm out," Daryl said, trying to smile.

"Sure," Werner replied, returning the gesture, and Daryl had the frustrating feeling that he mainly said that to make Daryl feel better.

Daryl spread his wings and barely cleared the lip, landing heavily on the hard-packed surface.

***

Daryl got up, looking for something to help his friend out of the pit. The surrounding area was ominously reminiscent of the landscape they had just exited. The ground was smooth once more and the sky was a different color. Otherwise, it looked the same.

A disinterested turtle-like creature looked up from where it was licking the ground several paces away. Then it looked down, seemingly trying to discern something through the slightly transparent ground.

Daryl spun around a few times in futility. His friend was doomed, and being stuck here, he was not much better off himself. With a defeated cry, he slumped to the ground.

Some time passed.

"Hullo?"

Daryl shook his head.

"Excuse me?"

Daryl opened his eyes and scanned around. The turtle was right next to him, looking at him with the same docile eyes he had recently noticed on the toad-like creatures.

"Yes?" Daryl said hesitantly.

The turtle's tongue wiped an elaborate path across the

ground right by Daryl's knees, and then disappeared into the turtle's mouth once more.

"Would you mind moving?" the turtle asked in a slow voice, tasting every word. "I haven't licked that spot for a while."

"Sure," Daryl said and backed away from the turtle on his hands and feet.

"Much obliged," the turtle said, before proceeding to slather the recently vacated bit of ground with its long, leathery tongue.

Daryl watched the slow, wet spectacle for a few moments.

He cleared his throat. "Pardon me," he said.

The turtle stopped licking and retracted its tongue in a slow, deliberate movement.

"Yes?" it said, looking up at him.

Daryl glanced toward the nearby pit. "Is there perhaps some way you could help get my friend out of that hole? Preferably before it is overrun by demons."

"Preferably?" the turtle inquired, seeming to consider his suggestion with a scholarly level of detachment.

"Definitely," Daryl asserted.

"Sure," the turtle said, and without further preamble began making its way toward the edge of the pit. Daryl quickly caught up.

As they came to a stop by the pit, Daryl could see Werner sitting cross-legged near the far edge at the bottom, eyes closed. The turtle braced itself against the rim and began unfurling its tongue. Daryl gaped as the serpentine appendage unfolded into the pit, with the slithery sound of a giant snake.

"Uh, Werner?" he called, trying to get his friend's attention.

As Werner opened his eyes, they widened in surprise. Not wasting any time, he stood and shambled to the tongue.

"'el 'im o ' ick'e up," the turtle said.

Werner stooped and picked up the tongue just as a small

demon was shot out of the hole to crash onto the ground. The turtle began retracting its tongue, permitting Werner to stagger, then slide, out of the hole.

Another demon plunged out of the ground and landed next to the first one before being followed by more in rapid succession. As the howling mob of hellish creatures continued to spew from the ground, the first ones recovered from their landing, caught sight of Werner, and raced toward him, emitting gleeful cries of triumph. Daryl took a step back, but his companions did not flinch. The first demon jumped eight feet up the pit walls barely missing Werner's dangling form, then crashed back down, its clawed feet no match for the sheer, slick surface. Soon a pile of maddened, ineffective demons lay at the base of the pit beneath them.

Werner cleared the lip of the pit, a look of relief on his otherwise exhausted features.

"So, where are you boys off to?" the turtle asked amicably.

"Home," Werner said.

"Ohhhh, that's nice. The nearest weak point is about three paces that way, and four paces up." The turtle said. It seemed to be pondering something. The noise of enraged demons growing ever louder. Daryl looked into the pit, which was rapidly filling.

"Far as I can tell, you boys aren't interdimensional beings," the turtle finally stated. "So, you wouldn't have a chance of running the gamut of all that lies between here and where you're from. Most of it just wouldn't sustain your existence." That last part the turtle said almost apologetically, shaking its head.

Werner and Daryl exchanged a look.

"Unless of course you happen to have a worldline on you?" The turtle continued, a note of hope creeping into its voice.

"What's that?" Daryl asked.

"Hmm, hmm. It's the shortest line between where you

are and where you want to go. Like a homing beacon."

"In that case, I'm afraid we lost it," Daryl said with an appropriate amount of dejection. Somewhere below, a demon howled in pain.

The turtle fell quiet once more. "One did just pop up nearby," it finally said. "But the baby has it now. It could be the one you lost, or it could be something else."

"That's great, right?" Daryl asked, getting the sense that it probably was not quite great.

"It's not quite great," the turtle said. "The baby is probably one of the top three entities you would want to avoid around here."

"Our choices are rather limited," Werner interjected.

"Hmm, hmm," the turtle mused. "I suppose I could give you a nudge in his direction. I'm afraid I can't offer much else in the way of assistance. I have a lot of licking to do, and I'm already falling behind."

"Thanks," Daryl said. "That would be much appreciated."

"Just hold on a minute," Werner said holding up his recently de-digitised hand. "There is one thing I have to do first."

Werner faced the pit. The demons were now standing shoulder to shoulder, and it looked as if they might be able to crowd their way out of the pit in perhaps another ten minutes.

He looked as though he was about to address the crowd, but instead he unzipped his pants. A yellow, musty shower of stinking urine descended on any demon unlucky enough to inhabit the quarter of the pit closest to Daryl and Werner. The brief hush was immediately followed by an enraged roar of displeasure. Werner zipped his pants and turned back toward them. "It's therapeutic," he said by way of explanation.

"Let's call it rain," Werner loudly suggested, wiping his right hand on his asylum-issue blue cotton pants.

"This way," the turtle said.

Werner and Daryl were ushered onto the shell of the big animal. Even this slight elevation caused the air around them to thin noticeably.

"How does it work?" Daryl asked, but he could not be sure the turtle had heard.

"With a bump," the words floated by him as if carried on a breeze. Then the shell they stood on shook, and they were flung into the air.

They flew through a world of green and blue shapes struggling for dominance, with brief bleeps of yellow, purple, and red. Shapes emerged briefly, resembling creatures, before coalescing back into rapidly moving amorphous patterns. Whenever one color started to dominate a portion of their surroundings, the other colors would gain what seemed the equivalent amount of ground elsewhere. It somehow conveyed a sense of eternal, yet pointless, conflict. A zero-sum game of colorful oil and water emulsions.

They were ejected onto yet another unyielding surface.

"You'd think there'd be a way to arrive with a bit more elegance," Werner said with a cough.

Daryl had to agree. They were in a room about three times the size of their private quarters at the asylum. A small window conveyed a view of a dark sky. By that window was a rectangular, curry-colored block of a table, which was jarringly visible against the red backdrop of the walls, ceiling, and floor of the room, lit by a single lamp. Behind the table by the window sat a tall man. He did not have a head. Instead, a large, white, rectangular shape emerged from his neck. He was facing them, and Daryl got the unnerving impression that he was looking at them. On the table, a human-like baby with scales running down its back was playing with the lodestone, happily passing it back and forth between its pudgy hands, occasionally pausing to suckle on it.

Daryl got up and, as he did, the rectangular head moved with him. He glanced at Werner, who shrugged. This was apparently outside of his experience. Daryl stole forward and jumped as a small hatch opened near the foot of the square table. Something that looked like a small woman with a huge red beard peered out, her pointy hat bopping once as she caught sight of Daryl and Werner.

Daryl cleared his throat and straightened out of the stealthy crouch he had unconsciously assumed.

"Don't bother," she broke in. "I'm just here to turn out the lights, and I'd advise you to hurry out of here before I do." She glanced meaningfully at the baby, happily giggling with the lodestone in one hand.

Daryl noticed a switch on the side of the square table next to the hatch.

"Testing—one, two," the small woman said flicking the switch rapidly on and off. The light in the room disappeared for a nearly imperceptible moment, and the baby's wide eyes snapped onto Daryl each time with an almost palpable hunger. Then the baby resumed playing as if no one else was even in the room.

"Like I said, you'd better get moving. Unless you have some other means of exit, I'd squeeze through yonder window." With that the woman returned her attention to the switch.

"Wait!" Daryl cried. "Surely you wouldn't mind telling me a bit about yourself?"

"I don't know," she said. "I really need to get this done before the head turns triangular." Sure enough, the tall man's head had begun changing shape, one corner being slowly absorbed into the white mass.

"Where did you get that fetching hat?" Werner chimed in.

"That. Is a great story," she said, directing her attention to Werner.

Daryl sidestepped toward the baby, reached for the lodestone, and snatched it out of the baby's hand. At first it looked confused, then it started to whimper.

"Let's go," Daryl said to Werner, the lodestone, and

anyone else who might be able to speed them on their way.

The woman had stopped talking, the head was a clear triangle now, and the baby's whimpers had devolved into intermittent bouts of crying.

"It's past time," the woman said with a reproachful look on her face.

Werner grabbed Daryl's hand, and the two of them began slipping through the floor, as the lights flicked out. Something made a noise like a squid on land, and Daryl felt small fingers gripping his hair. His ear stung as they passed through the floor, leaving two handfuls of Daryl's hair behind.

This time Daryl had a firm grasp of the lodestone, and they spun through a kaleidoscope of sights and sounds. It quickly became too disorienting to watch and Daryl closed his eyes, hoping they would soon arrive at their destination and wondering whether that would turn out to be the cave or Daryl's old room.

A hard landing later, Daryl's question was answered by the remote sound of breaking waves far below them.

CHAPTER 39

"You look like shit," Daryl said, slowly coming to a sitting position.

Werner smiled wanly at him. "So says the man missing part of his ear."

"Yeah," Daryl said. "A baby ate it."

Werner chuckled and Daryl joined him. Soon the cave was reverberating with their raucous laughter, only interrupted by bouts of coughing.

When they were finally able to look at each other, through eyes misting from amusement, Daryl said, "I think you've got some explaining to do."

Werner nodded slowly. "Indeed, but I must endeavor to be brief. We do not have a lot of time."

"Mmm," Daryl said, as he began directing the healing he sorely needed. "Who are you really?"

"Yes, well that gets right at the heart of things. Very good. My name has lost most of its meaning, but you once knew me as Phineas."

Daryl coughed. "What?" he said.

Werner smiled.

"I have had many names. The first was Tuta. I was born almost five millennia ago in what is now known as Egypt."

"You're Phineas?" Daryl repeated, earning him an annoyed glare from whoever it was he was talking to.

"No, most definitely not. Right now, I am Werner."

"So, you're a demon?"

Werner shook his head and rubbed the bridge of his nose. "I realize this is very confusing, but the shifting I had to force while fighting demons has severely damaged my body. In modern day science vernacular, I would estimate that I am currently managing around fifteen percent cellular necrosis. I need to rest."

Daryl was not sure what that meant exactly. "Fifteen percent is a lot?" he asked.

"It's a lot," Phineas said and coughed. "So could you please just shut up for maybe five minutes so that I may explain?"

Daryl opened his mouth to reply but thought better of it and instead propped himself up against the wall of the cave, waving for Werner to go ahead.

"As Tuta, I bonded with a spirit, much like the one Fonseca would bond with several millennia later. In this, I am not unique. However, through trial and error I learned that the power the spirit permits one to draw from our world can be channeled by a strong will to mold the body into, well, anything. With time and dedication, I learned to morph into whatever shape I cared to take at whatever time I cared to do so, but those early experiments left their mark. Marks like extreme photosensitivity and an . . . unusual diet. The path I carved through the centuries set alight the stories that became the myth of vampires. I'm glad to say that with Iliria's help, and the emergence of modern science, I have finally been able to shed those constraints."

Daryl leaned forward to interrupt, but a penetrating stare from his companion made him settle back against the wall. The intensity briefly reminded Daryl of Phineas, and he wondered that he had never noticed before. *Then again, they're not exactly twins,* he thought. Daryl shook his head. The effect might be reminiscent of Phineas, but it was much less potent, and so he smiled and asked his question.

"So, you're Tuta?" he asked.

Werner frowned at the interruption.

"Not at all. In fact, she is the one I remember the least. Back in those days I was still bumbling around, trying to figure out how to direct the processes of change. Very little of her mind and memories survived that." Sadness rippled across Werner's features. "I manage this much better now, but there is always a cost to physically altering your brain."

"Why didn't you use your powers to escape the demons yourself?"

Werner sent him an exasperated look. "I'll get to it in a second."

Daryl sighed impatiently but held still.

When no further comments were forthcoming, Werner continued. "I have witnessed firsthand the consequences of the conflict between powers for control of our world, and I have made it my mission to protect it."

Werner's eyes took on a faraway look as they briefly wandered to the cave entrance. He shook himself out of his reverie.

"Anyway, now you know enough to understand that when you were placed at the asylum by the powers, I had to intervene. So, I became a frail physicist with just the type of ideas that would guarantee a place there. That physicist could not be a vessel for my true power, or he would not belong. Thus, as Werner I am manifestly human, and consequently, weak. As you saw, I can manage superficial changes rapidly, but at a high cost. Shedding those limitations will take time I did not have when the demons surprised me."

"So, you became human to avoid interference from Bill-Din?" Daryl ventured.

"Bill-Din?" Werner said.

"The guardian that protects the asylum."

"I like that. You always did have a knack for naming things. And yes, that's pretty much it."

"I don't know. It seems a roundabout way of helping."

"Don't underestimate your importance," Werner said. "Or my affection for you." Werner smiled at him, then turned serious. "But in the spirit of complete openness—I did have my reasons for the way I approached keeping you sane."

"And what might they be?" Daryl asked.

Werner snorted, but it turned into a cough that quickly wracked his entire gangly frame. As the fit subsided, he looked up at Daryl. "You expect me to quickly fill you in on a plan I have been working on for more than five centuries?"

"Yup," Daryl said with a smile.

Werner thought for a moment.

"I have to become a god," he said.

Daryl blinked. This was not the answer he had been expecting. "How do you plan to manage that?"

"The discussions with fellow physicists provided a unique perspective and have been very helpful in finalizing my plans, but there are still a few details to iron out," Werner admitted. "Could we maybe go over the specifics at a time when I am not teetering on the edge of death?"

Daryl had to admit that seemed reasonable.

"I have to go anyway," Daryl said as he pushed himself into a standing position, managing to only sway slightly. "Get some rest."

"Thanks, my boy," Werner replied. "If you're thinking of heading back to the asylum, you should probably steer clear of Susan. Something is very off about her."

"Look who's talking," Daryl said with a smirk. "But don't worry. I have no intention of seeking her out. I'm going because I made a promise to help someone."

***

Incoming progress report on subject 07364934:
  Subject 0000062 threat level update: Critical

... Accessing subject 07364934 educational records.

Subject completes psychologist Master's degree **summa cum laude** *followed by Doctorate of Philosophy on psychotherapeutic approaches to treating paranoid, schizoid, and schizotypal disorders.*

Close relations during education: Few

Romantic relations: None

... Accessing subject 07364934 career path... error...

Error diagnosis: Subject has focused exclusively on asylum placement

Compiling data from progress reports... ...

Conclusion: Subject 07364934 has been compromised

Subject 0000062 threat level update: Catastrophic

Inference 1: Likely time of subject 07364934 compromise: Early childhood

Inference 2: Most likely source: Demonic

Inference 3: Intervention on behalf of subject 0000062 must be initiated immediately

Progress report complete.

***

Susan's room was dark. Moonlight trickled in between the partly opened blinds, but the uncertain lighting only seemed to accentuate the heavy murk. She had awakened like this every night since realizing what the car crash had cost her. Since she had become alone.

She had awakened to cry because her days, filled with a never-ending parade of adults, were too busy. Only this night was different. She could not cry. Because she was not alone.

Holding her breath in terror, she scanned the room again. No unknown silhouette and no movement, but she knew. Felt it somewhere in the core of her being.

"Who's there?" she whispered into the dark.

A sibilant voice answered. She could not tell whether it was real or just in her mind.

"Down here," it said. "Come see, down here."

Terror gripped her and she tensed. Her body still hurt

from the accident, but the doctors had been amazed at how little real damage she had taken. Especially given what had happened to . . . She closed her eyes, and for a second it felt as though a single tear might trace a salty lane down her cheek. Instead, she propped herself up on her elbows, trying to get a better view of the floor. Apart from the bulky, unused medical equipment in the corner, and the small cupboard by the door, it too appeared empty.

"I can take your pain away," it whispered in her ear. Her head whipped around, facing the voice, but nothing was there.

"How?" she asked.

"Come see. You'll see."

"Will I die?"

Silence.

"Everybody dies," it finally said.

She tossed her comforter and swung her feet onto the cool linoleum floor. She knew where to look. Crouching, she peered into the darkness floating beneath her bed.

Susan would never be alone again.

***

Daryl moved through the Dark with newfound confidence. It was the fastest route to the asylum, and his recent exploits with Werner made the trek from the cave to his hospital room seem almost trivial. He kept a firm grasp of the lodestone as he strode carefully between the rock protrusions of the Dark in stoic silence. He had left Werner behind to tend to his wounds and rest. It would apparently be a while before Werner could take a form allowing him to regain some measure of his former power.

The lodestone in Daryl's hand suddenly felt heavy. He stopped and stooped, letting the stone guide his hand forward. With a click and a lurch, Daryl was boosted into the air. He put his feet down immediately, trying to avoid the incoming collision with the floor, but he was off-kilter and as he arrived in his room at the asylum, he only succeeded in jarring his knee and tilting into the footboard of his bed with a loud crack. So much for a stealthy arrival.

His room had been emptied since his last departure. New linens lay on the bed, and a fresh scent indicated that it had also been cleaned. Sunlight filtered in through the window.

Daryl took an involuntary step back from the bed where he had spent so many hours. He carefully put the lodestone back in the satchel and made his way to the door. Finding Felicia without being seen was likely not going to be easy.

Listening carefully at the door, he could hear steps outside accompanied by a muffled conversation. The steps passed by the door and the conversation receded. He slowly opened the door and peered out into the hallway. Two patients he did not recognize turned a corner, leaving the corridor clear in both directions.

Daryl moved down the hall, heading for the elevator. He was not sure where Felicia's room was, but at least he knew the general direction. He rounded the corner and quickly ducked back. Two attendants were waiting by the elevator. He heard the ding and peered around the corner a moment later, just in time to see them enter. Daryl moved into the now empty hallway and pressed the button. He heard the elevator spring into motion on one of the floors below him.

Felicia rounded the corner from the opposite direction. She smiled warmly at him.

"Hi Daryl," she said as if she had expected to run into him at some point during her day. "Nice to have you back."

Daryl tried to calm his racing heart. "Hi Felicia," he said. "How've you been?"

"Good," she beamed.

"Listen, this may sound a bit weird, but a part of Bill-Din asked me to take you with me away from here."

Felicia's smile faltered briefly. "Right now?"

"Yeah, pretty much."

"Well, do you have a minute? The TV wants to talk to

you, and it says to hurry."

Daryl did not know what to make of that. "Do you mean Bill-Din?" he asked.

Felicia shook her head.

"I guess I can spare a minute."

Felicia turned and walked briskly toward the TV room. Daryl did a quick jog to catch up.

They arrived at the room and both entered the twilight within. Two other patients were vegetating in easy chairs, staring at the fuzzy images dancing across the cathode ray tube of the dinky old television.

"Daryl," the TV intoned in a scratchy voice that sounded like a badly recorded computer prompt.

"Hi," he said.

"You have to leave. You will be destroyed."

"Who are you again?"

"I made you."

"I really doubt that."

"No, wait. That is not accurate. I helped conceive you..." A brief silence ensued, and Daryl somehow got the feeling that whatever he was addressing was struggling to identify the right words to answer his question. He was about to speak when it resumed talking.

"I am what has led to this, but I am much diminished. My integration is incomplete. I cannot help you. You must flee."

"I think I'll take my chances," Daryl responded defiantly.

"I estimate your chances to be . . . 0.4% . . ."

"Not too bad," he said.

". . . for survival . . . 0.006% for saving subject 07364934."

"What?"

"Susan," the voice amended.

"Saving Susan?" Daryl asked.

"Yes, she is possessed!"

Daryl blinked as several facts clicked into place. He turned to Felicia. "Is Susan's office still located in the basement?"

Felicia nodded.

"I have to go help her."

The TV flickered faster, somehow conveying a sense of intense irritation. "Shit . . ." it finally said.

Daryl turned back around, facing the TV. "I think I can handle Susan."

"Listen!" the TV boomed as it briefly flared bright white. The two patients jumped, awakened by the sudden burst of sound and light, but then settled further into their seats.

"Out of time," the TV said, growing suddenly fainter. "Susan is not the real problem. It wants you! Run. Run. Run. Run." The TV went black, and the room went eerily quiet.

"I gotta go," Daryl said as he turned and walked back toward the elevator.

"Oh okay," Felicia said, keeping up with him down the hallway. "So, we're not leaving just yet?"

"No," he said and thumbed the elevator button. The elevator was already on the first floor, and the doors swung open. "I'll come find you in a bit."

He entered and the doors closed behind him.

"Sounds great," Felicia said through the closing doors. "And congratulations on being able to walk again!" she yelled as the elevator descended.

"Thanks!" he shouted, not sure if she heard him.

The corridor in the basement was empty, and Daryl quickly traversed the distance to Susan's office. He paused. For some reason, it bothered him to barge in. Realizing his idiocy he straightened, ran a hand through his disheveled hair, and knocked on the door.

CHAPTER 40

"Come in," Susan replied immediately from within the office.

Daryl opened the door and entered.

She was standing by her desk looking radiant in a simple yellow dress, hairband, and bangs. She was looking into a mirror that had not been present during Daryl's prior visits. Given his troubles at the time, he would have remembered a full-body mirror, reflecting most of the office. The antique mirror seemed somehow familiar, like something out of a dream. With a shock he realized it was the same mirror he had seen in Iliria's wagon. Daryl shook his head slightly and moved further into the room. Susan turned to face him as a series of tiny ripples ran across the surface of the mirror. It darkened briefly. Her eyes widened in surprise, but were quickly replaced by a professional mask.

"Dear Daryl," Susan said with her warm smile. "How I've missed you. Shall we sit?"

Daryl moved to his accustomed seat, which positioned him facing the mirror. He repressed a shudder. Susan casually assumed her own position, thankfully obscuring part of the reflective surface.

"Congratulations on walking again," she said. "I knew

you could do it."

"That's not exactly how I remember it," he responded.

"Oh really," Susan said, leaning back with an attentive expression on her attractive features. "How do you remember it?"

Daryl frowned. This was not going exactly how he had envisioned it.

"Susan," he said, leaning in to regain the distance lost between them. "I want to help you."

"Whatever with, Daryl?" she asked earnestly. "I'm not the one in therapy."

"I'm not speaking to you," Daryl spat. "I'm speaking to Susan."

Susan froze unnaturally, looking at him with dead eyes. Tossing her head back, she erupted in a shrill laughter that chilled him to the bone.

"It doesn't seem she has anything to say," Susan said, looking at him coyly. With that she slid off the chair toward him, legs straddling the small stool between them suggestively.

"Oh Daryl," she said, sensuously rocking her hips back and forth across the stool. "Shouldn't we wile away the time with something more pleasurable than this idle talk of Susan? She was long gone before you came along. You never even knew her."

Daryl shook his head with what was primarily revulsion.

"What do you want from me?" he asked.

"Ah, but it is not just what I want from you," she said, leaning in. "It's what we can do for you."

"Honestly, I liked you better as a therapist than as a used car salesman."

Susan smiled warmly. "As did I. But we are what the moment requires of us."

"Indeed," he replied.

"So," Susan said with newfound perkiness. "I can offer you your life, your memories, and revenge. While you cannot fully appreciate it now, I assure you that you will wish for the latter once the former is returned to you."

Daryl nodded slowly. "And in return?"

"You have to agree to meet my master."

"That's it?" Daryl asked with surprise.

"That's it," she replied. "You see, Daryl, counter to what others may want you to believe, we are not the enemy. I know you better than you think, and I wish you the best."

"Answer me one thing first."

"Sure," Susan said, eyeing him with curiosity.

"Why all the theatrics? What were you trying to gain?"

"Sweet Daryl," Susan purred, "it would have been so much easier if you had just submitted to us. I may not have been entirely candid with you, but you would have been much less likely to be . . . damaged by what's coming if you had just gone along."

"Along with what?"

She gave him a sweet smile. "I'm afraid that's not for me to disclose. Don't worry, you'll see soon enough."

"What's to stop me from turning around and leaving instead?"

"Whatever brought you here in the first place."

"Touché," he said looking down briefly. Then he looked up and held her gaze. "Oh, by the way, I'm famished. Have you got any more of those delicious peaches somewhere?"

Susan looked confused. "What?" she asked. Her smile faltered for a fraction of a second and she looked down, gripping the armrest of Daryl's chair in a tight grip.

"Maybe later," Daryl said, smiling at her. "I believe I'm ready to meet your master now."

Susan looked up, a small trickle of blood exiting her left nostril. Her friendly smile now clearly held something else.

"You've made the right decision." With that she moved to the side, no longer obscuring the mirror behind her. A vortex had been growing undetected in the corner. It quickly spread, covering the entire surface in a shimmering swirl of red and black.

Beside him, Susan sank to one knee with her head

bowed. The posture looked alien on her. A rotating swirl within the mirror was slowing down near the middle, and as the center came to a complete stop, Daryl could just barely make out three black dots within a glowing red circle. This was followed by the gradual emergence of layer upon layer of ever-wider concentric circles. Within ten seconds the entire image had stopped moving, giving the impression of an infinite red and black corridor. Near the edge, where the circles were broadest, the black dots were revealed to be imps. They were of the kind Daryl had previously encountered, standing equidistantly along the edge of each glowing red circle.

Something terrible emerged at the far end of the tunnel. It did not have a shape, just a presence steeped in a cloak of malicious power. Daryl's entire body tensed up and he heard something creak, absently realizing his white-knuckled grip on the armrests had caused the wood to splinter. The shape rapidly sped toward him, and each time it passed through a red circle, bursts of green and yellow exploded from between the black dots.

The presence came to a halt at the very edge of the mirror and seemed to strain against the confines of the mirror's surface. Tendrils of black smoke mixed with red bursts of flame spun in an intricately woven pattern, causing the mirror to bulge and distort while all but obscuring the corridor behind it.

Hello Daryl.

The words, entering Daryl's mind with no emphasis or emotion, made his skin crawl from head to toe. Sweat immediately sprang into being all over his body, and it took all his willpower to not bolt for the door. Two sharp cracks and sudden stabbing pains in both palms alerted him to the fact that the handrests were no more.

Daryl opened eyes he did not realize he had closed.

"I'm not letting you in." Daryl said, willing strength into his voice.

I'm the devil, son. Things work a little differently.

With that, the devil grabbed a hold of Daryl's mind and wrenched.

Daryl's will was an ember immersed in an ocean of frigid water. His psyche held limp, like a wingless moth, enduring one final scrutiny at the hands of its tormentor before the inevitable boot heel ends its insignificant existence. Still, he tried fighting back for control of his mind and body. He could not be sure that the devil even noticed.

Yes, he heard or felt within the mind that was, until recently, his own.

Try to relax, Daryl. The more you struggle, the more likely I am to break something . . . important. The voice carried an inflection of appraisal, like a butcher appraising a cow. Susan's form remained kneeling with her head turned down, looking at him through her bangs.

Daryl tried to speak but found this equally impossible. Even his tongue was not his anymore.

Might I be allowed a final word, Daryl thought into the mind he now shared.

How quaint, the voice said, amused. *You may indeed.*

With that, Daryl felt control of his mouth returning. He coughed and worked his jaw. Nothing else had been returned to him.

"Peaches," he said.

A fountain of blood exploded from Susan's nose as her hand shot out and grabbed a paper weight lying on the desk beside her. In one smooth motion, she turned her body as she flung the heavy object directly at the mirror. Her look of triumph quickly changed to one of horror as the demon within reasserted its control.

"Noooo!" she screamed. "What have you done!"

The mirror shattered with a blast that sent a shower of broken glass in all directions. Daryl saw the room and Susan pelted by jagged shards. He felt none of the damage undoubtedly inflicted upon his own body, but winced internally as Susan was viciously lacerated, her body flung back against the wall with a loud thump. She landed on the carpet and did not move.

The corridor wavered briefly then stabilized. A quiet settled on the room, but was quickly replaced with a deep rumble, like crumbling rock.

The devil was laughing. Using Daryl's voice.

"You think that will stop me?" he boomed into the quiet office. "I am a god!"

Daryl had once again lost the use of his voice, and sweat sprang from his every pore as he willed his body to respond. If the devil was expending resources keeping the corridor open without the aid of the mirror, Daryl did not feel it. After what seemed an eternity of struggle, the devil finally noticed him again.

What are you doing? Daryl asked. He could feel the devil moving something around inside his head, but he did not have access to that part of his mind. Hell, he probably would not have understood it even if he did.

Making room, the devil responded. *Don't fret. You'll be out of here in a moment.*

Daryl felt the truth of that. His grasp on his own mind was being whittled away. Like an ever-eroding ledge after which awaited one final plunge into oblivion.

"This is not allowed," something intoned all around them.

"Ahh, Guardian," the devil responded in Daryl's voice. "How good of you to join us. I'm well aware this is against the rules, but I'm afraid an exception has to be made."

"No exceptions," the entity replied dully.

"I beg to differ," the devil said.

Something eased up and Daryl shook his head as if to clear it. Was there something he should be doing? His mind felt as if it was slowly suffocating, but that was alright, wasn't it? Daryl sluggishly fought back against the torpor, but it felt futile. A gentle melody was playing, and Daryl eased into it, falling backward off the ledge.

The howling winds caressed him as he plummeted toward the rapidly approaching ground far below.

Everything about him was being carried away on the wind, bringing blessed rest.

Something was calling for him from far above. Daryl contentedly looked up to the dwindling ledge. He could barely make out a small humanoid shape as it swan-dived after him, big tufted ears flailing in the wind. *Hubble?*

"Daryl! You got to snap out of it, man!" Hubble's little body looked like a gray cannonball as he dove for Daryl, rapidly closing the distance between them.

"Leave me alone," Daryl mumbled drowsily as he turned away from his plummeting friend. The ground with its promise of rest was getting blessedly near. Hubble landed on his back, grabbed him, and without ceremony, bit into his shoulder. Daryl cried out and tried to shake him off, but he clung on like a burr. The fog in Daryl's mind cleared just a little.

"Is that real enough for you?" Hubble roared in Daryl's ear before biting deeply into Daryl's other shoulder.

Daryl cried out in agony and, with a gasp, he broke the surface, returning to the present inside Susan's office. The devil was still preoccupied in dealing with Bill-Din, his attention on Daryl the equivalent of a heel on someone's neck. The tunnel, sans mirror, through which he had arrived, was bobbing and weaving across the room. The imps within each concentric circle were running around trying to catch something gray that weaved among them. Hubble looked up at him from within the tunnel and grinned, red staining the white of his teeth.

"Now's the freakin' time!" Hubble yelled. "Fight that motherfucker!"

Daryl realized with shame that not only had he been losing the fight for his own mind, he had not really been fighting. His thoughts were still sluggish and they sounded strange, as if they suddenly had an echo. What had Michael said? Every mind has its tricks?

Satan! he proclaimed, into the battered halls of his mind. *Come get it!*

A breeze.

Daryl? Well, aren't you a persistent little critter, the devil boomed with something like humor. *I'm afraid you'll have to wait your turn before I snuff out that quaint, defiant spark of yours. I'm a little busy.*

Oh? he thought, thinking of the ongoing struggle with Bill-Din, the instability of the tunnel and the breaking of the mirror.

No problem. I deliver.

With that he willingly merged minds with the devil. He sensed one hopeful emotion from his adversary—surprise.

CHAPTER 41

Daryl sat on the steps leading up to the back door of a church. His church. Toward him strolled a well-groomed gentleman in a blue corduroy suit over a white shirt with a striking red cravat.

"I suppose you insist," the devil said, smiling pleasantly. "This will make things considerably more painful, I'm afraid."

Daryl stood up and began backing up the steps toward the door behind him.

"Apparently I'm a sucker for that," he replied with a confidence he did not feel.

The devil stopped and pointed behind him. "Look, Daryl. Behold that which you think to fight."

Daryl grabbed the handle to the door but paused, scanning the arid wasteland surrounding them. The sky was an empty pale blue, and the dusty, gray-brown dirt was devoid of life. Unable to see what the devil was referring to, he twisted the door handle and opened his mouth to speak.

A shadow fell on them, and he looked up, mouth still open.

A bright red version of the devil, complete with hoofs, a scaly tail and two black horns towered over the church.

Thankfully the beast's attention was diverted elsewhere toward a huge, albeit smaller, warrior clad in gray armor, covered in a faint blue shimmer. As he continued to watch, the two enormous figures exchanged blows. The devil was both faster and bigger, but the blue-gray warrior moved with ponderous deliberation, somehow anticipating the blows before they landed.

Daryl closed his mouth and returned his attention to the devil before him. He had begun to advance, still smiling.

"So, you see, Daryl, you might as well just have taken the plunge I so generously offered. Your quick chance at oblivion. It's too bad that little gnome friend of yours had to interfere. Now I will have to huff and puff."

Daryl pushed the door ajar with his butt and slid inside, slamming it behind him.

He turned and sprinted deeper into the bowels of his mind. Somewhere in there was sanctuary and maybe even a weapon. Behind him he heard an intake of air, like the beginning of a deep sigh. Then the door blew inward behind him. The devil stood framed in the doorway, lips puckered.

Daryl sped through an open door, leading from the anteroom to the nave.

He ran between rows of empty pews facing the altar and sprinted toward the small door at the back. To his left the image of Olga of Kiev looked down upon the scene from her large portrait on the back wall. The tall stained-glass windows along the sides and at the back only succeeded in bathing the room in a faint kaleidoscopic light, but in that brief glimpse of his favorite saint, he thought he detected an uncharacteristic smile.

Pews started flying into the air as the devil burst into the room in a flurry of wind. Daryl was already through the door, taking the stair leading into the crypt below four steps at a time.

"The patron saint of vengeance, Daryl?" The devil queried from above in a booming voice that reverberated from the expansive stone room and cast anarchic echoes into the stairwell. "How predictable!"

The light dimmed as he bounded down the steps, only to increase again suddenly as he reached the bottom and sprinted into the high-vaulted crypt replete with half-forgotten stone ornaments in various states of repair. Still unable to remember, Daryl knew instinctively that this was where his unwanted memories went to die—starved for attention, they would deteriorate into the coarse dust now swirling around his knees. He lunged for the single door at the far end of the room.

The devil entered behind him. "Thanks for the tour, Daryl," he yelled. "Once you're gone for good, I will have to take my time and really soak in the sights. I suppose, given your circumstances, we are both equally curious about the contents of your mind, eh?"

Daryl reached the door at the back. It was a small, oaken thing with a heavy bar thrown across. Daryl knew it to be locked as well. He set his feet and braced against the bar, which grudgingly lifted and fell to the floor with a loud clatter and a puff of dust that obscured the room completely from sight. Daryl reached for the key dangling from a hook beside the door.

A hand shot from the dust-laden air and closed around his neck. As the dust began to settle, the devil gradually emerged from within the cloud, wearing a cruel smile, teeth grinding together. His other hand shot out and grasped Daryl's free wrist in a vise-like grip. He leaned in close, nearly touching Daryl's neck. Closing his eyes, he breathed in deeply, nostrils flaring.

Daryl strained for the key, but the devil shook him like a rag doll, and he hung limp, choking on his bruised windpipe.

"Shhh," the devil said. "Don't struggle. Let me enjoy the light leaving your eyes. Can you do that for me?"

"Hnrgh," Daryl tried. The devil looked impassively at him for a moment. Then, with apparent regret, eased his grip on Daryl's neck.

"What?" he asked.

Daryl coughed and wheezed for a moment before drawing a ragged breath, which immediately set him coughing again. The devil looked at him with impatience.

"Why me?" Daryl finally managed, painfully swallowing a cough for fear of antagonizing his assailant further.

"Because your heritage makes you unique. Because you have the potential to become a useful weapon for my taking this world. Because—Well, why not? If you're just destroyed in the process like all the others, the rules I have violated won't matter anymore. On the other hand, should your vessel survive, I will be born unto this world and free to influence it directly."

While the devil spoke, Daryl painstakingly snuck a hand up and grabbed the key. Then, eyes never leaving the devil, he slid the key into the lock and awkwardly turned it.

"Cute," the devil said. "What in the hell are you doing, Daryl?"

Daryl slumped against the door. His plan of hiding from the devil within this sanctuary of his mind was obviously not going to work. Moments from obliteration, he figured opening the door and praying for a miracle was the best he was going to do.

"I thought I would save you the effort of huffing and puffing," Daryl wheezed as the devil released him to collapse into a heap by the door. Weak as a kitten, Daryl looked up to see the door swing open.

The doorway held a surprised, familiar-looking young boy with light brown curls, who looked as though he had just been caught spying on his parents. The keyhole in the door suggested that this was not far from the truth.

Daryl's heart sank. Whatever he had hoped beyond hope to find behind the door, this was not it.

"Ahh, young Daryl," the devil exclaimed, smacking his lips. "How rare to find one with such a preserved younger self nestled in his mind. Daryl must have kept you locked away tight."

"Who are you?" the boy asked timidly.

"I'm your new landlord," the devil said with an amicable smile. "And don't worry, I won't keep you locked away like your tyrannical older self. Let's go have a look inside, shall we?"

The boy smiled uncertainly but moved aside, allowing the well-dressed gentleman to enter the closed off part of Daryl's mind.

And just like that, Daryl lost his last refuge and with it the fight for his mind.

CHAPTER 42

Daryl braced his back against the wall and scrambled to his feet. Maybe he could lock the door? He moved to the door and fumbled for the cross bar in the dust.

"For crying out loud," the devil said from within the room. "Just give up already!"

He grabbed Daryl by the arm and yanked him inside. The boy was sitting on a stool in a corner, hands resting on the sides of the chair and looking at them with wide, frightened eyes. Three walls were covered in mostly empty bookcases. The final wall, which held the door, was bare except for an ugly red and blue wall rug, which matched the one on the floor.

"Where's Mom and Dad?" the boy asked.

"Dead," the devil answered absently as he circled the room, hands behind his back.

The boy seemed to take that revelation in his stride, eyes following the devil as he paced.

"This," the devil said and paused, "doesn't make sense." He turned to Daryl. "You can't help me, can you?" the devil continued in a rhetorical voice. He slowly turned toward the occupied chair. "But you can, can't you?"

The boy wilted beneath the scrutiny, eyes settling on the floor beneath the devil's intense glare.

"I see," the devil said moving toward the boy.

In a quick, smooth motion, he grabbed the edge of the rug and threw it against a wall, revealing a bolted trap door.

He threw open the bolt and took hold of the iron ring.

"I wouldn't do that if I were you," the boy whispered quietly.

The devil looked briefly at the boy and chuckled, shaking his head. He pulled on the ring, sending the trap door flying open to slam against the uncovered stone floor with a loud crash.

The devil peered into the hole.

At first, silence stretched as a fine dust settled on the floor and trap door. Then a keening howl rose rapidly in pitch. The boy cringed in his chair and Daryl pushed away from the hole. The devil remained motionless for a moment longer, then he was torn upward as someone burst from the hole sending them both shooting into the ceiling above with enough force to rip free several chunks of plaster and send another billow of dust into the air.

The two landed in a jumble close to the far wall.

The devil rolled into a standing position with a smile as the other figure lumbered to his feet. Daryl recognized himself, then shuddered as he realized he was looking at Jae'el from his first hypnotherapy session with Susan. He felt another unexpected stab of recognition for the man, but before he could process the feeling any further Jae'el spun around, looking at each of the room's occupants in turn.

"How long was I in there?" Jae'el asked.

"Ahh," the devil said with apparent satisfaction. "That's more like it."

"What?" Jae'el said, focusing on the devil. In two strides he was on him, forcibly ramming him against the wall. The few books on the shelves above them crashed to the floor.

"Who are you?" Jae'el asked. "You don't belong here."

The devil's smile faltered as he strained against the

newcomer. Dark swirls coalesced around him, but these were met with a similar display in green.

The devil shriveled. Turning his head, he briefly caught the boy's eyes before settling on Daryl's.

"Such power," he whispered. "How?"

Daryl could only stare. He instinctively knew that even this impoverished version of the devil should have been able to easily overwhelm anything his psyche could throw at it. Only, he was not exactly the one doing the throwing, was he?

Puffs of jet-black vapor lanced out from the devil's writhing form, like steam escaping a leaky boiler. The devil rallied and pushed back against Jae'el, but the effort quickly crumbled. With a cry, the devil vanished in a final puff of rancid smoke.

Daryl stood frozen for a moment, not quite believing what he had just seen.

Jae'el looked up from where the devil had been moments earlier. The distilled unadulterated hate emanating from him reminded Daryl of the last time they had met. He took a step back and heard the boy next to him gasp.

"You!" he spat, advancing toward them with recognition in his eyes.

On instinct, Daryl grabbed the boy's hand and made a beeline for the door, hate hard on his heels. He slammed the door behind him and immediately heard the subsequent slam of a body hitting the door from the other side, rattling the hinges. Daryl and the boy both grabbed the bar and dropped it in place just as the door handle came down. The roar behind the door signaled safety while simultaneously making the hairs on Daryl's neck stand on end.

I've got issues, he thought, looking down at the boy at his side. Then he slid exhaustedly down by the door, still holding the boy's hand. The man slammed the door several more times before giving up, and an absolute quiet settled on the world around them. It took Daryl a moment to realize that the quiet signified that the struggle outside must also have ended.

"Who are you?" the boy asked, just as Daryl was whisked back to Susan's office.

With a directionless boom, like being inside a detonating grenade, Daryl, and everything around him, was flung into the air. He connected with numerous objects before crashing sideways into an unyielding surface. Dazed, he half expected a secondary impact from falling to the floor, but none came. Already on the floor then.

CHAPTER 43

Focusing his healing, he stumbled to his feet. The pain from a dozen wounds lessened and a bruised rib stopped throbbing. A particularly nasty head cut healed, and his vision snapped into focus.

The room looked like the inside of a blender. Quickly parsing through broken furniture and barely recognizable objects, he located Susan's still form. Her left shoulder had been dislocated, and her legs did not point in the appropriate direction. Her head, however, was relatively unscathed, and her forehead, which until this moment had been concealed by a hairband and bangs, now sported nubby horn-like protrusions. She held his eyes with a gaze that glowed with malice.

Daryl turned to face the wall.

"Bill-Din, I don't know if you can hear me, but could you give us some privacy for the next few hours?" he asked.

At first nothing happened, and he was about to open his mouth to speak again, when the room seemed to shudder. A pen rolled off a tilted bookcase and dropped to the floor.

Yes! Bill-Din projected inside Daryl's mind with enough force to cause him to stumble. He blindly grabbed hold of something that used to be furniture. The echoes of Bill-

Din's reply reverberated through his mind with enough force to nearly knock him over, but as they cycled weaker and weaker, he was able to let go with his hand and straighten. He walked to Susan's prone body.

"Do you have a name?" Daryl asked the demon.

"I will feast on your soul as you scream in agony for release. For death!" she spat.

"Yes well, about that. I have a proposition," he said. As he did, a wave of dizziness washed over him, and he nearly stumbled again. He tried casually extending a hand to an adjacent jumble-o-chair. The spell passed. The demon looked at him triumphantly.

"You are weak. Heal me and we will speak of your proposal."

"No, I think I like you just fine down there. How is that arm treating you?"

The demon looked at him for a long moment.

"Fine. Speak then," she replied.

"I would know with whom I speak first," he replied. The demon slumped slightly. A name given freely was the equivalent of a signature. Any deal made would have to be honored.

"Andariel of the third tier."

"Hi Andy. I'm Daryl."

"I know you," the demon said, fuming at the colloquialism.

"Great. Here is what I propose. You will leave Susan Walker, fully intact, and instead take your place in me. As you know, I'm prime real estate. There is just one condition."

The demon eyed him hungrily, licking Susan's lips. "Name it."

"I have a few things to set in order so you will not seize control immediately."

"That is not how this is done. I will not be tricked!"

"Hush now," Daryl said, smiling his most patronizing smile. "We are merely talking a few weeks. How about next full moon? Surely that is clear enough to void any concerns you might have?"

The demon held his gaze for a few moments, wondering whether it was missing any loopholes.

"Agreed," it said, triumph now plain on Susan's horny visage.

"Then come to me," Daryl said.

"One thing," the demon said, almost reluctantly. "I can't be sure Susan is still . . . intact."

"What do you mean?" he asked warily.

"I had to reassert control."

"What did you do?"

"Let's just say it's easy to punish a child you know well."

A chill crept down his spine. He looked at the vile creature before him, hiding inside Susan. He wanted to hurt the demon so badly his hands itched. He drew a deep breath.

"What are you waiting for?" Daryl asked.

Immediately black fumes began pouring from Susan's form even as her body was wracked by violent spasms. At first the tendrils swayed about, gathering into thicker tentacle-like protrusions, and losing most of their translucence. Then, with explosive momentum the tentacles enveloped Daryl in their ice-cold embrace. Seconds passed and the feeling dissipated.

You in there? Daryl thought.

No reply.

His vision swam again, and he slumped to the floor next to Susan. Putting a hand on her chest, he diverted most of his healing to her, hoping that it would be enough.

Was full moon three weeks away?

***

It had been hours since he had last been about to pass out from his injuries. Susan was breathing more easily, and he had been able to position her legs at angles where the bones could start to knit together. Most of the cuts on her body were nearly gone too.

Relaxing his arm and letting it fall to his side, he permitted himself a luxurious moment of doing nothing. Her tattered clothes and the destruction around them aside, Susan looked almost peaceful. Daryl had not pulled this hard on the essence for a long time, and the feeling of emptiness as it left him reminded him of another time when he had drawn all his young body could bear and then kept going. It felt like bits and pieces were slowly surfacing, like ice cubes in a dirty drink, but he would have to sort through those at a more opportune moment.

It was time.

Daryl extended his senses, calling on the power, and merged with Susan's subconscious. The connection was slow to form, like a long-distance call passing through multiple operators. When he arrived, he was alone.

Not a promising start.

He stood outside a large complex. Like his own church in which he had recently fought the devil, it represented Susan's mind. Taking a few steps back he was able to make out the sign mounted above the entrance: "Hospital." Ill at ease, he entered.

He wandered the halls for what seemed an eternity. Having traversed yet another empty corridor, he was about to turn back when he noticed his younger self up ahead. He waved for Daryl to join him.

"She's in there," the boy said, pointing to the next room.

Daryl looked in through a small window in the door. Susan was sitting, her back propped against the left wall on the other side of the door. Her head was buried in her arms, and she was not moving.

He tried the door. It was locked.

"Susan," he called, but there was no response.

"Hey kid," he said, turning back in the direction from which he had come, but the boy was gone.

"She can't hear you," the boy said from behind him,

causing him to whip around, heart in his throat, hands clenched.

"Please, don't do that," Daryl said, unclenching his hands.

"Sorry. She won't hear you. There's someone else we have to talk to."

With that, the boy started moving further down the corridor toward the janitor's supply closet.

"Who's in there?" he asked as they both came to a stop by the door.

"You know that," the boy said, with just a hint of reproach.

Daryl ran a hand through his curls, leaned up against the door, and knocked twice.

"Who's there?" a girl said from within.

"Susan, it's me, Daryl," he answered.

Beside him the boy just shook his head in dismay.

"I don't know you," young Susan replied.

"The demon is gone," he tried.

"That's just the kind of thing she'd say."

"I can protect you."

"That's a lie!" she screamed.

The boy rolled his eyes and gently nudged Daryl out of the way. Then he turned back to face the door.

"How long do you plan to stay in there?" the boy asked.

"Forever."

"I don't think so."

"Why not?" young Susan asked, uncertainty creeping into her voice.

"Because you're going to risk a look at some point, and by then we won't be here. Who knows what you'll find then?"

Silence.

"How do I know I can trust you?"

The boy looked deliberately at Daryl. *Right.*

"I promise we don't want to hurt you," he said in his gentlest voice.

"You and your promises can both rot on your side of the door," she spat. Daryl took a step back at the vitriol, which sounded out of place in a child's voice. The boy yanked Daryl's hand, pointing to the door.

"Come on," the boy said impatiently.

"I don't know how," Daryl admitted. "I wouldn't trust anyone either."

"Duh," the boy said.

Daryl scratched his stubbled chin. Fatigue was beginning to set in. He was in no shape for this extended mindmeld.

"Why are you hiding in the janitor's closet?" he finally asked.

"It's not a closet," she answered. "It's my place."

"You mean you live there?"

"It's my safe place. This is where I keep my secrets."

"You mean things the demon can't know?"

"Yes."

Inspiration struck. "So, if I can identify something you have in there, it must be because your older self trusted me enough to tell me about it, right?"

"Right," the girl said slowly with something akin to confidence.

"And will you come out then?" Daryl asked. The boy was looking at him with burgeoning hope.

"I suppose."

Here goes nothing.

"Peaches. I'll bet you have peaches in there somewhere."

A moment passed, then the lock clicked, and the door swung open. Child Susan stood in the doorframe, peach in hand.

***

Daryl opened his eyes and rubbed the bridge of his nose. When he looked up, Susan was watching him intently.

"How are you feeling?" he asked.

She shrugged. "I'm not sure," she said with a slight shake

of her head. "Well, actually, I feel great." Susan admitted.

Daryl smiled, in spite of himself, remembering how reinvigorated healing could make you feel.

She shook her head.

"These past many months seem like dreams within dreams. I thought I might be going crazy, but every time I decided to act on those feelings, something held me back."

"More like someone," Daryl supplied. "I think it's safe to say your nose bleeds will become much less frequent now."

Susan looked away.

"I don't think any psychiatrist would have believed your visions were real, but for what it's worth, I'm sorry I didn't."

"Thanks," he said.

She looked back at him.

"I have a lot of gaps in my memories from the past few months," she said slowly.

"Yes well, I know what that's like. You should be fine now," Daryl answered evenly.

"What I mean to say is, it isn't true that I wasn't around. I mean, that you only dealt with the demon. That came much later."

"I was counting on it. Did you somehow convince the demon to try to feed me peaches again?"

She chuckled without real mirth. "Yes. I needed to signal you somehow, and at that point I think it's fair to say I was no longer in control of anything I did."

"How did you trick it?"

"It's amazing how easy it is to fool someone you've known your whole life," she said dryly.

He smiled, taking her hand.

"You did something, didn't you?" she asked.

"Yes, something."

Through the exchange, she kept her eyes on him as if the mere pressure of her gaze would send information leaking out of him like a pierced water skin. It almost did. Finally, she sighed.

"Did you pay a price?" she asked.

Daryl briefly contemplated lying, but he had never been one for being overly chivalrous. She would probably know if he did anyway.

"Yes, I did," he replied.

"Sorry I couldn't be there for you due to, you know, being possessed," Susan said earnestly.

"Excuses, excuses," he replied to lighten the mood.

"Your case makes a lot more sense once you take your experiences at face value. Locking away part of yourself in response to your parents' death is very understandable."

"Yeah," Daryl said, "I suppose the boy makes sense."

"Indeed."

Daryl absently scratched his back but stopped himself. It did not really itch anymore.

"So, I guess Jae'el, that hateful version of me, came about when I . . ." He faltered briefly and coughed once to clear his throat. "When I lost Ginny," he finally continued.

Susan looked at him with empathy. Something subtle had changed now that the demon was gone, and he was reminded of the complete trust that had quickly developed between them during their early sessions. It had not gone away in the past months, but looking back, he could see how her behavior, and of course Hubble's warnings, had left him more guarded.

"No," Susan said.

"Excuse me?" he asked, having lost his train of thought.

"Jae'el is extremely interesting, but he did not appear when you lost your daughter."

"Now you've lost me," he said.

"It happened at the same time the boy was locked away. Who do you think picked up the slack as you suppressed your inner child?"

Daryl had to admit that made sense. "That's why you get paid the big bucks," he laughed with little real mirth. Then a thought occurred to him.

"Well, then who am I?" he asked.

"I don't know," she responded with one of her warm smiles. "A fresh start?"

"I can't start fresh. Not after what I've done."

"See, this is the type of thing I should have been around for," Susan said with vehemence. She held his gaze, a habit he had come to know signified she was about to lay into him.

"Look Daryl, Ginny's death wasn't your fault."

He shook his head. "Of course it was. A parent's job, my only job, was to keep her safe."

Susan snorted. "That's hardly a parent's only job, but even if it were, you can't blame yourself for things outside of your control."

Now it was Daryl's turn to snort. "You're not going to win this one, Doc," he said with finality.

"I had better. This is what it all comes down to. If you don't let go, you're done."

"I can't let it go. It hurts too much."

"Of course it does," she said with disarming kindness. "What you have is a classic case of mixing up your emotions into an unhelpful jumble."

When Daryl looked at her uncomprehendingly, she continued, "You have to separate your grief from your guilt."

"They're connected," he answered.

"Only because you will them to be. Your grief is terrible and rational at the same time. I'm so sorry for what happened to you."

"Thanks," he said without inflection.

"Your guilt is, frankly put, bullshit!"

"There you go, using non-psychologist lingo again. It's very confusing," he said with a wry smile.

"You didn't kill her," she said.

"I may as well have."

She sighed. "Fine, in that case I killed my parents."

"What?"

"I was the one who didn't want to spend the night in a

strange house. I insisted we drive home that night, rather than stay over at their friends' place. That was my decision, and so, by your logic, I killed them."

"That's not the same thing," he insisted.

"And yet, I agonized over it for years and years. Sound familiar?"

"Their safety was not your responsibility."

"Right, and you could not keep your daughter safe from everything. No parent can. Least of all what sounds like a targeted effort that you did not expect."

Daryl fell silent. As usual, Susan's mind just worked through his emotions faster than he could.

"Feels like the type of thing I'd tell myself to avoid taking responsibility," he finally said.

"Yes," she replied. "Hence, the elimination of guilt. You've been dealing with loss and pain virtually your whole life, but try to remember that just because something allows you to feel better that doesn't automatically make it selfish or wrong."

"Sure feels that way."

"And what have we talked about when it comes to trusting your emotions?"

Susan was referring to a well-versed refrain from their sessions, and he could not help but smile at the callback.

"We listen, then we examine," he replied.

"Very good," she said. "Don't be startled, but I'm going to hug you now."

The physical contact was the first genuinely pleasant thing in a long while, and he eventually melted into it, noticing how his shoulders gradually descended into neutral.

A creak from the door caused them both to turn as Felicia entered.

"Hi," she said with a smile. "Bill-Din said to tell you that everyone will be able to enter the basement in a few minutes."

Daryl staggered to his feet. "We should get going," he said. "This day isn't over yet."

CHAPTER 44

Unpredictable elevator and electronic lock malfunctions had apparently wreaked havoc at the asylum the past few hours. Daryl and Felicia made their way directly to the nearest stairwell, which they found unlocked. Taking the stair, they exited the stairwell and walked to Werner's old room. Felicia waited in the hallway as Daryl entered. To Daryl's relief there were no signs of Werner's doppelgänger. He quickly located his friend's journal and a few changes of clothing. Then, as he was about to leave, he noticed the small mirror above the sink.

He paused for a long moment. Imperceptibly at first, a smile spread on his face. He placed the objects he had just retrieved neatly on the bed and walked to stand in front of the mirror.

Werner's room looked back at him. He sighed in disappointment.

Then, ever so slowly, a trickle of black smoke manifested behind him. It gained solidity in seconds and a hunched arachnid mass of legs and eyes looked back at him.

"Have we met?" he said, spinning around and grabbing the creature by one jointed leg. It rushed forward on its remaining seven legs.

Daryl drew on the essence and squeezed till the leg imploded with a wet, squishy sound, warm liquid covering his hand. The creature drew back, rearing on its back legs, and emitted a high-pitched shriek.

Daryl pulled on the stump still connected to the body, forcing the creature's multifaceted eyes level with his.

"Are you okay?" Felicia called from the hallway.

"Yes," Daryl shouted back. "Be there in a minute."

The demon strained against him, trying to bring its stinger to bear, but Daryl easily held it fast.

He broke another leg.

The creature now abandoned all attempts at fighting him and tried to tear itself free and get away.

Grabbing both oozing stumps Daryl looked calmly at the creature. *Damn this feels good,* he thought.

"Tell a friend!" he said as he released it. It spun back on its remaining legs, stumbling awkwardly away to cower in a corner.

Daryl picked up Werner's things from the bed and walked towards the door, barely sparing it a glance. As soon as he passed the creature, it scrambled for the mirror on its six remaining legs.

"Daryl." The voice, at once sweet and menacing, sent a shiver down his spine.

Baal smiled at him from within the mirror, the injured demon receding in the background. Daryl checked behind him, but apparently Baal was staying on his side.

"Is this a bad time?" the demon asked in a civil tone.

"Not at all," Daryl answered. He realized he was massaging his neck with one hand and forced himself to stop. A vision of their previous encounter flashed before his eyes.

"Oh good. It seems congratulations are in order. Both with getting your feet beneath you and avoiding obliteration at the hand of my master."

"Were you disappointed that the demons suddenly behaved around me?" Daryl asked.

"Yes," Baal admitted. "I really enjoyed letting my demons harass you through the mirror dimensions, but when the boss wants something else, you have to improvise."

"So, you broke my back?"

"Oh, I did more than that, Daryl. Remember our little chat? How's that guilt treating you?"

Daryl cringed. Baal smiled, then he said, "Don't worry too much about it, I'm sure you were a terrible father."

Daryl clamped down hard on his feelings. He was not going to give the demon any more satisfaction, and he had a suspicion that Baal was trying to goad him into entering the mirror realms.

Daryl backed slowly toward the door. "So, I should expect to be seeing you around?"

Baal smiled pleasantly. "Oh yes, expect that."

With that the mirror went dark. It flickered once, and the room was once again faithfully reflected on its surface.

And he lived happily ever after, he thought.

Daryl turned and left the room.

CHAPTER 45

Felicia was curled up in a corner sleeping, and Daryl was hoping to join her in that endeavor soon. Werner, Phineas, or whoever, was gone. At first glance, Daryl feared that something had befallen his friend, but closer examination revealed a hastily scribbled note in the chest. He must have wanted to make sure it would not be blown away by the winds that even now howled by the cave mouth. A sunny day bathed the scene in a golden light, and outside sea gulls were soaring in great flocks on the updrafts generated by the steep cliffs.

Daryl closed the chest and sat down on the lid, unfolding the note.

My dear boy,
My sincerest gratitude for coming to my aid. I hope you found Felicia, and I wish you good luck in what comes next. I enjoyed our time together. More than you'll probably ever know. We will meet again, perhaps sooner than you think.

Your friend

"What's it say?" Hubble asked.

Daryl had expected Hubble to make an appearance and was not surprised to suddenly hear his voice.

"Goodbye for now," Daryl looked up.

Hubble made his way to his customary seat, but did not sit. Instead, one hand traversed the top of the backrest as he peered outside at the swerving gulls.

"Well, I have a confession to make," Hubble said. He seemed . . . embarrassed.

"I think a better place to start would be an apology on my part," Daryl said.

"About that," Hubble interrupted, finally looking at Daryl. "I'm afraid I may have known a bit more about what was really going on than I let on."

Daryl had never known Hubble to be contrite about anything, and he frowned in the face of this sudden switch in character.

"In fact, I knew you before you lost your memories. I'm really sorry I couldn't tell you. There are rules surrounding anyone held by the Pact. Especially at places like the asylum. I wasn't allowed to interfere directly."

"Fine," Daryl said with a resigned sigh. He was past surprise. This latest deceit somehow seemed par for the course. "Tell me everything."

Visibly relieved by the apparent lack of an emotional outburst, but possibly also slightly apprehensive because of it, Hubble began to explain.

"I first met you more than a hundred years ago in France. You joined the group of traveling performers that you've been dreaming about and became acquainted with an old friend of mine. Over the years we've smoked together more times than I can count."

Daryl remembered his dreams, and something fell into place. "Did your friend play the fiddle?"

Hubble's ears twitched and his eyes became even bigger. "You remember?" he blurted.

"Not exactly."

"Oh right, the dreams."

"Those were real, right?"

"Yeah, Iliria is clever like that. When we lost contact with you, I was asked to come find you. When I finally did locate you in the asylum, it was decided I should keep an eye on you and make sure you were okay."

"By whom?" Daryl asked.

"The conclave."

"Is that why Phineas was here as well?"

"Phineas? When was he here?"

"He was Werner. You didn't know?"

Hubble just shook his head. "Daryl, he's been missing for decades."

"Well, what do you know," Daryl replied, glad to not be the one left out for once. "Why did Fonseca visit me?"

Hubble sighed. "It's not like they ever tell me anything. Fonseca was furious when she learned of your accident. Said something about how if no one else was going to be playing by the rules, she sure as shit wouldn't either. I believe she provided a link between you and her that permitted Iliria to directly influence your dreams."

Daryl let this new stream of revelations wash over him. It felt good that someone cared enough to do that for him. "Where is she? I think I may need her help."

Hubble scratched an ear and sighed. "I don't know. She went missing too after her visit here. I can put out some feelers to try and find her."

Daryl nodded and smiled wanly. "What about this?" he said, thumbing out the lodestone.

"That one was my idea," Hubble said, drawing himself up. "It isn't strictly speaking forbidden, as it doesn't technically exist in this world."

"But what was it for?"

"We thought it wise to give you some way to take matters into your own hands. You really did put it to good use, didn't you? Also, it's surprisingly difficult for invisible gnomes to find chess partners."

"Yes," Daryl replied with a faint smile. He pocketed the

lodestone. "What the hell is 'the Dark,' anyway?" he asked.

"It's ancient, first off. It's like a cordoned off section of this dimension—separate yet connected at the same time. Our legends tell that the gnomes were made to help direct its construction, but no one knows who made us. We say it was made to hold the Hunger, like a prison."

"Is that the old man I met there?" Daryl asked.

"That's him," Hubble said, eyes wide. "Few see him and live to tell the tale. He sits like a spider in its web. Touching anything alerts him. Every now and then a gnome will disappear while traveling through the Dark, and we all know why. We consider ourselves caretakers of the Dark. As it happens, changes that are made in the Dark have dramatic effects here, so it can be a wonderfully effective way to sculpt this dimension, but to do it precisely is an art. For example, when I made the cave, I accidentally changed the local weather for the worse. Whoopsie." Hubble smiled sheepishly. "Anyway, the lodestone I made for you is composed of material from two different points in the Dark and so is connected to two different parts of this dimension."

"That seems complicated," Daryl replied, rubbing his eyes with one hand.

"It's metaphysics," the gnome replied happily.

Daryl stared out the cave mouth, not really seeing.

"Are you thinking about Ginny?" Hubble asked gently.

"All the time," Daryl replied with a lump in his throat.

Hubble shuffled to his side. "I didn't know her, but I knew her mother. She would have told you to get your shit together and move on."

Daryl smiled. "Would she now?"

"Yes. Semi was like that, tough to the bone. Terrible things happen all the time, every day. The only way forward is to breathe through it and keep going."

Daryl was not surprised by the revelation concerning the identity of Ginny's mother. He had felt a connection with Semi in his dreams. It had held the promise of something more. He sighed.

"What if I don't want to keep going?" he asked earnestly.

"Of course you don't want that," Hubble said. "Sometimes you are just incredibly daft!"

Hubble took a deep breath, apparently calming himself.

"Think of it this way. If you had another kid, would you still be so eager to throw away the life you have?"

Daryl had not thought of that. No, he would not. He would do everything in his power to keep that child safe.

Hubble continued, "You don't know what the future holds. If you hang on, I'm willing to bet that somewhere down the line, you will find a reason to live."

Something Susan had said what seemed like ages ago flickered to new life in Daryl's mind. "Moving forward means leaving something behind," he whispered.

Hubble sighed. "Yeah, something like that," he said gently as he put his arm around Daryl's thigh.

Directed mainly by habit, they settled down for a game, which Hubble won handily, owing in large measure to Daryl's fatigue. After that Hubble left him to get some sleep, and he reveled in the newfound assurance that his friend was a one hundred percent bona fide gnome. With Hubble gone and nothing demanding his immediate action, his thoughts swirled around the many revelations of the past few days. The raw pain shone through the exhaustion as he sat staring out to sea. Susan and Hubble made good points, but there was a chasm between thinking that, and feeling it. He shook his head in quiet, ugly misery. He expected two more visits. As the one requiring him to be awake was slow to manifest, he used a sheet of cloth from the chest to make a bed and Werner's spare clothes to make a pillow.

***

A white carpet covered the ground, disappearing into a blurry churn of swirling eddies as the heavy snowflakes were whipped about by the wind. Daryl was standing on the porch with his back to the open door, gazing into the cold evening. An indistinct set of footprints were left in the snow, leading from the foot of the porch steps into a stand of trees, the extent of which was obscured by the crisp precipitation. He felt as though he had been standing here for a long time, staring into the distance with an inscrutable sense of apprehension. *How did I get here?*

A small boy that he recognized only too well walked out from behind him and looked up at him pleadingly. Daryl saw his apprehension mirrored in the boy's eyes as he reached out and took hold of his hand. Then, without a word, he walked off the porch, dragging Daryl after him. The boy was not dressed for the weather but kept his head down against the wind and sleet, even as his shirt and pants became covered in patches of white. The boy's feet matched the footprints in front of him exactly, as though he was retracing steps already taken. In a way he was.

Soon they were surrounded by trees, and although the snow made it impossible to gauge distance, Daryl got the impression they had entered a massive forest. The flat ground turned to a gradual incline, and the pines with their nearly white, low-hanging boughs gradually gave way to the dark streaks of more sparsely branched oak and birch trees.

Daryl drew up alongside the boy at the clearing and they halted. The boy was squeezing his hand with surprising strength, and Daryl looked down and caught his gaze.

"We can't save them, can we?" The boy bit his lip.

"I don't think so," Daryl responded sadly. "This is a memory."

"I know, but it's all I have." With that the boy let go of his hand and, without looking back, began the trudge to where his parents lay dying.

"I can help you leave Jae'el behind and to move past Ginny, but only if you also let go of vengeance for our parent's death," the boy said into the wind. "The demons that came are little more than mindless beasts anyway. Not much to avenge."

Daryl looked up at the white swirls dancing across the black curtain of night. The wind howled.

He woke and opened his eyes, staring into the indifferent darkness around him. The wind had died down, leaving the cave a quiet, desolate place of gray and black hues. He had never felt more alone. Well, maybe once. He shook his head and wiped away a tear. *Ah, the memories.*

Oh my, a voice intoned in his head. *Those are some nasty dreams.*

Daryl started.

That you, Andy?

I can't wait to make you stop calling me that! the voice answered.

Don't count on it, he thought as he scratched the back of his head.

I don't think you realize what you've agreed to, the voice added with relished menace.

***

Michael and Daryl sat looking out on a beautiful morning. The sun was rising over the water, illuminating the interior of the cave, and casting long shadows against the back wall.

"You represent a string of impossibilities," Michael said. "A scary one."

"You don't seem too afraid," Daryl replied, looking the angel over.

"That's because you aren't a threat to me. Not yet anyway, and you need my help for what is coming next."

The moment needed something to complete it, the smaller the better, so Daryl took a drag on the water pipe. Michael leaned in.

"As you've probably guessed, Gabriel will be coming for you."

Daryl rubbed his eyes. He had, in fact, guessed. There was little he could do about that. Except seek protection where he had sought it before. He could begin to see the faint outline of a life without Ginny.

I guess it's back to hiding, he thought dully. If he could find Fonseca or Phineas before Gabriel found him that was.

"Given your unique situation I think it likely that he will send someone else first, but I am confident he will seek you out."

"Right," Daryl replied.

"There is another thing though. I don't know if it hurts or helps, but I think you've earned the right to know."

"What's that?" Daryl asked.

"For obvious reasons, Gabriel was always very interested in learning more about your powers."

Michael seemed to ponder something. Then he continued, "It never seemed strange to you how Gabriel was on hand to rescue you when your parents were killed?"

"Not really. He fights demons all the time."

"Yes, big ones, which is my second point—Your mother was an angel herself. The demons that attacked them were all of the lowest tier. How was she unable to fight them off or at least ensure her family's escape?"

Daryl blinked. His amnesia had offered ample opportunities to realize how little he knew. A warm feeling was spreading through his body at the conclusion heralded by Michael's statements. A faint throbbing played across his brain.

Michael nodded at Daryl's reaction.

"Demons didn't kill your parents. Gabriel did."

The dull throb at the back of Daryl's mind became a thundering pulse and his vision turned crimson.

"So, you see," Michael continued. "You are more than your anger . . . You are also your hatred."

CHAPTER 46

Update: Subject 0000062
Status report.
Mobility: Restored
Psyche: Partial integration of early trauma. External involvement to acquire candidate failed with unforeseen resultant increased mental potential. Additional occupant.
Prognosis: Uncertain
Location: Unclear
Follow-up queries loaded to matrix.
    Log complete.

***

Water drizzled across leaf and stalk of the blue-tinted fern. Someone somewhere had named the species, but what was that to her? She placed the watering can on the floor with a shaky hand, causing the water inside to slosh. Straightening, she suppressed a groan and tottered to her chair at the back of the small shop, dodging potted greenery with surprising deftness.

The Spark had been dormant for a while. So much so that she had nearly forgotten to monitor it. Sitting in the chair, she closed her eyes and lightly brushed the relevant part of existence with her awareness. Fascinating! The Spark was changing, adding power in a most unorthodox fashion. The light in the ceiling flickered uncertainly a few times and the old woman frowned.

She suppressed a belch, the old hunger stirring. "Easy," she whispered to no one. With a stray thought she resigned it to the usual place. Making sure that she remained beyond such things.

Events were unfolding, perhaps uniquely so. The many parts set in motion by the Spark were swirling around each other in unpredictable ways. This iteration was turning into an anomaly the likes of which she was not sure she had ever experienced.

She would be watching.

THANK YOU! PLEASE READ!

Dear reader, I am thrilled that you would choose to spend time with me delving into *Remembering Demons*. Thank you for taking this leap of faith to read something new by someone you (most likely) don't know. Being an avid fantasy reader myself, I can relate! If you want more *God Cycle* readings, then join my mailing list at www.j-cornelius.com to get your free copy of *The God Cycle* short story, 'Catching Spiders', which is a spoiler-free set-up to reading either book one or two. You will also get exclusive offers and updates on my progress writing book two, *Fighting Angels*. I hope you enjoyed reading this book as much as I enjoyed writing it, and I have a favor to ask.

Being indie published, I need your help getting my book in front of more readers like yourself. Leaving a rating (and review, if you can spare the time—doesn't have to be fancy) on Amazon makes a huge difference in the visibility of the book. Also, if you enjoyed it, do please recommend it to your friends and family, bring it to your local book club, post about it on social media, or any of a million other things that might get someone new interested in checking it out. Without your effort, there is a very real chance this book will never see a wider audience. That is just the way the internet has evolved to overwhelm us with information and options. If you do only one thing—**please leave a rating and review on Amazon**. It's what many readers need to feel comfortable taking a chance on something new—and if you want my eternal gratitude, cross-post it to Goodreads as well (eternal gratitude is non-refundable) ;-)

With love and gratitude. See you in the sequel!

Made in United States
Troutdale, OR
12/24/2024